A series of te
seconds apart, glow
name, the second a.. .....ss in Bryn Mawr, one of
Philly's priciest hoods, and the third a picture of a
shady-looking dude in a fancy pinstriped suit. The final
text listed a price.

Frank's stomach dropped. Last night, over their
customary dinner of ramen and beer, Rauch promised
to give him three months of back rent by the end of the
week. Frank didn't ask how his best friend planned to
get the money. Since they'd first met in juvie, he'd
known Rauch ran "errands" for the mob, and that was
all Frank cared to know. Avoiding grisly details became
their own watered-down version of *omertá*, the mob's
sacred code of silence.

After a final glance at the address, Frank dropped
the phone, donned his black face mask, and dashed out
the door. Usually his nocturnal escapades involved
herding drunks, chasing down purse snatchers, and
attracting enough attention to make the drug dealers
slither out of the street corners and into the shadows of
a different neighborhood. But not tonight. Tonight,
Lambda Man would devote his attention to saving his
best friend's soul.

Every hero needs a pal, even if he's a delinquent
like Rauch.

Praise for J. L. Delozier

"…fast-paced ride full of entertaining characters, rich settings and a plot that will keep you on the edge of your seat…mob bosses, spy tech and caped crusaders abound…clear your schedule—once you start Con Me Once, you won't want to put it down…."

~Sarah K. Stephens @skstephenswrite

Con Me Once

by

J. L. Delozier

Con Me Once

COPYRIGHT © 2020 by Jennifer Lynne Delozier

Cover Art by *Abigail Owen*

The Wild Rose Press, Inc.
PO Box 708
Adams Basin, NY 14410-0708
Visit us at www.thewildrosepress.com

Publishing History
First Mainstream Thriller Edition, 2020
Print ISBN 978-1-5092-3010-5
Digital ISBN 978-1-5092-3011-2

Published in the United States of America

Dedication

To life's heroes without capes—
thank you

Chapter One

Rauch sat on the edge of the pool with his foot on the drowning man's back and wondered if he had time for a smoke. Turns out you really can drown someone in three feet of water—if you knock him out first.

He'd thought it would be more difficult. Not the physical punch—he was as tough as they came—but the emotional wallop. Despite an extensive criminal record for a variety of minor offenses, he'd never whacked anyone before, and he expected a rush of fear or horror or…something.

Instead, he felt numb. The way he saw it, if the mob wanted this poor guy dead, he wasn't a stellar citizen to begin with, and when you're hungry and months behind on the rent, well, the truth is, money makes a great anesthetic.

The neighbor's hound dog howled a warning. Rauch jerked, splashing water over the top of his grungy canvas sneaker. He cursed under his breath and scrambled to his feet. The scraggy brown hedge separating the two suburban houses rustled. Darkness, interrupted only by the dim glow of a dozen solar lights tracing the kidney-shaped pool, obscured the source.

The rustling grew louder, more violent. He tapped the cigarette back into its pack and pulled out his gun. Tonight had been easy so far—too easy. He should've known better. Things were about to change.

Chapter Two

Bam.

Lambda Man bobbed and weaved as he struggled to avoid the wooden cane of death. A teacup poodle attached itself to his ankle pads. He fought to shake free of the clinging beast but tripped on the hem of his flowing green cape and hit the ground instead. With a whimper, he curled into a fetal position and succumbed to the stinging blows.

"Ma'am, please. Ma'am, I was only trying to help." Frank Lambda's pleas fell on the deaf ears of a woman old enough to be his grandmother.

"You're crazy, you hear me? Nutso." The elderly woman took one final swing at the back of Frank's head, breaking the cane over his shoulders. She snatched her purse off the sidewalk, gathered her snarling poodle, and hurried away, shrieking as if the devil himself was nipping at her orthotic heels.

Based on the glimmer of lights flickering in the previously dark upper story tenement windows, the whole neighborhood had heard her screams. With a groan, Frank staggered to his feet to make a quick getaway. Someone giggled from a shadowy corner.

"Julia, is that you?" Frank peered into the darkness and retrieved his fallen Taser.

A curvaceous figure detached itself from the crumbling storefront and sauntered into the light. "Bad day at the office, Lambda Man?"

He rubbed his sore neck. "You could say that. Third beating of the night and it's barely twelve. People don't seem to understand I'm only trying to help."

"It's a rough neighborhood, sweetie. People are used to fending for themselves. But if it makes you feel any better, you'll always be my hero." She awarded him a bubble gum-scented peck on the cheek and strolled away.

Frank swiped the pink lipstick from his mask. Julia once worked for a pimp who'd aimed to transform their South Philly neighborhood into a prostitution mecca. Driving him out of town remained Frank's greatest achievement. Julia was self-employed now and using the extra money to put herself through nursing school. Someday, they'd no longer meet on this corner.

He gimped back to his apartment, cranked up the tunes, and removed his ski mask before assessing the damage. The leather patches he'd sewn over the neckline protected him a little, but a quick glance in the mirror told him by morning the ugly red welts marking his shoulders would be all shades of purple and green.

Mrs. Pagnotto, the old lady from upstairs, thumped her walker as she crossed the floor. Frank scowled. Deaf to normal conversation, she somehow never managed to miss a snippet of neighborhood gossip, and she never *ever* failed to object to his loud music.

With a resigned sigh, he lowered the volume. The thumping stopped. He could ill-afford to get evicted. His boss was great, but housing in Philadelphia was expensive, and working at a used book and comic swap was a minimum-wage endeavor. His roommate's income was sporadic at best, so even with splitting the rent for their tiny apartment, Frank lived paycheck to paycheck—except for the months Rauch managed to cough up his fair share. If it's true that crime doesn't pay, crime fighting pays even less.

A cell phone buzzed on the plastic storage bin they used as a coffee table. The device vibrated wildly, boogying off the bin's lid to land on the white shag carpet they'd scrounged from a pile of garbage outside the hipster apartment building on Walnut Street. Frank muttered under his breath as he stooped to retrieve it. Rauch routinely leave his dirty socks and underwear scattered around the apartment; he rarely forgot his phone.

A series of texts, sent from different numbers seconds apart, glowed on the screen. The first was a name, the second an address in Bryn Mawr, one of Philly's priciest hoods, and the third a picture of a shady-looking dude in a fancy pinstriped suit. The final text listed a price.

Frank's stomach dropped. Last night, over their customary dinner of ramen and beer, Rauch promised to give him three months of back rent by the end of the week. Frank didn't ask how his best friend planned to get the money. Since they'd first met in juvie, he'd known Rauch ran "errands" for the mob, and that was all he cared to know. Avoiding grisly details became their own watered-down version of *omertá*, the mob's sacred code of silence.

After a final glance at the address, Frank dropped the phone, donned his black face mask, and dashed out the door. Usually his nocturnal escapades involved herding drunks, chasing down purse snatchers, and attracting enough attention to make the drug dealers slither out of the street corners and into the shadows of a different neighborhood. But not tonight. Tonight, Lambda Man would devote his attention to saving his best friend's soul.

Every hero needs a pal, even if he's a delinquent like Rauch.

Chapter Three

Rauch stretched both arms in front of his chest and tightened his shaky grip on the dinged-up revolver. The rustling stopped as quickly as it had begun, replaced by the soothing sound of water lapping the pool's edge. His shoulders relaxed, but the barrel of his gun stayed trained on the hedge. He may be a newbie to murder, but he was nobody's fool.

"Ouch." The hedge's brittle branches snapped as a spandex-clad arm and leg broke through the six-foot tall barrier. The flailing continued until, with a final heave, a masked man hurtled onto the manicured lawn and rolled to a rest on his back.

Rauch lowered his weapon. "Jesus Christ, Frank, you trying to wake the whole neighborhood or what?"

He slipped the gun under his belt, covered it with the tail of his Phillies team jersey, and shook the water off his shoe. Dammit. He knew he should've worn boots. His sock was soaked, and his sneaker squished as he sauntered toward Frank, ruining his attempt to look casual—and innocent.

He leaned over his roommate who lay motionless with his eyes closed. "Frank, buddy, you okay?"

Frank groaned and tried to roll on his side, but his cape snagged on a spindly branch and pinned him to the ground. He engaged in a brief tug of war, wrenching at the cloth with both hands until the fluorescent green fabric tore free. Exhausted from the effort and with his legs tangled in the tattered cape, he thrashed around like a bunny snared in a net until Rauch took pity on him and set him free.

"Frank, dude, you're embarrassing. Good thing there's no one around to witness how lame you are." Rauch grabbed him by the shoulders and hauled him to his feet.

Frank hunched over, gasping like it might be his last breath. "I'm Lambda. Man." He lowered his voice, forcing Rauch to lean closer. "I told you not to use my real name when I'm on patrol."

"Last I checked, 'Lambda' *is* your real name. Whatever. Are you okay, Lambda Man? Apparently, shrubbery's your kryptonite."

Frank straightened upright and gagged at the sight of the dead body bobbing in the shallow end of the pool. "My God, Rauch. What did you do?"

Rauch dropped his gaze to stare at his wet shoe. "Don't ask, don't tell, Frank." He looked over his shoulder. "How'd you find me?"

"You forgot your phone. They texted the address. From a burner phone, I hope."

Rauch nodded. "They're pretty smart, these guys. They keep a whole bunch of them lined up, and—"

"Send the info from different numbers so each text taken by itself appears harmless. Yeah, I get it. Helps cover their asses, but it doesn't do shit for you, Rauch."

"I still think it's pretty smart. Maybe not to you techie types—"

"I am not a techie. I'm a tech school dropout."

"You know more than me."

"The Dalai Lama handles tech better than you. He

uses Twitter *and* Instagram."

"Ain't nothing in my life worth tweeting about, Frank. You know that." He scuffed the toe of his soggy sneaker on the patio's textured concrete.

They stood in the darkness next to an inflatable rubber ducky and a dead man wearing nothing but red silk boxers. A siren wailed, and the neighbor's dog resumed barking. Next door, a porch light clicked on, casting a sickly yellow glow across the hedge.

Like a feral animal scenting trouble, Rauch raised his nose in the air. His eyes narrowed. "We need to go."

"What about him?" Frank waved one arm toward the corpse, and the tattered cape fluttered in the thick air of a late Indian summer.

"Now, Frank. We'll talk about him later."

Rauch grabbed his best friend by the elbow and dragged him through the back yard and across the driveway to the front of the house. They hustled down the block to where a curvy black convertible, splattered mud obscuring its license plate, sat parked in the murkiness between two street lights. The door automatically unlocked as Rauch approached the driver's side. He jerked it open and plopped behind the leather-wrapped steering wheel.

"Wow." Frank ran a gloved hand over the sleek lines of the hood. "Tinted windows, retractable soft top, leather seats…how much do you think this baby runs?"

"A cool one-fifty. Get in. We gotta go."

Frank whistled.

Rauch grinned. "I know. They lent it to me. Can you believe it? Little ol' me, driving a ride like this, if only for tonight."

"Just don't look in the trunk."

"Frank, it's a roadster. It barely has a trunk."

"That's a good thing, considering what I saw floating in that pool. I'd hate to think there were more."

With a push of a button, the engine roared to life. Rauch tapped the gear shift, and the car pounced forward like a panther released from its cage.

Frank grabbed the edge of his seat. "I didn't know you had a driver's license."

The sirens grew louder. Rauch adjusted the rear view mirror. Several blocks back, flashing red lights illuminated the dark sky and were approaching fast. Were they coming for him? Rauch didn't know, but he sure as hell wasn't gonna sit around and find out. He revved the engine and took his foot off the brake.

"I don't, so buckle up and hang on, Lambda Man. We're going for a ride."

Chapter Four

Once Rauch and Frank were sure they hadn't been followed, they cruised around the neighborhood, taking a few laps to enjoy the booming bass of the roadster's superior sound system. When the gas gauge dipped below a quarter tank, Rauch eased the car onto a narrow side street and parked in front of a rundown pawnshop.

The red letters on the shop's overhead sign had faded and bled from years of exposure to the elements. An intimidating grid of thick iron bars blocked its filthy windows. Bullet holes, now smooth from age, marred the sooty granite walls. Rauch dropped the key through a mail slot in the heavily fortified door.

Frank loitered on the corner, watching for trouble. He shook his head as Rauch, with a final wistful glance for the roadster, approached. "Who spends that much money on a security door, then ruins it with a mail slot?"

"The same people who'd lend a one-hundred-and-fifty-thousand-dollar car to the likes of me." Rauch chuckled. The pawnshop was known for selling everything and anything to anyone with the proper amount of coin, and none of it was pawned. "There ain't a soul in South Philly stupid enough to rob Pacifico's. The bars are for the outsiders—competition, like the Irish."

A pigeon swooped off the building and landed at

the curb, stirring a pile of papers to life. Frank jumped. "Come on. Let's get outta here."

They hurried down the empty street toward more familiar territory. Once they'd reached their home block, Frank's pace faltered. He cleared his throat. "Rauch—"

"You know you'd be seen as aiding and abetting, right?"

"What?"

"If you turned me in. Pacifico's has surveillance cameras. They installed them the last time the Irish sprayed the place with bullets. I disabled the security system at the target's house, but stoplights have cameras, you know. If any one of them caught sight of you—and let's face it, Frank, you're kind of hard to miss—you'd be considered my accomplice."

Frank stopped dead. "I would never turn you in. You're my best friend."

"I'm your *only* friend."

"That's beside the point. I still wouldn't."

"I used to believe that until you started prancing around in a cape and calling yourself a hero. Heroes are supposed to catch criminals, Frank, not ignore them."

Their heads turned in unison as a strange rustling emanated from a cardboard box on the corner.

"If it ain't Booger Man and his sidekick, Snot." The neighborhood wino staggered to his feet. "I don't suppose you've got a fiver crammed in the crotch of those girlie tights you're wearing, do ya?"

Carmine was a nice guy when he was sober, which wasn't often. He swayed toward Frank, who steadied him with a gloved hand. "Go home, Carmine. It's late. Linda's probably worried sick about you."

Carmine snorted, sending a stream of alcohol-infused spittle dribbling from the corners of his mouth. "She kicked me out again. Won't let me drink in the house. Can you imagine? In my own goddamned house. I'm the *man*, for Christ's sake." He wiped his mouth with the back of his hand and eyed the pack of cigarettes in Rauch's pocket. "Got a smoke?"

Rauch grinned. "If you lit up now, you'd burst into flames."

Carmine waved his hands in disgust before stumbling back to his box. "To hell with ya then. The both of ya."

They continued their walk with Frank glancing over his shoulder every few feet. "Maybe we should go back and take him home. It's supposed to turn cold tonight."

"He'll be fine. Carmine can find his own way home."

"Yeah, but—"

"Frank, it's been a rough night, and I just want to go home and go to bed. If you want to be a hero and drag that drunk home to his dragon-lady wife, be my guest. Maybe she'll give you a cookie or something."

They completed their walk home in silence. Frank tugged at the edge of the knit mask where it met the polyester collar of his costume. It was soaked with sweat. Indian summer in the city could be stifling, and this one had been a doozy. The unlit corners of the sidewalks teemed with skittering black masses. Frank grimaced and swerved around them. The cockroaches were enjoying the last of the warm weather.

Accustomed to sharing the night with lesser humans, the boldest insects refused to move out of

Rauch's path. He crunched one under his heel, grinding the exoskeleton into fine bits. When he and Frank reached their apartment building, he paused to scrape the goo off his sneaker and onto the bottom step.

"You're like that cockroach, Frank—either too dumb or too brave to get the hell out of the way when things go down around you. You're gonna end up like a splat on the sidewalk if you keep this up, and I might not be around to save your dago ass."

"Don't call me a dago. It's rude. And I can take care of myself, thank you very much."

Rauch snorted. "I tried to teach you Survival 101 a long time ago in juvie. I guess I should've let that gorilla pound the shit out of you. Maybe then you would've learned your lesson the first time.

Rauch jogged the three flights with ease while Frank labored behind, struggling not to step on the hem of his flowing cape. He sighed. In some respects, Rauch was right. At fifteen, he'd ended up in juvie for stealing a rare comic book, while Rauch, already a repeat offender, was in for assault. Rauch had never had a break in his life; Frank's life had imploded overnight. Wide-eyed and naïve, he'd been easy pickings for the facility's gang of bullies who loved nothing more than to initiate scrawny newbies into their brutal club.

To this day, Frank never understood why Rauch decided to intervene and make quick work of Frank's assailant. The unlikely duo bonded, and no one bothered Frank again. Frank introduced his new friend to the world of fantasy—role-playing board games, comic books, and cheesy '80's action films. Rauch taught Frank how to survive in their real world of foster care and neglect. When they both turned eighteen, they moved into a tiny apartment and never looked back.

Frank finally conquered the stairs and wheezed into the apartment. He ripped off his mask and raised his flushed face toward the measly wafts of air produced by the ceiling fan's barely spinning blades. "Look, I know you don't understand why I do what I do, and I'm sure the guy you k…k…" He stuttered over the word.

"Say 'whacked,' Frank. That's what the mob soldiers say. It sounds better."

"I'm sure he was no innocent. That's who I'm here for. To give the good people hope and protect the innocent." Frank glanced at a framed photo of his family adorning the otherwise bare walls.

Rauch noticed. "Carmine is not innocent. I'm not innocent. I'm not sure an innocent creature exists, at least not in our neighborhood. Even if they do, you can't save them all, Frank. You're not responsible for the sins of your father, and you're sure as hell not responsible for me."

"Okay—that's enough. We're so not going there."

"Suits me." Rauch yawned. "It's late, and the only place I'm going is to bed. You're the one who started this stupid conversation anyway." He paused at his bedroom door. "At least I know who I am."

Chapter Five

When Frank rolled out of bed, the sun was shining and his bedroom smelled like a cheap tobacco shop. He followed his nose to the living room where Rauch stood by the open window smoking a cigarette. As foretold, the air had cooled since last night. October had slid into November, and just like that, the warm weather was gone, probably for good. A sudden gust blew a cloud of smoke in his face, and he coughed.

"You know you're not supposed to smoke in the apartment. It triggers my asthma, and the landlord will blow a hemorrhoid if you set off the fire detectors again. We can't afford another fine."

"It's how I maintain my girlish figure."

"You'd be in better shape if you ran up and down our three flights of stairs to smoke outside. Or better yet, if you quit entirely."

"Thanks, Mom." Rauch ground the butt of his cigarette on the sill and closed the window. "Aren't you late for work?"

Frank glanced at the clock on the microwave. "Crap." He dashed into his bedroom and pulled on a faded Spiderman T-shirt and a pair of jeans. No time for a shower.

"The old man's gonna be pissed."

"Nah, Roy's chill." Frank's boss was the only person other than Rauch who knew about Lambda Man.

Frank grabbed a windbreaker from the back of the ratty plaid couch and hopped toward the door on one foot, trying to don his shoes and coat at the same time.

Rauch, holding his cell phone, followed him to the door. "Say, uh, Frankie—you saw those texts on my phone, right? The ones from last night?"

"The ones you should've deleted by now? Yeah, I saw them. You're such a lousy criminal, Rauch." He eyed his best friend from the top of the stairs. Rauch never called him Frankie unless a pigeon the size of Texas was about to crap on their heads.

"We had the correct address, didn't we?"

"Sure we did. We went separately, remember? We both couldn't have read it wrong."

"Did you take a look at the picture?" Rauch, his skin pale, held his phone's screen in the air.

"Yep. Typical *paisano* in a swanky suit. Why?"

"I think I might've whacked the wrong guy."

Chapter Six

For the sake of speed, Frank usually rode the subway to work, but after Rauch's bombshell, he'd dashed out of the apartment and past the subway station without thinking. He had no memory of his sprint through the city. He kept replaying his conversation with Rauch in his head.

"How could you kill the wrong man? I mean, how could you kill anyone, but especially the wrong man?" He'd paced and sputtered like a maniac, horrified not only at what Rauch had done, but by the nuclear fallout that was sure to come.

"I'm not sure I did. I'm just saying maybe I did. It was dark, and it's not like I checked him for ID. All he was wearing was a pair of red boxers, for Christ's sake. With chili peppers on them."

"Forget the goddamned boxers. Do you know what the mob will do to you? They don't tolerate mistakes, Rauch. They *bury* them. And you're not even one of their soldiers. You're just an associate, and associates are disposable. They make examples of associates."

"Like you're such an expert on the mob."

"My father was a soldier. I may not have your street cred, but I'm a dago, remember? I know enough about *La Famiglia* to be scared for your life. And you should be, too."

"I'll take care of it, Frankie." Rauch had said it a

17

dozen times over, as if repetition equaled conviction. But he didn't say how.

Frank chugged along with his racing thoughts, fighting to ignore the cold air which made his chest tight and his nose run. East of South Street, the tidy Italian neighborhoods transitioned to the "tree" streets—Pine, Locust, Walnut, and Chestnut—of the swankier historic district. With brick-paved alleys and three-hundred-year-old row houses to the north and the Delaware River to the south, Baum's Books occupied an expensive piece of real estate, especially for a used book and comic swap.

The front of the shop housed stacks of coffee table books, meticulously organized comics, and shelves overflowing with dusty dime novels. But in the back room, behind a curtain made from the same cheap black velvet reserved for cheesy oil paintings of Elvis, Roy Baum hid his treasures. A scarce, perfect copy of *Marvel Comics No. 1*. A first edition of *I, Robot* signed by Asimov himself. A program from the original Comic-Con International in 1970.

Once upon an ugly time, Roy had Frank arrested for shoplifting a rare copy of *Batman No.1*. Roy kept tabs on him during his incarceration. Frank's parole officer told him so. They even exchanged a few letters about the latest news from Marvel and DC.

And as soon as Frank was sprung from juvie, Roy, impressed by Frank's encyclopedic knowledge of all things comic-related, offered him a job.

Except for a brief and ill-fated stab at an associate's degree from a local tech school, Frank had been Baum's Books' lone employee ever since. Last year, after a health scare landed Roy in Mercy Hospital, he gave Frank the ultimate compliment—his own key and the code to the shop's security system.

Attached to the key was a note: *To the only lad who knows as much about heroes as I do. Now don't screw up.*

Roy sat in his customary place behind the polished walnut counter when Frank hustled through the alley entrance. "You're late," he said, without looking up from his project.

The day's shipments lay scattered across the counter in boxes and envelopes of various sizes, but Roy's focus was on the large cardboard container sitting before him. He squirted his hands with sanitizer and rubbed them dry. Then, with the delicate precision of a surgeon, he removed a layer of air-pillow cushioning and a snowy mound of white tissue paper and dropped them on the floor.

"I know. I'm sorry."

Roy stopped rustling through the box long enough to inspect the dark circles under Frank's eyes. He clucked his tongue. "You need to take better care of yourself, boy. Even heroes need to sleep."

Frank flushed and grabbed the pile of mail. Junk. Junk. He tossed one unopened envelope after another into the trash.

"Care to talk about it?"

"Huh?"

The shopkeeper pointed to the letters in Frank's left hand. "I know I have cataracts, but I'd swear to sweet Molly Brown you're reading those envelopes upside down."

"Oh." With a sheepish grin, he flipped them to the proper position. "It's one of my super powers, I guess."

"Uh-huh. I have just the thing to cheer you up. Better than a shot of Irish whiskey." Roy reached into the cardboard box to resume his extraction. Frank, a foot taller and half as wide, watched over his shoulder. With a flourish, Roy removed the first item and held its colorful pages to the light.

"Wow." Frank whistled. "*Watchmen #1.*"

He knew Roy considered the series to be more than just an ordinary set of graphic novels. To him, the *Watchmen* series was one of the most significant works of twentieth-century literature—the pinnacle of comic creation. Coming from a man who peddled the written word for a living, that was serious praise.

"First edition, signed by Alan Moore, Dave Gibbons, and John Higgins. And that's not all. Look in the box, but don't touch."

Frank peeked between the remaining billowy sheets of tissue. Nestled in the box were four stacks of comics with bright yellow titles.

Roy beamed. "All signed first editions. The complete set of eleven volumes in perfect condition." He turned his rapturous face to the ceiling and quoted. "The accumulated filth of all their sex and murder will foam up about their waists and all the whores and politicians will look up and shout 'Save us!'…and I'll look down and whisper 'No.'"

"Rorschach."

"Rorschach," Roy echoed, with a reverence only reserved for a saints.

The bell on the front door tinkled, interrupting their adulations. With a whoosh of cold air, a whirlpool of leaves and errant bits of paper breached the shop's threshold, ushering in a woman with long glossy hair.

The maelstrom lapped around the ankles of her black leather boots until she closed the door with a firm shove. Deprived of its energy source, the swirling wind died, the leaves collapsed into a heap on the floor, and the brass bell fell silent.

Roy buried his latest treasure deep in the box and closed the lid. "Can I help you, miss?"

"Just looking, thank you." Her voice was cooler than the autumn air and as smooth as her ivory skin.

Roy and Frank exchanged glances. Baum's loyal clientele consisted of a cadre of regulars who wandered in at least once a week to get their fix. The shop also got the occasional tourist, mostly over the summer. This woman was neither. Frank knew from experience that newcomers who claimed to be "just looking" often left with a comic shoved under their shirts or in their pockets. Or, in this woman's case, potentially stuffed inside a knee-high boot.

Roy knew it, too. "Why don't you give the young lady a tour of the place while I put this in the back?" He hefted the box and shuffled toward the velvet curtain.

Frank nodded and rounded the counter. She disappeared in fiction, between fantasy and crime. He caught up with her in horror. "Um, so you obviously found the fiction section. This half of the store is all used books. The first ten rows are fiction. The rest are non-fiction. The other side is graphic novels and comics, and they're organized alphabetically. If you want something special, ask. He keeps the rare stuff under lock and key. It's guarded by a three-headed dog and a cosmic Cthulhu."

She smiled. "Do you consider *Captain Britain Volume 1, No. 8* to be special?"

Frank raised an eyebrow. "I don't, but Roy might, given it's over forty years old. Let me see if he has it on display." He guided her to the other side of the store. "Like I said, the rows are more or less alphabetical. I recommend you look in these two here."

She bent her head and started rifling through the C's. In the harsh overhead light, her long hair, which had appeared black in the shadowy rows of books, glowed a lustrous deep purple—a striking contrast to her olive-green pea coat, which had lots of nice, deep pockets, perfect for stashing stolen merchandise.

Without turning his back, Frank slipped behind the counter and yelled for his boss. "Hey, Roy. The lady wants to talk about *Captain Britain*."

The curtain rustled, and Roy reappeared. "Really? What does she need to know?"

"I don't need to know anything except whether you have volume one, number eight in stock." She abandoned her browsing to join them at the counter. "Keira." She extended her hand.

Roy, with uncharacteristic reserve, hesitated before extending his own. As she withdrew her fingers from his tepid handshake, she rotated her palm face down. A gold Claddagh ring encrusted with two huge emeralds caught the light, sending green sparks dancing across the counter. Roy blinked and looked away, as if their brilliance hurt his eyes.

She watched his reaction, and her smile hardened. "A gift from my father before he passed. The emeralds signify me and my brother, Jack. I can't wait to tell him about this place. He's been dying to check it out. Now, about that comic…"

Roy pulled a handkerchief from his pocket and

mopped his damp forehead. "Yes. *Captain Britain.* I have it in the back. It won't come cheap, but I suspect you already knew that." He swept the curtain aside and invited Keira into his inner sanctum. "After you."

It was Frank's turn to blink. No one got into the back room to see the wizard. Not nobody, not no how.

"Mind the door for me, will you, boy?" The curtain swished shut, and Roy disappeared before Frank could stutter a reply.

He double-checked the date on his cell phone. Yup, November fifth. Figures.

On November 5th, 2006, he'd developed a fear of movie theaters. He went into foster care on November the fifth. One year later, he was sentenced to juvenile detention—on November the fifth. Every bad or bizarre event in his life had occurred on November the fifth. It was Frank's Friday the thirteenth. So the fact that his bestie whacked the wrong mob target and his boss was spellbound by a purple-haired chick who behaved like a mutant sorceress was simply par for the course.

He jotted Rauch a quick text but got no response. He strained to overhear the murmurs of conversation from the back room but only managed to pick out a few random words and phrases. The negotiations took longer than usual. Roy knew the worth of every single item, and he always bargained hard. Sometimes Frank wondered if Roy intentionally overpriced his favorites, secretly hoping they wouldn't sell. If this shop was his life, its contents were his babies, and no father sells a child without soul-crushing remorse. No worthy father, anyway.

When the velvet curtain finally parted, Keira emerged clutching a flat paper bag, a big smile on her face. Roy followed, only he was wearing a frown.

She breezed past the counter, leaving a subtle trail of perfume in her wake. Frank closed his eyes as the clean scent triggered a memory, a rare happy memory, of a family vacation long ago. He heard his little brother Joey giggle and his mom laugh as they ran down the Atlantic City boardwalk and onto the sand. He felt the water on his bare chest as he crashed into a wave and rode its swell back ashore. He tasted the ocean on his lips and sniffed the salt air. Keira smelled like the sea.

Her voice intruded; he opened his eyes, reluctant to let the warm memory go. "It was nice meeting you, Frank." She stood by the door with her hand on the latch, and her kohl-rimmed eyes met his. "We'll meet again, I'm sure."

The bell clanked, and with a second whoosh of cold air, she was gone.

"She bought it then?" It was a stupid thing to ask, considering Keira had left with a comic book-sized package in her hands. But her departure created a leaden void in the shop, and it was the only way Frank could think to fill it.

"Yes, she did." Roy's sober demeanor was not that of a man who'd just made what would likely be his biggest sale of the week.

Frank shot him a quizzical look. "Did she pay you what you wanted?"

Roy's eyes brightened, though his smile retained a tinge of sadness. "And then some. I jacked up the price by ten percent when I saw that whopper of a ring."

Frank grinned. Roy had a gentleman's heart, but he made sure to never let it get in the way of a good business deal. Shrewd and sharp as flint despite his advancing age, he never missed a trick.

"As a matter of fact, I've decided to close early." Roy waddled to the front door, turned the sign in the window to closed, and set the lock.

"But I just got here. We just opened." Frank's eyes widened. Not once during the tenure of his employment had Roy closed early. Not even the day of his heart attack. "You feeling okay, Roy?"

His boss shrugged. "Business is typically slow on Thursdays anyhow, and I made enough on this one sale to cover the day's expenses, including your salary. You go home and catch up on your sleep, and I'll catch up on my paperwork." Roy clicked off the overhead lights and ushered Frank past the curtain and into the back.

Like the front of the store, Roy's inner sanctum held rows and rows of shelves. But these shelves held secrets. Colorful cigar boxes, duct-taped shut to prevent prying eyes, concealed the unknown. Plastic bins sat dormant, coated with such a thick layer of dust that Frank doubted even his boss remembered what hid within. Frank's favorites were the vintage wooden tool chests with felt-lined drawers—and brass locks. Roy was the only one to hold the keys, and they were always in his pocket.

Roy yanked a photo album off the shelf closest to the door and flipped through its oversized pages. "I've been meaning to give you something…here it is." He pulled an old black-and-white print from the album. Without another word, he thrust it in Frank's hands.

The photo captured a snarling boxer's right hook the second before it impacted his bloodied and cowed opponent's jaw. Sweat sparkled in the air, suspended forever in time. Cameras flashing in the seats gave the appearance of star bursts hovering over the expectant audience's heads. The boxer's left eye was swollen almost shut from a cut above his brow, yet the ferocity of his expression as he dealt his opponent a vicious final blow was terrifying.

The photographer had labeled the print with a single word: *Malice*. On the back, he'd written the boxer's name: Primo Lambda.

The lower right hand corner of the print revealed three young men dressed like dandies in fancy suits and ties seated in the audience. One of these men was Roy.

Frank pushed the photo toward Roy. "I don't want it. What would make you think I want anything to do with this? You know what my father did."

Roy refused to accept it back. "It's part of your history, boy. And the past has a funny way of coming 'round and demanding attention or payment or penance—whatever it is that you owe—when you're least able to afford it. Best to be prepared."

"My father died in prison two years ago. I doubt he'll be knocking on my door anytime soon. And, for the record, I owe him nothing."

"Maybe. I never told you, but I knew your daddy. Not well, but well enough. He was a brutal man."

Frank's fingers tightened into a fist, crumpling the photo in his grasp. "Wait—what? You knew him? How come you never said anything?"

"I know you don't like talking about him, that's why. I can't blame you." Roy paused. "No matter what happens, I'm not like him. Never was." He patted Frank's cheek. "And neither are you."

Roy herded Frank out the back door and into the

alley. "Now go on. I've got some invoices to finish. Take the subway home. It's getting dark."

"It's not even noon, Roy."

"Doesn't matter." He rooted around his pocket and extracted a shiny subway token, which he pressed into Frank's palm. His fingers, gnarled with age, trembled, and with a firm push to Frank's shoulders, Roy sent him on his way.

Frank stood puzzling over Roy's strange behavior until the lock clicked and the deadbolt slid into place. He knew his boss's health had been failing. Maybe the old man was getting senile. Or, perhaps, as Roy's days dwindled, the threat of his own mortality had triggered the sentimental outburst. It was a side of him Frank had never seen and wasn't sure he understood. Despite long hours spent working side by side, he knew nothing about Roy's life outside the shop. Frank didn't think Roy had one. Apparently, he did once, back when he knew Frank's father.

The alley acted as a wind tunnel for the breeze off the river, and a chilly gust stung his face and urged him to be on his way. A row of green trash bins lined the narrow passage, and the smell of rotting garbage assaulted his nose, further encouraging him to move along. He navigated around teetering piles of cardboard boxes and a maze of metal cans to reach the main street.

He stuffed his hands into the pockets of his thin jacket and hurried down the block to the nearest subway station. He shivered. Tonight, he was breaking out his warmer coat. The sudden change in climate had caught him unaware.

The calendar claimed six more weeks of autumn, but Mother Nature had thrown him a sucker punch.

Winter was hitting early this year, and it was only November fifth.

The worst was yet to come.

Chapter Seven

As soon as Frank left for work, Rauch threw together a plan. He wasn't prone to panic—couldn't say he'd ever panicked in his life—but when he went to delete the texts and photo from his phone, something seemed wrong with the face. It'd taken him two cigarettes to figure it out. The face he'd busted against the concrete patio had a scar on its right cheek. The face in the photograph did not.

He considered what this might mean. The faces—typical Guidos with black wavy hair, brown eyes, and olive skin—were damned close to being identical. Everything might still be okay. Maybe the picture they'd texted him was an old one, taken before the misadventure that had given the target his scar. Or maybe in the dim reflective light of the pool, Rauch had been mistaken and there was no scar.

He crinkled the empty pack of cigarettes and watched it slowly re-expand in his hand. If he had whacked the wrong man, the poor dude had to be a blood relative, probably the target's brother. Not that it made any difference. An easy mistake is still a mistake. And as Frank pointed out, the mob buries mistakes, or more accurately, those who make them.

First he'd do an online search to see if the murder made the news. If it did, he might be lucky enough to find a photo identifying the name of the victim. If not, it was business as usual. He always claimed payment in person, and they never paid low-level associates in advance. Now he knew why.

Rauch slipped his gun into his waistband and walked around the apartment, making sure he'd leave nothing incriminating behind. Despite his tough talk about aiding and abetting, he didn't want to cause Frank any trouble. He considered leaving a note in case he never came back, but what would he say? Live long and prosper? He shook his head and tossed the pen on the kitchen counter.

Upstairs, Mrs. Pagnotto clicked on her television, sending a fervent chorus of amens vibrating through his kitchen ceiling. A televangelist promised salvation and a multitude of blessings for a donation of only twenty dollars. Maybe the preacher man could heal the old bat's deafness. Now *that* was worth twenty bucks.

The clapping gained in intensity as the congregation called upon Jesus in earnest. Their boisterous prayers were his signal to leave. He threw on his weathered leather jacket and jogged down the stairs to the relative quiet of the city street.

Rauch had heard that outside the city you can see the stars glow at night. A guy he knew from juvie, a drug runner who regularly traversed the small towns lining the I-80 corridor between Philly and Pittsburgh, once told him that in the wee hours of the morning, the streets were so quiet, he'd heard crickets chirp and the grass grow.

Rauch wasn't stupid enough to buy the last part, of course, but he'd love to experience the rest, if it were true. In his neighborhood, the quietest time was now—a weekday morning when the good people worked and the bad people slept. The night belonged to gunfire and sirens, not crickets.

He loitered outside his building and typed his target's name and neighborhood into his phone, browsing for news about the murder. Nada. He varied the search every way he knew how, but still came up empty. No news; no photo. He shoved his phone back in his pocket and stared across the street at the bus stop, where a middle-aged man sat with a folded newspaper under his arm. Rauch had never read an honest-to-God paper, but apparently some folks still did. They were still being printed, right? Maybe he'd find something in one of them.

The closest place to get a local newspaper was the convenience store on the corner of Delaware and Columbus, a brisk fifteen-minute walk. He fished around his pockets for money and pulled out a few coins. Forty cents. He had forty cents. Probably not enough to buy a paper. Definitely not enough to buy a pack of smokes. He'd been meaning to quit anyway.

Rauch lowered his chin and raised the collar of his leather jacket so it shielded the bottom half of his face. Except for the sleepy-eyed clerk tapping on his phone, the store was empty, which was not cool since he planned to lift a paper. The more distractions, the better.

He wandered around the store and pretended to scan the rows of snacks before tucking a paper under his arm and darting out the door. The clerk never looked up from his phone. Rauch put some distance between himself and the store, just in case. Most hired help wasn't paid enough to care, but sometimes, if the clerk happened to be the owner…Rauch had never been to prison as an adult, and if he was going to go, it wouldn't be for stealing a stupid newspaper.

Once he reached the safety of his home turf, he leaned against the wall outside Mama Vittone's hole-in-the-wall bakery and flipped through the paper. Online, a single murder rarely made the front page. He doubted it was different in print. The headlines were reserved for more sensational news, like a reality TV star's latest over-the-top fashion statement.

He scanned every page twice but found no mention of his crime. He folded the paper neatly and wiped his inky fingers on his jacket. Behind him, the bakery door cracked open, releasing the tantalizing aromas of toasted almonds and warm sugar. His stomach cramped. No food since the ramen noodles with Frank yesterday. Or was it two days ago? It must've been. Yesterday, he'd been too nervous to eat.

An elderly lady in a tatty wool coat pushed against the door and struggled to balance a box of cookies in one hand and her cane in the other. Rauch finger-brushed his short hair and rushed to help her with the door. "I'll trade you today's paper for a cookie." He dangled the paper in front of her face, knowing its cheap print could never be as enticing as one of Mama's freshly baked amaretti.

The old woman sized him up with the shrewdness of a long-term urban dweller. "Keep your paper. I'll give you the cookie." She opened the box and held it away from her body as if she expected him to snatch the whole thing and run. "Take two; you look like you could use them."

Rauch claimed his two cookies and no more. "Thank you, ma'am."

Her craggy face crinkled into a broad smile.

"You're a nice boy. Your mama must be very proud." She patted his cheek and hobbled down the street.

As far as he knew, his mother was dead. He hadn't heard from her since Children and Youth took him away as a young teen, and he didn't expect to. He was born in the Devil's Pocket, where she used to turn tricks for a local pimp. Before the gentrification, the area was so violent a horrified priest claimed the local children were tough enough to "steal a chain out of the devil's pocket." The name stuck, and Rauch had always strived to live up to the notion.

Now, much to the chagrin of the Italians, the area was an outpost for the city's Irish population, which had previously been confined to the northeastern corner of the city. With the redevelopment, he couldn't afford to buy a beer there, much less live on his old block. Not that he'd want to. He wasn't even sure he could find it anymore.

He crammed both cookies in his mouth at once and used his sleeve to wipe away the bits of almond clinging to his upper lip. Time to face the *capo*. If he had to die, at least he wouldn't die hungry.

He tossed the newspaper in the trash and slogged down the block. Past the neighborhood laundromat, a three-story brick building housed a thrift store run by Catholic Charities, an indoor bocce ball league, and the local chapter of the Sons of Italy. Three businesses, four back doors.

No one entered door number four without an invitation and an escort.

Rauch traversed the tight space between the buildings and entered the rear alley. Door number four loomed at the bottom of six concrete stairs, steeply angled and lacking a handrail to deter visitors. He took a deep breath and descended the narrow stairs sideways. A red dot of light flashed across his ankles, and he spun to face the high-resolution camera he knew was mounted high on the wall of the opposite building. He didn't need to knock. The basement door opened, and Skinny ushered him in.

Skinny stood six-four and packed a solid two-forty into his black nylon track suit.

"How ya doin', Raunchy boy? You packin'?"

Rauch nodded.

"Then you know the drill. Nice and slow now."

Rauch removed his leather jacket and dropped it to the floor. Skinny, too lazy to bend over, stomped over the pockets and kicked it against the wall.

"Hey, take it easy, will ya? That's the only coat I've got." He resisted the urge to rescue his jacket from the floor. Skinny was right; he knew the drill. They weren't done yet, and any sudden movements on his part might result in a couple of broken ribs. He rotated in place so Skinny could inspect the gun crammed in his waistband.

Skinny claimed Rauch's weapon and emptied it of its bullets. He cocked his head toward the coat, and Rauch snatched it off the floor, brushing away Skinny's footprints with his palm.

The room was more of a foyer, a dark square of a holding cell. A second, heavier door with a round peephole stood across from the first. Beside the door was a metal box with a card reader. Skinny removed a lanyard from around his neck and swiped the attached card. The box opened to reveal a fingerprint scanner. He placed one stubby finger on the screen, and the lock on the door clicked.

Skinny hung the lanyard around his neck and held the door open so his guest could pass. Ever since they'd first met, Rauch had fantasized about strangling the bastard with his ugly orange lanyard. And Rauch was not a violent man. At least, not as violent as Skinny. He'd once witnessed Skinny pulverize a poor schmuck with a pipe wrench for allegedly disrespecting the boss. Rauch had never been hit in the face with a pipe wrench before, but he'd been whacked with a ratchet, and that was pretty much the same thing. Either will break your nose on the first try. Subsequent blows were for the assailant's amusement.

"We've got a special surprise for you today, Raunchy boy."

Rauch's stomach dropped, and he fought to appear nonchalant. "I hope it has sprinkles. I only like surprises if they have sprinkles on top."

Skinny's high-pitched giggle raised the hairs on Rauch's neck. With a laugh like that, he must've been bullied as a kid. No wonder he'd over-compensated.

Rauch shuffled into the room and blinked. No matter how many times he walked through that security door, he still gaped at the unexpected opulence of what should be a moldy basement with a dirt floor. Instead, cherry paneling lined the walls. Soft, recessed lighting and a patterned Oriental rug brightened the room. A massive sectional leather sofa faced a magnificently carved desk worthy of a king. And this wasn't even the boss's—the don's—primary office. This annex was usually staffed by the under-boss or a trusted *capo*—a captain—who himself managed a squad of soldiers and associates.

All of Rauch's dealings with the Italian mob from his early teenage years to the present had been with an ever-changing group of *capos*. For unspoken reasons, the turnover rate was high, and usually the only face Rauch found familiar was Skinny's. He'd never met the big boss, the don of Philadelphia's entire theater of operations. An associate like himself, someone not of Italian lineage who was considered to be at most a contractor, was typically not given such an honor. Today was his unlucky day.

The don remained seated behind his mahogany desk as Skinny and his guest entered the room. "Step closer, Mister…" He looked to the underling seated to his right for assistance.

"Rauch," the man whispered. "Just Rauch." He licked his lips and glanced at Rauch. Their eyes met, and Rauch knew they were in trouble.

Big Mike, the local *capo*, was an asshole of the highest order—a cocky son of a bitch too lazy to do his own dirty work and too cheap to pay his soldiers what they were worth. That's why he'd hired Rauch. And right now, Big Mike looked like he was about to either crap his pants or cry. Maybe both.

The don waved toward a posh velvet chair across from his desk. "If you please, Mr. Rauch."

Rauch took a seat.

"Would you like a drink? Some wine, perhaps? We have a nice bottle of Nebbiolo already opened. It'd be a shame to see such a fine vintage go to waste. A bottle of wine is like a family secret. Once you expose it to the air, it turns dirty." The don smiled, revealing a set of perfect teeth. They glowed impossibly white against his smooth olive skin.

Rauch's mind raced for the appropriate response. He didn't give two shits about wine, and what he knew about it could balance atop the don's huge diamond ring. Yes or no?

"Yes, sir. Thank you."

The don appeared pleased. Rauch's shoulders sagged with relief. Skinny poured him a glass and with a smirk, shoved it in his trembling hand. As Skinny leaned over, the lanyard around his thick neck dangled in front of Rauch's nose. He curled his fingers around the glass's delicate stem to keep from grabbing the orange cord and giving it a twist. That would not go over well with the don, for sure.

Rauch made a show of swirling the wine in its glass and lifted it to his nose like he'd seen the fancy pants do on TV.

The don raised his own glass in a toast. "*Cin cin.*"

The burgundy liquid touched Rauch's lips, and he raised his eyebrows. It was good. Earthy and tart, not too sweet…he'd based his entire opinion of wine on the cheap stuff he'd guzzled out of a paper bag to get drunk. It beat sniffing glue, but he'd never really enjoyed the taste. Now he understood why the rich drank it for pleasure.

The don watched his reaction with a keen interest. "You like it?"

Rauch nodded.

"Good. I like a man who appreciates nice things. I expect our friends to conduct themselves with class."

He finished his own glass, and Skinny, moving faster than Rauch thought possible for a man of his size, refilled it. "Mikey here—" The don waved his bling at the fidgeting *capo*. "—Mikey tells me you've been doing fine work, really fine work, for us for years. Is that so?"

"Yes, sir. I mean, yes, I've been running small errands for years. As far as the quality of my work—"

"No need to be humble. Mikey trusted you enough to give you a job he should've assigned to a soldier. A soldier is a made man, Mr. Rauch. Do you know what it takes to be a made man?"

Rauch shook his head. Despite its fine furnishings, the basement remained musty. The dank air hung heavy with an unpleasant blend of Skinny's cheap cologne, body odor, and fear.

"To be a made man, you need to be Italian. You need to take an oath, the oath of *omertá*. But most importantly, you need to commit or witness a hit in the presence of another member of our Family. That way, both parties share the secret or else they'll both go to jail. Then, and only then, do you become a soldier, like Vito." He pointed to the burly bodyguard hovering over his shoulder. "Make sense?"

Rauch nodded. Vito sauntered from the don's side to loom threateningly over Big Mike in his chair. The *capo* choked on a sob, and for a split second, Rauch felt sorry for the lazy bastard. The second passed quickly, and he raised a palm to wipe his damp brow. Whether from the wine or his overwhelming sense of impending doom, his stomach churned with nausea, and his forehead beaded with sweat. He didn't want to be educated on the ways of the Family. He liked being ignorant. The more secrets he knew, the more likely they were to kill him.

"You never whacked anyone before last night?"

"No, sir."

"See, that was Mikey's mistake. I know you've been doing good work, Mr. Rauch, and I can see you needed the money, but Mikey should've never hired an unmade man to do a soldier's job."

The don pushed a button on his desk, and a section of the paneling slid open to reveal a hidden room. Skinny grabbed Mikey by the collar and hauled him to his feet.

"Please." Mikey's knee buckled, and a sob gurgled low in his throat. "I wasn't the one who killed the wrong guy. It was him."

Vito helped Skinny drag him through the door. Rauch caught a glimpse of a stained concrete floor with a drain in the middle before the paneling slid shut. The three men disappeared from sight. The wall, he soon discovered, wasn't soundproof.

The don pointed to Rauch's half-empty glass. "Finish your wine."

"I killed the wrong man. I killed a man for nothing." Though Rauch's gut had already told him as much, the confirmation sickened him more than he expected.

A blood-curdling scream exploded through the wall, adding to his queasiness. He tossed back the last swallow of cherry-red wine and prayed it would stay down. His chair sat in the center of the plush Oriental carpet, and it sure looked expensive.

"The target was out of town. His wife was not. You killed his brother, with whom she was having an affair. You did him a favor. Now, you'll do one for me."

Rauch stared at the colorful rug and focused on his breathing. His shoulders heaved.

The don rescued the crystal goblet from Rauch's

fingers before it hit the ground. "Careful, now. I'd hate to ruin the set." He placed the glass on his desk before returning to his fine leather chair. "No need to worry, Mr. Rauch. The target's being investigated for the murder, and my sources tell me he doesn't have an alibi. With such strong motive and a sprinkle of money here and there, he'll end up in jail. After that, he'll be dead within weeks. All's well that ends well, or so they say."

Another agonizing scream echoed through the room. The wine glass shuddered on the desk. Rauch cringed. He stood, placing a hand on the back of his chair for support. "Thank you for your understanding, sir. Can I...may I go?"

"Not quite yet. About that favor..."

The don hit the button on his desk a second time, and the paneled door slid open. Vito and Skinny stood in the corner washing their hairy arms and hands at a giant cast-iron sink. Big Mike lay dead on the floor. He looked a whole lot smaller with a couple of pieces missing. Bile rose in Rauch's throat. He swallowed compulsively, willing himself not to vomit.

The don interlaced his fingers. "I received a phone call today, an anonymous tip that another of our long-term associates is a mole. Turns out it's true. Working for the Irish, no less. Betraying the Family is punishable by death. *Capisce?*"

Rauch nodded.

"Mikey had faith in you, but he was careless. He gave you bad information." The don pushed an unmarked manila folder across the desk. "Open it."

Once opened, the file contained two black-and-white photos. One was a storefront. The other was its owner. "You know him?"

Rauch nodded and looked away. "Not very well, though."

"Good. That makes it easier. You help us with this, I bend the rules and make you a soldier."

I don't wanna be your goddamned soldier. Rauch's mind floundered, looking for an excuse, a way out, and found none.

His hesitation lasted too long. Skinny placed a hand the size of an ape's on his shoulder and squeezed until it hurt. He reeked of blood and soap.

Refuse. All you have to do is say no, and he'll kill you now and get it over with. Rauch gritted his teeth and blurted out the first thing that came to mind. "Did you scrub under your fingernails?"

The don laughed and Vito laughed. Then Skinny laughed.

The don waved him to the exit. "Skinny will know what to do. You have until midnight tonight."

Chapter Eight

Due to the off-hour, the subway station was quiet. A mumbling panhandler teetered dangerously close to the edge of the platform. A busker wearing a mysterious smile played his violin, the sweet strains swelling to fill the subterranean chamber. A businessman in a shiny black suit avoided them both. When the doors to the car opened, Frank climbed aboard and found himself alone. Another November the fifth anomaly.

As the train zipped south under Broad Street, he stretched out his legs and debated how to spend the rest of his free afternoon. His eyelids grew heavy from too many late nights and the gentle sway of the train. He should catch up on his sleep, as Roy had suggested. But Rauch's predicament and his boss's bizarre behavior had left him too uneasy to rest.

He'd texted Rauch while waiting for the train to arrive and checked his phone every five minutes thereafter, hoping for a response. So far, nothing.

Frank had fallen into a routine of bickering with Rauch, then working at Baum's, and patrolling his neighborhood as Lambda Man. But along with the sudden drop in temperature, the pattern had changed overnight. A faint disquiet hung in the polluted air, as gray as the city sky. Though Frank sensed its hazy presence, he had no idea what it meant.

He exited the subway a block from his apartment. A Porsche parked outside his building caught his attention. His lips pursed in a silent whistle. He circled the car, crouching to admire the sensuous lines of the curved, iridescent purple hood at eye level. Not something you see every day. Not in his neighborhood, anyway. Too flashy for the mob. Its owner was lucky it hadn't been jacked. For a prize like that, the local criminals might risk a midday heist.

He snapped a picture and texted it to Rauch.

—*Looks like we're moving up in the world, huh*?

After the long climb to the top of the stairs, he paused to check his phone. No response to this or any of his earlier texts. His heart, already racing from exertion, fluttered with anxiety. Rauch typically spent most of the daylight hours napping and playing video games. Whatever his errands were, they began at dusk. The ongoing silence was alarming.

Frank entered the apartment on autopilot, tossing his keys over the sofa and onto the plastic bin of a coffee table. His leather mask muffled their fall. He froze, eyes fixed on the mask. He always kept Lambda Man locked in the bedroom closet. All senses went to red alert. Some foreign odor, clean and faintly salty, tickled his nose. He backpedaled toward the door and without turning around, groped for the knob.

Keira, carrying his cape in one hand and knee pads in the other, strolled out of his bedroom. "Hello, Frank. Don't look so surprised. I told you we'd meet again."

Frank blinked, mouth agape. "I…I didn't think that meant later today." He clenched the doorknob. "How'd you get in here?"

"I used high-powered suction cups to scale the

building, then a laser mounted on my ring to cut through the window."

He glanced at the window's intact glass, and she laughed. "Made you look. I picked the lock, silly. Sorry—Lambda." She traced the Greek symbol on the front of his cape with a shiny violet fingernail.

"Lambda *Man*."

"Of course. My bad. You couldn't have picked a prettier color than slime green?"

Frank scowled. "It's not supposed to be pretty. It's supposed to be intimidating, like a glowing radioactive beacon." He moved to pry the cape from her grasp but she scampered over the sofa and out of reach.

She held it high in the air. "You know capes are highly impractical. They get snagged on everything. It's Superheroes, 101."

"I like it, okay?"

He rounded the sofa to confront her face-to-face. An awkward standoff ensued. Awkward for him, at least. Keira didn't appear uncomfortable at all. She tossed his knee pads next to the mask. "Manners, Frank. Why don't you invite me to sit down?"

"You're standing in the middle of my apartment, fondling my stuff. You don't seem to be the sort of girl who needs an invitation." He snatched his cape out of her fingers and folded it into a neat square

She arched one brow. "A fair assessment, with one major correction. I'm a woman, not a girl. Just like you're Lambda Man and not Lambda Boy. Words matter, Frank. It's a respect thing."

"Awesome. Won't you please sit down, Keira-woman-who-broke-into-my-crib, and tell me what it is that you want? And while we're at it, would you like a nice cup of tea?"

"I prefer Tieguanyin oolong." She grinned. "Do you have any?"

"Hell, no."

"Then I'll graciously decline."

Keira perched on the corner of the threadbare sofa before folding her hands in her lap. "I'm here to recruit you."

"I already have a job, and Roy's a good boss."

Her eyes narrowed. "I'm sure he is. I meant for this." She scooped the mask off the coffee table. "I'm recruiting Lambda Man."

What was this chick's game?

An explanation dawned, and he nodded his head. Of course. "Okay. I get it. This whole thing's a Guido Fawkes's Day joke. What did Rauch do—give you his key?" Rauch was the only person on the planet who knew about both Lambda Man and Frank's fifth of November curse.

Keira's smile faltered. "Who's Rauch? You mean your roommate?"

"Oh, you're good, lady. Like Black Widow good." Frank pulled out his phone and texted Rauch a fourth time.

—Game over, buddy. I'm on to her. Good one—

"This is not a joke, Frank. I recruit wannabe heroes, cosplayers like you, and train them for special missions."

"And let me guess—you find these recruits by hanging around comic book stores."

"Absolutely. And word of mouth, of course. There aren't as many of you running around as you'd think. Not ones who truly want to help humanity and believe in the hero ideals. Most just want to show off their costumes and get laid." Wide-eyed and earnest, Keira leaned forward in her seat, causing the sofa to groan. "I've been watching Lambda Man for weeks. He'd be a perfect addition to this year's class. Room and board are included."

"Oh, come on. Do I look like a sucker to you?"

"You dance around in hockey pants and a puke-green cape. Do you really want an answer? Or would you rather learn some skills to back up that suit?"

Frank snickered and shook his head. "You're unreal. Thanks, but no thanks. I told you—I already have a job, and at least I know Roy is sane." He held the door open and gestured for her to leave.

Keira rose and pulled a business card from one of her pea coat's many pockets. She stuffed it in his hand on her way out the door. "In case you change your mind. Job security isn't what it used to be." She paused at the top of the stairs. "I'll be awaiting your call."

Frank locked the door behind her and ran to the window, watching for her to exit the building. With a toss of her glossy purple hair, she sauntered to the Porsche, looked up at the window, and waved as she slid behind the wheel.

Heart pounding, Frank ducked behind the curtain until the sexy coupe purred away. He stood there a long time, trying to make sense of the last twelve hours, which, even by November the fifth standards, had been radically insane.

Keira's business card had fluttered to the floor during his mad scramble behind the curtain. He retrieved it, holding it by two fingers as if the ink might be toxic to the touch. The thick card's glossy finish glowed the same shade of purple as her hair.

A lone telephone number graced one side. On the other, centered and typed in bold green font, were two words: Heroes2B, Inc.

Chapter Nine

Every time Rauch's phone buzzed with a text, Skinny took his eyes off the road, barely missing two garbage cans, one cat, and a stepladder that fell off a utility truck. "Who the fuck keeps texting you?"

"How should I know? You told me not to touch my phone until after the job is done. Something about breaking my fingers if I do—"

"Turn it off."

With a theatrical sigh, Rauch pulled the phone from his pocket. He stole a glance at the screen before powering it off. "It's my boyfriend, and no, no matter what you say, I'm not sharing."

Skinny came within inches of sideswiping a minivan. "Are you shittin' me?"

Rauch shrugged. "Does it matter?"

"Shoulda known you was one of those goddamned faggots."

"Better keep your distance, then. It's contagious."

Skinny muttered something in Italian, then clicked on the sound system. Dean Martin crooned a boozy tune to which he added his own off-pitch falsetto.

Rauch winced. "Are we going to discuss the plan?"

"Shut up. I'll tell you when we get there." The city bus in front of them slowed to a halt at its designated stop, and Skinny laid on the horn.

Rauch slumped into the supple leather seat and

stared out the tinted windows at the Delaware River. The choppy waters reflected the cloudy gray sky. As a child, he used to dream of escaping the Devil's Pocket by swimming across the river to freedom. That was before he knew it led to Jersey.

The roadster slowed as they approached the target's address. Skinny surveyed the area with an expert eye. "Where's the best place to park?"

"Depends on whether you're planning to go in the front or the back."

"We go in the front door, nice and regular."

"You know it's the middle of the afternoon? Like, broad daylight? The store's probably crawling with customers, not to mention the regular employees."

Like Frank.

"Thanks for the heads up, chicken shit. Here's lesson number one: Soldiers got class. No skulking around in the shadows for us. Got it?"

Rauch eyed Skinny's nylon track suit and bright orange lanyard. "Class. Sure. Got it."

"Good."

Skinny eased the car to the curb and removed his lanyard. "Lesson number two: You can't just kill them snitches. You gotta work 'em over first. They need to be made examples of. Keeps all the other potential snitches from, you know, snitching."

Rauch's throat tightened. "What about the people in the store?"

"We'll see. The boss don't like us hurting women and children." Skinny heaved himself from the car. "All righty, Raunchy boy. Tighten your nuts. It's showtime."

****

Closed.

The sign on the door to Baum's Books read closed. Rauch blinked, hoping the lettering would miraculously change. If not, he was dead for sure. But at least there was a chance Frank had gone home.

Skinny's face flushed a deep red, and his huge hands balled into fists. "You said he'd be here."

"He should be. The store's always open this time of day." Rauch pointed to another sign in the storefront's picture window. "See? The hours are posted right here."

"You tipped him off."

"How could I? I've been with you the entire time since we left the don."

They pressed their faces to the glass and peered into the dark store. A glimmer of light shone around the velvet curtain hanging behind the counter. Rauch stepped away from the window. "The owner's in the back room. He must've closed early for some reason. Maybe a pipe broke or something." He glanced longingly at his phone, wishing he could sneak a peek at Frank's texts.

Rauch wasn't the praying type, but if he knew for sure that dropping to his knees right there and then would guarantee Frank's safety, he'd do it without hesitation. Roy was the mole, the don's target. Killing an old man was bad enough, but if Frank were present, he'd be a witness in need of silencing, collateral damage to the likes of Skinny. And Rauch would have to intervene. Then things would get really ugly. Rauch had already had enough ugliness to last a lifetime.

Skinny's hot breath left a crescent of steam on the window. "You said you know the code for the security system to the back door, right?"

"Yeah, but I don't have a key to open the door. It's not a keyless entry."

"You'll think of something."

They rounded the building. Past a row of foul-smelling trash cans, they found the windowless service entrance. The steel door had a keypad to its right.

"Well?" Skinny, his hand clenched on the door's handle, cocked his head toward the key pad. "Do your thing, Raunchy boy."

Rauch hesitated. If Frank's code was unique, using it would implicate him in his boss's murder. "I told you—I don't have a key. Deactivating the alarm doesn't do shit to help us if the door stays locked. I'm just gonna knock and hope he lets me in. He knows me."

"Yeah, but how much does he trust you?"

"About as much as you do."

Skinny chortled.

Rauch pounded on the door. "Frank, hey Frank. It's Rauch. I need to talk to you. It's important. Open up."

Skinny shot him a look. "His name is Roy, you goon."

"I know. Frank's one of his employees. He's the one who gave me the code." Rauch stuffed his hands in his pockets and waited.

No response.

Skinny jiggled the handle, and the door popped open. He raised his unibrow at Rauch, who shrugged. The alarm stayed silent. Skinny pulled his gun, yanked the door open wide, and shoved Rauch into the narrow passage between the pair of dusty shelves lining the entrance. They thundered into the room together.

Roy sat napping on a chair upholstered in cheap

red vinyl. His back faced the door, and his head lolled over a cluttered desk strewn with papers. He didn't so much as twitch at their approach.

"Deaf and dumb," Skinny whispered with a grin. "Wait 'til he gets a load of us. Watch this, Raunchy boy."

"Skinny, wait. I smell—"

Skinny crept behind the chair and smacked Roy's cheeks between his huge palms, like an organ grinder monkey clapping a pair of cymbals.

Roy tipped sideways, taking the chair with him. He landed on the floor with a sickening thud. Skinny used his foot to roll Roy away from the fallen chair and onto his back. A shower of blood clots splattered off Roy's sopping white shirt and into the air. They rained to the ground in a fine red mist and slithered across the floor like tiny amoebas.

Skinny jumped backward. "Jesus fucking Christ."

Roy had been gutted from stem to stern.

The air reeked of blood and feces. Rauch clung to the corner of the desk for support and gagged until tears streamed down his cheeks. The room spun, and he hunched over, his vision narrowing to a blurry white blotch on the wide-plank floor. He blinked his watery eyes, fighting to regain control. When his focus returned, the white blotch on the floor became an envelope.

The letter had been sealed with green wax embossed with a single mark: λ. Rauch recognized it from Frank's costume, which had the same symbol stamped on its chest. From the letter's position, partially tucked beneath the edge of the desk, the envelope appeared to have fluttered out of Roy's fingers, perhaps when he was attacked.

Rauch dropped to one knee and forced himself to emit a series of loud and disgusting retches. Skinny looked away. Rauch slid the envelope from under the desk and crammed it in the inner pocket of his leather jacket. Whatever it was, it was meant for Frank.

He rose to his feet and noticed an open pill bottle tipped on its side lying on the desk. He pulled his shirt sleeve over his fingers and grabbed the bottle for closer inspection. The label had been meticulously peeled away, and the bottle was empty. "Skinny, look at this." Rauch held the bottle to the dim light.

"Shut up. I'm trying to think here. Between the stink and you yammering…" Skinny ran a hand over his greasy hair. "The old guy took medicine. Big effin' deal. Someone beat us to our mark, and you're worried about kyping some oxy?" He scanned the floor. "There—I thought so. You see that? Next to his left hand." He pointed to a blood-spattered playing card inches from Roy's fingertips.

"Jack of clubs. So what?"

"It's Jack McConnell's calling card. He's the new boss of the Irish mob, but even before that, when he was just mob royalty, he liked doing his own hits. Always leaves a card. It's his way of saying he's untouchable. I guess Jack didn't like the old man playing with us Italians any more than we liked him dealing with the Irish."

Skinny snatched an invoice off Roy's desk and slid the card onto the stiff paper, which he folded like an envelope. His forehead beaded with sweat. He pulled out his phone and snapped a few photos of Roy's intestines while Rauch averted his eyes. "C'mon, let's scram. You didn't touch anything, did ya?"

Rauch placed the pill bottle back on the desk.

Skinny made a move toward the door, then stopped and looked over his shoulder at the floor. "Don't step in any of that muck. You'll leave footprints."

"I wasn't planning on it."

They hustled out the door and wiped the handle clean. Skinny tossed the paper with the bloody card in the nearest garbage can on their path down the alley.

Back in the car, Skinny slipped the ugly orange lanyard over his thick neck. He pushed Rauch's knee aside to root around in the glovebox. "You smell like blood and shit. If you tracked anything into this car, so help me God, I'll pop ya." He removed a business-sized envelope. The red sealing wax bore the personal imprint of the don himself.

He handed it to Rauch. "Open it."

"What's in it?"

Skinny furrowed his unibrow, and Rauch decided against asking further questions. He cracked the seal and opened the envelope. It was stuffed with banded packs of hundred-dollar bills. "Ten large," Skinny said, when Rauch began to count. "It's your payment for the two hits."

"But—"

"Listen carefully. This is how it's gonna work. As far as the boss knows, we killed Roy Baum, not the Irish. Otherwise, you don't get paid, and more importantly, I don't get paid. The other option is I blow your head off and keep all the dough for myself. But then I'd have a lot of explaining to do, questions to answer, not to mention the clean-up. It's easier if we keep this between you and me. You with me?"

"Absolutely. I am absolutely with you, Skinny. For ten grand, I'll even buy you a new lanyard."

Skinny laughed and slapped Rauch on the back so hard he almost hit his head on the windshield. "What's the matter with my lanyard? You've got no class. C'mon, I'll drive you home."

"I'll walk, thanks. I could use some fresh air."

Skinny sniffed and lowered the car's tinted windows. "Now that you mention it, so could I, Raunchy boy. So could I."

Chapter Ten

Frank finished his crime-fighting prep in front of a cracked bathroom mirror and vanity lights that flickered in time to the theme from *Rocky*. His mood soared with the pounding rhythm. He stretched his sore, bruised muscles and shimmied away the stress of the day, swishing his neon green cape like a bullfighter. Smoke bombs—check. Taser—check. Knee pads—he'd put them on before heading out. They chafed.

His usual hobbies had failed to distract him from crazy Keira's bizarre offer and Rauch's ongoing absence. Video games, a Netflix binge, the graphic novel he'd been doodling on for years and would probably never finish—nothing had worked. By early evening, he was as jittery as a meth head. His streets, where vigilance was paramount to survival and distraction equaled death, beckoned. And, as Roy had said, it was getting darker earlier these days.

He boogied from the bathroom to the living room, clicked off the music, and bounded down the stairs like an exuberant puppy. First, he'd check on Julia. Then he'd patrol what he considered to be his home turf, which spanned ten city blocks in the cardinal directions. That should be enough to keep his feet moving and his mind occupied.

He strutted down the street, receiving more attention than usual due to the earlier hour. The strange looks and occasional profane sexual slur no longer bothered him. Most came from outsiders passing through on their way to the sports arenas or other venues. The locals knew and tolerated him. A few, like Julia, truly appreciated him.

Once, shortly after he'd donned his shiny new costume for the first time, he'd even been asked to pose for a selfie with a tourist. Dude claimed he was from the planet Dural and liked the costume's shade of green. Go figure. But Frank was happy to oblige.

His footsteps slowed as he approached Julia's corner, which was vacant. He frowned. What day of the week was it? Thursday? Friday? Julia usually tried to catch the rush hour commuters on their way home after a long, emasculating week of work. Easy pickings.

She lived in an apartment above her corner. He entered the tenement through its creaky front door and paused at the base of the stairs. The elevator was perpetually broken, and Frank wouldn't have trusted it even if it weren't. The entire building was held together by duct tape and the prayers of its tenants.

He gazed up the stairwell. High above, a bare bulb flickered, causing the graffitied walls to play out their painted scenes like the jerky reel of an old polychrome movie. His chest tightened with anxiety. Frank hated movie theaters. He averted his eyes and plodded upward.

Each floor reeked with a different combination of the same foul odors. Stale beer. Weed. Dirty diapers. Body odor. When he reached the sixth floor, a sudden outburst from apartment 6B made him cringe. Angry words preceded a baby's wail and the sound of a woman weeping. The building exemplified his childhood in one ugly, giant block of concrete. But he only had one more flight to go. He gritted his teeth and carried on.

He knocked on Julia's door. Nothing. He knocked again. "Julia, it's me, Fr—Lambda Man. I missed you downstairs. Just checking to make sure you're okay."

A faint rustling preceded the scraping of metal against metal as the deadbolt turned. The door creaked open, and he winced. "Oh my God. What happened?"

With a fearful peep behind the door, she ushered him into the dark room. A few stray beams of sunlight peeked around the tightly drawn curtains, enough for Frank to assess the spare but tidy room. They were alone.

Julia cranked the door's lock and clicked on the floor lamp beside the couch. Frank gasped as the harsh yellow light brought the full extent of her sickening injuries into view.

Her lower lip was split and swollen twice its normal size. The area around her left eyelid glowed a deep purple, and her neck wore a choker of fingertip-sized bruises. Streaks of black mascara painted her damp cheeks.

"Who did this to you?" Frank's voice quivered with horror and another emotion to which he was less accustomed. Rage.

Julia raised her fingertips to her mouth and choked back a sob. She blinked rapidly in an unsuccessful bid to prevent further tears. Her knees collapsed, and Frank caught her, cradling her head against his chest until the sobbing ceased.

"I'm sorry." She sniffled and swiped the tears from her cheeks, further polluting her face with mascara.

"I...I stained your shirt."

"Julia, it's okay. Forget the shirt. Tell me what happened."

She snatched a tissue from the kitchen counter and twisted it between her fingers. "There's these three guys—I don't know their names, but I've seen them hanging around the block off and on for about a month now. They've got tattoos covering their necks. I don't recognize the symbols, but I'm sure they're part of a gang trying to muscle into new territory."

She paused and took a steadying breath. "You should've seen...you should've..." Her face contorted with pain, and she buried her cheeks in her palms as she broke down a second time. She managed to wail out the words between sobs. "You should've seen what they did to Carmine."

"Carmine?"

"He was drunk, and he got mouthy. You know how he is. They killed him. Kicked the shit out of him right in front of me. This—" She pointed to her battered face. "This was my warning. I'm lucky. They could've done worse. The other girls have told me stories."

While Julia sobbed, Frank's anger grew. It grew like a dying star, a supernova of hate, swelling until it reached critical mass, then collapsing on itself to form a cold, hard core of determination deep in his chest. "Do you know how I can find these guys?"

Julia's crying stopped all at once. "Lambda Man, no. These are hard-core gang bangers. They'll set you on fire and laugh while you burn."

"They need to be taught a lesson, Julia. Not here. Not on my streets. Not to my people."

"I won't tell you anything."

"I'll follow the trail of blood, then." He touched her cheek and let himself out of the apartment. "Lock the door behind me."

"Be careful, Frank. Please."

He was three flights down when he realized she'd called him by his real name.

****

Frank heard them from half a block away, cussing and bragging about the wino they'd stomped for shits and grins. He ducked into an alley and watched as they swaggered past a boarded-up liquor store. The tallest guzzled from a cheap bottle of wine Frank assumed had been Carmine's.

They had dark hair and wore a tangle of gold chains around each of their thick tatted necks, but their accents indicated they weren't Italian. Which meant they were stupid. Everyone knew this quadrant of South Philadelphia belonged to the Family. They wouldn't last long no matter what he did or didn't do. But Carmine and Julia deserved vengeance.

An idea formed. Frank opened the pouches on his leather belt and removed a flash bomb, a smoke bomb, and a lighter. Next, he detached his Taser and set it to max. He pressed his spine against the cold brick wall and exhaled.

One. Two. Three. He poked his head and arm around the corner and threw the flash bomb first. It exploded in a burst of blinding light. A flurry of gunshots spewed blindly into the street. He tossed the smoke bomb before they could reload. As he'd hoped would happen, the disoriented gang bangers stumbled in his direction, retracing their steps in a blind retreat. Hugging the wall, Frank crouched in the alley's dark shadows with his stun gun's cartridge locked and loaded. The trio staggered past, hacking and wheezing from the thick, acrid smoke.

The dart flew. The thug closest to Frank twitched and hit the ground. His friends hesitated. Lambda Man stepped from the alley, and their bloodshot eyes widened. The burliest of the two readied his gun.

Frank pressed one boot on their fallen friend's neck and lowered his voice to his best Batman rasp. "His name was Carmine, and he was my friend."

Flashing blue and red lights lit up the street. The burly one stuffed his gun into the waistband of his saggy jeans, and the two men turned and fled.

Lambda Man dragged his helpless prey into the alley. He detached a lint roller from his belt and rapidly rolled it over the sidewalk, removing the bright yellow confetti discharged by his Taser. The tiny scraps bore the serial number of his device, rendering it traceable. The police didn't appreciate vigilantes, but thus far, the local precinct had turned a blind eye. Frank wanted to keep it that way.

Satisfied he'd covered his tracks, Frank propped the quivering thug against a filthy metal garbage bin. Wild-eyed, he struggled to focus as Frank thrust his masked face inches from his own. "You tell the others if Lambda Man ever sees their ugly mugs in South Philly again, there will be no mercy. Understood?"

The thug gurgled. A stream of drool trickled from the corner of his lips. Frank took that as a yes.

A police radio crackled, and Frank peeked around the alley's corner. Two officers approached. With his green cape fluttering behind him, he bolted down the dark alley, praying it wasn't gated or worse yet, a dead end. A pile of flattened cardboard boxes obstructed the exit. He bounded over the top, fell, and rolled down the heap. Fur brushed his face as squealing rats scurried from the corrugated mound and scampered to safety. His boots landed on a glass bottle which shattered underfoot. He was besieged by the stench of garbage and cheap gin.

He ran until the cold air made him wheeze, and he could run no more. A block from his apartment, he hunched over to catch his breath. He'd done it. Lambda Man had done it. Rah-cha-cha. If he weren't so winded, he'd dance the rest of the way home. Tomorrow evening he would pay Linda, Carmine's widow, a visit and console her, as he had Julia. But for tonight, Lambda Man needed a bath and a good night's rest.

He'd earned it.

Chapter Eleven

Rauch walked with his bare hands in his pockets and his head down against the bitter wind. Every now and then, he stopped to pat the envelope of cash in his left inside pocket to make sure it was still there. His eyes scanned his path, watching for suspicious characters. He'd never been mugged in his life—at least not successfully. Watch today be the day. Hopefully Frank's November fifth curse wasn't contagious.

Behind the wad of cash, Roy's letter sat closest to Rauch's heart. The embossed seal rubbed over his ribs, irritating him through the thin fabric of his shirt. It nagged him enough to warrant a stop at the liquor store on his way home. He'd figure out what to tell Frank over a nice bottle of—what had the don called it— Nebbiolo.

He plunked the bottle in front of the register. The clerk at the state store had seen him often enough to be surprised by his purchase. She raised her overly tweezed brows and bagged the wine with a supercilious grin. "That'll be ninety dollars." She crossed her arms as if expecting him to protest.

He handed her a C-note. "Keep the change."

"I'm…I'm not allowed." She glanced over her shoulder at the security camera mounted in the corner. "We're run by the state, you know."

Rauch grabbed the brown bag off the counter.

"Keep it anyway." He sauntered out the door.

Rush hour traffic in the city is a bitch, even for pedestrians. By the time he made it to the apartment, the sun hung low over the river, and the light had begun to fade. Rauch stood in the stairwell and debated cracking open the wine, but a quick peek in the bag put the kibosh on his plan. No screw top for Nebbiolo; this bottle had a real cork. He'd have to face Frank without the benefit of alcoholic fortification. Maybe, despite Frank's prior texts, he wouldn't be home. It would only delay the inevitable, but at least it would give Rauch time to consider his options.

To say nothing about today's events was the easy way out. Frank would discover Roy's mutilated body tomorrow at work, and Rauch wouldn't even be part of the equation. But how would he explain Roy's letter? He'd have to throw it away, unopened and unread.

Or he could tell Frank the truth and spare him tomorrow's horrific surprise. *Your boss was a mobster, and now he's dead, and oh, by the way, I'd planned to whack him myself. But great news—I didn't have to. The Irish did it for me. Now have some wine.*

Neither option appealed. Clenching the door key in his hand, he made one firm decision. He couldn't throw Roy's letter away. A dead man's last words—there's something sacred in that, an unspoken rule which states he who is privy to the message must ensure its delivery. It played out in the death scenes of every movie Rauch had seen and loved. Even Darth Vader had gotten into the act. *Whoosh. Tell your sister. Whoosh. You were right. Whoosh.*

Even if Frank hated him for the rest of their lives, Rauch had to deliver Roy's letter. He hoped it was worth it.

****

The apartment was empty when Rauch entered, granting him the reprieve he craved. He centered the bottle of wine on the coffee table next to a business card in a God-awful shade of purple. Heroes2B, Inc. He flipped the card over in his hand and frowned. The phone number was unfamiliar. He'd visited Baum's Books at least a dozen times over the years with Frank, and he'd never seen either Roy or Frank handing out cards. Strange.

He stared at the kelly green print and removed Roy's letter from his coat pocket. Coincidence, maybe, but the tint of the lettering on the card exactly matched the wax seal on the letter, and they both appeared to be made of quality paper, which was not Roy's MO. Rauch had never known cheap, ol' Roy to spend good money on anything except books and comics.

Heavy boots trudged up the stairs, and he stiffened, tucking the letter in his pocket behind the envelope of cash. The apartment was secured by a half-dozen locks, not that they mattered. The laminate door was as thin as the ceiling. Sound carried, and anyone could kick it in.

He relaxed when Frank cursed under his breath and fumbled with the locks. Rauch shook his head. The man carried a Taser, yet he could barely handle his keys. The final lock clicked, and the door flew open. Frank tumbled into the room.

Rauch waved at the unopened bottle of wine. "Ta-da. Now tell me we own a corkscrew."

****

Frank slammed the door and rounded the couch. "Where the hell've you been? I messaged you all damned day. I thought they'd killed you, Rauch. Sealed you in an oil drum and tossed you in the Delaware River."

"Surprise. I'm still alive. I texted you back about an hour ago." Rauch sniffed. "Jesus, man. You stink like garbage."

"Yeah? You smell like shit, so we're even. If you'd had the screwy day I've had, you'd understand. It was weird and then even weirder and then sad and then fantastic. You're not going to believe what I did. I wish you would've been there. That's why I missed your text. I was busy saving the day." Frank paused to take a breath and survey his friend's somber face. Rauch looked twice his age and tired.

Rauch nodded at the coffee table. "Who's the card from, Frank?"

"That was one of the weird things. This ultra-fine chick strolled into the shop today and bought an expensive comic book, expensive enough for Roy to treat her like royalty, which I'm sure made her day. He took her to the back room and everything. You know the photo of the Porsche I texted you earlier? That beautiful baby is hers. The funny thing is, I think she went to Baum's just to scope me out because—get this—she showed up here at the apartment a little while later and tried to recruit me for some ridiculous superhero training camp. 'Complete with room and board,' she said. Woo-hoo. Not sure how she knew about Lambda Man, but—"

"Frank, everyone knows about Lambda Man. You used your real last name, for Christ's sake. It's not a stretch."

Rauch carried a scar above his left eye, a constant

reminder of the only fight he'd almost lost. When he got tired or tense, his eye twitched, and the scar danced the tarantella, as it was doing now.

Without another word, Frank grabbed two ceramic mugs and a corkscrew from the kitchen and plopped on the sofa. He popped the cork and poured them each a cup. "Since when do you drink wine?"

"Since now. Savor it. It's expensive."

They each took a swig, and Frank nodded. "Nice. Smells like roses. Go ahead. Tell me what happened. Obviously, the mob didn't kill you for your mistake, but you don't look overly happy to be alive, either."

Rauch pulled the thicker of the two envelopes from his coat pocket and tossed it on the plastic bin. A wad of Benjamins spilled onto its bright blue surface.

Frank choked on his wine. "How much?"

"Ten grand."

"For one hit?"

"For two."

"For two." Frank cradled his mug between his hands and stared Rauch in the face.

Rauch squirmed. "I didn't actually kill the second guy. Things got real complicated real fast, Frankie. You should've seen what they did to the *capo* who hired me. And…and they mentioned Roy."

"Roy? Roy Baum? As in my boss?"

"They want him dead, Frank. They said he's a mole, and someone ratted him out. They didn't give details, but the don and Roy definitely had business dealings. I'm guessing he was running an illegal import/export business out of the shop. He wasn't just working with the Italian mafia, either. He was also working for the Irish. It's all a front, Frank—the store, the comics, everything."

"No way. There is absolutely no way Roy Baum is working for the mob. He's a good man."

"Who says?"

"I say, Rauch, I've worked side by side with the man for a long time. I'd know. He's like my father."

"Really? Because last I checked, your father died in jail after pounding your mom and baby brother into hamburger. Was he a good man, too?"

A police siren wailed from the street below. Flashing red lights strobed through the window, casting ghoulish shadows over Frank's taut face.

He placed his mug on the bin and stood. "While I was at the movies. You forgot that part. May as well finish the story. While I was at a goddamned movie."

"Frankie, I'm sorry." Rauch averted his eyes. "Look, I'm thinking you and I need to blow town for a while. Between the mob and your freaky, comic-addicted stalker chick, things have gotten pretty hot around here lately. We could take the money and start over somewhere else."

"Where would we go—Hoboken? Ten grand isn't gonna take us far."

"It'll take us far enough."

Chapter Twelve

They stayed up late and finished the bottle of wine, along with a six-pack of beer Rauch had received as payment for running one of his "errands." Once the specter of Frank's father dissipated in an alcoholic haze, Lambda Man regaled Rauch with the story of his triumph over the gangbangers. He skimmed over the traumatic details about Julia and Carmine. Even while carrying a good buzz, Rauch's eyebrow scar continued to dance, and Frank didn't want to hear any more talk about leaving town.

Rauch tried a couple of times to steer the conversation back to the idea, but Frank cut him off with brutal efficiency. Finally, Rauch relaxed and enjoyed the high. As the night waned, he held the empty wine bottle upside down over his mug, trying to coax a few more drops to fall.

"Nada." He slammed the spent bottle on the coffee table. "I do believe it's kicked."

The bottle tipped on its side and rolled to a rest next to Keira's card. He plucked it off the table and slurred its words out loud. "Heroes2B, Inc." He flashed Frank a boozy grin, and they giggled. "What kind of person names their business Heroes2B, Inc.?"

"A person named Keira who drives a purple Porsche." Frank's thick tongue stumbled over the words, and he frowned. He'd never been able to hold his liquor as well as Rauch. "With purple hair to match, no less."

"She's got purple hair?"

"Uh-huh."

Rauch waved his empty mug in the air. "Well, good for her. I wonder what other names she considered. The rejects must've really stunk."

"Now there's an interesting thought." Frank struggled to stand, gave up, and sank back into the sofa's thin cushions. "I vote for Superheroes Anonymous. Like Alcoholics Anonymous but with lots and lots of spandex."

Rauch chortled. "Awesome. That's just awesome. Wait, I've got something even better." He flashed his hands in the air. "CRUS—Cosplayers R Us." Frank snorted wine out his nose, and they dissolved into drunken hysterics.

Frank swiped the tears from his cheeks. "And that right there is why we're super friends, isn't it, Rauch?"

"Yep. Because we're the only ones pathetic enough to laugh at each other's stupid jokes."

"Plus, we have our video games and comic books and Lambda Man—"

"And don't forget D&D."

"Absolutely." Frank raised his mug in a mock toast. "To us. May we always have each other's back…and Dungeons & Dragons."

Rauch clanked his mug against Frank's. "Amen, brother. Amen."

****

Rauch was sleeping off the wine and snoring mightily when Frank left for work in the morning. He stepped outside, slipped, and promptly fell on his ass.

The sole of his sneaker glided over the slick concrete. Sleet. He should sue the slumlord for not salting the sidewalk. Guess he'd better take the subway.

He slipped and skidded from the station to Baum's, arriving with all four limbs intact but fifteen minutes late. Roy was a forgiving man, but two days in a row was liable to make him testy. Frank stood outside the alley door and prepared an excuse.

The alarm wasn't armed, so Roy had definitely beaten him to work, which wasn't a surprise. Frank slipped his key in the lock and paused. The deadbolt wasn't set. Roy never left the alley door unlocked—not with the trove of literary artifacts he had squirreled away in the back room. Perhaps he was worried the lock might ice over and the door freeze shut. It seemed the only plausible excuse. Or else Roy's bizarre behavior had carried over from yesterday. The old man was losing his mind.

Frank frowned and, setting the lock behind him, slipped through the door into the chilly narrow corridor. He hurried toward the warmth of the interior room. "Roy? Sorry I'm—oh, God."

The stench. They say smell is the most primitive of the senses, capable of evoking visceral responses to memories long-suppressed. It stopped him two steps into the room, close enough for Frank to see the glint of amber light reflecting off Roy's dead, glassy eyes. Those eyes, milky with age and filmy with death, locked Frank in place, rendering him unable to look away, unable to breath.

Frank swayed to the side, knocking one of Roy's mysterious wooden boxes off the shelf. It hit the floor and splintered. The clatter broke the spell. Frank covered his nose with his gloved hand and staggered backward to fumble desperately with the door's stubborn bolt. When the lock finally gave, he stumbled through the exit and vomited last night's red wine into the alley.

"Oh my God, oh my God." He snatched his phone from his pocket and slid, retching and hyperventilating, down the icy alley until he reached the sidewalk. He fell onto his knees at the curb and dialed nine-one-one. "Please. Please help me. Somebody killed my fa…somebody killed Roy Baum."

****

Frank huddled in the back of the police cruiser with a heat-reflective blanket over his shoulders and his hands cradling a hot thermos. The coffee was unbelievably bad, yet he found its bitter taste as fortifying as it was repugnant. They'd been kind to him. He was still on his knees by the curb when they'd arrived. Lips frozen, shivering, and too shocked to string together a coherent sentence, he'd wordlessly allowed them to guide him into the car while the first responders investigated the scene. Later, when his brain thawed, he realized he was locked in. The rear doors of police cruisers have no handles.

A parade of professionals from various city offices arrived and went about their macabre business. EMS, the coroner, detectives, forensics…in the silence of the squad car, he watched their lips move as they did their jobs with ease, smiling and joking among themselves as if it were just another fine day at the circus. And for them, it was.

But not for Frank. His whole world collapsed in an instant, just as it had the day he'd arrived home to find his family dead and his father in handcuffs. He'd rebuilt his world the best he knew how. Today, that world died next to Roy.

After Roy had his heart attack, he made Frank promise to keep the shop going without him, if it came to that. Frank assumed that meant he'd be at Baum's forever. He hadn't worried about the details. And then Roy recovered, and once again, all was right with the world. Until now.

A pair of cops unfurled a yellow ribbon stamped with the words "Police Line. Do Not Cross." Frank sobbed. Baum's would be closed indefinitely while the police investigated the murder. His promise to keep the shop open was as dead as Roy. Images of a future in flux tumbled through his reeling brain. He'd lost more than a father figure. No Baum's meant no pay. No money meant no apartment. He was adrift and, if the look on the lead detective's face was any indication, in serious trouble.

Another detective in a long wool coat chatted up the officer who'd given Frank her thermos. They pointed to the patrol car. He took a shuddering breath. Here came the questions. He'd have to leave out Rauch's mob theory, but he had nothing else to hide.

A stretcher loaded with a black body bag careened out of the alley and skidded to the open bay of a waiting ambulance. A backwash of stale coffee burned Frank's throat as he pictured the flies buzzing over Roy's stiff, gray body. He gagged at the bitter taste. He would not—*would not*—throw up in the patrol car. He knew better.

The door opened and a gust of frigid air made him shiver anew. "Mr. Lambda? We'd like to ask you a couple of questions down at the precinct…"

To protect Rauch, he gave Julia's address as his own. Told them he'd been with her last night, which wasn't a lie. It just wasn't the truth, either. She'd vouch for him; of that he had no doubt. He made a mental note to call her later.

For four hours, Frank answered their questions and reviewed graphic photographs of the scene. He learned one thing. On television cop shows, the pictures were always in black and white. In real life, they're in color, and that color is mostly red.

The detective placed yet another photo on the steel table. Thankfully, this one focused on Roy's cluttered desk instead of his mutilated body. "Do you see anything out of the ordinary?"

Frank pointed to the medicine bottle.

The detective's partner jotted a note. "Did you notice any unusual behaviors or occurrences before this event?"

He told them about Roy closing early and his strange response to Keira's purchase. He gave them the photograph of his father and the three men and told them they could keep it. He still had it folded in his coat pocket. Roy had refused to take it back. Now it was Frank's turn.

With his eyes fixed on the table, he recited his statement in the monotone of a shattered, shell-shocked man. He raised his eyes only at their final question, the one he figured they'd save for last.

"How was your relationship with your boss, Mr. Lambda?"

It made sense for them to consider him a suspect. They had to ask. He understood. "Roy was like a father to me." His voice cracked, and he lowered his gaze back to the table. "He gave me a chance when no one else would. I loved him for it then, and I love him now."

Chapter Thirteen

Rauch jumped out of bed once he heard Frank leave for work. He hung around his bedroom for a half hour or so—Frank was notorious for returning for something he'd forgotten, like his keys—until he was sure Frank was gone for good.

Out of habit, he checked on the envelope of money, which remained stashed in the pocket of his black leather coat. His fingers brushed the wax seal of Roy's letter. Only now, he wasn't convinced it was Roy's. His money was on Frank's mysterious and wealthy visitor, Keira.

He showered, shaved, and rooted through his sparse wardrobe for the least scruffy shirt he could find. He frowned at his limited selection. He had money now; he really should invest in a shirt with buttons. A black, long-sleeve tee seemed the most serviceable option. It was tight, but at least it lacked sweat stains and holes. And it showed off his pecs, which was important. He had no marketable skills, so maybe Keira would hire him based on his good looks.

The card sat on the plastic bin where they'd left it. Rauch stared at its glossy purple finish and solidified his plan. Frank would never leave this neighborhood. He was lucky those gang bangers hadn't blow him away. They'd be back to find him, and the next time, they'd be better prepared. These streets had never done jack shit for him, and they were getting meaner all the time. Yet Frank acted as if running around in a cape and a pair of hockey pants could somehow make them better. He was going to get himself killed.

Rauch didn't understand it, but that didn't mean he had to sit around and watch it happen. He punched the number from the card into his phone. She answered on the first ring. "Hello, this is Keira."

"Keira, this is Frank Lambda's assistant, Rauch."

"Frank has a personal assistant?" She sounded coolly amused.

"He does today. A situation has arisen which may persuade him to reconsider your generous offer. I've encouraged him to accept, and I'd also like to offer my services, if there's a suitable position available."

"Are you a hero, Mr. Rauch?"

"No, but neither is Frank."

"Then what is it that you do other than functioning as Frank's personal assistant?"

"I was hoping we could discuss my qualifications, as well as the details of Frank's potential employment, in person."

"Where did you have in mind?"

He detected a note of concern, or perhaps suspicion, in her voice, and he rushed to reassure her. "You can pick the time and place, but I was thinking the apartment would work. You know where it is, or so I'm told."

"When?"

"As soon as possible. I expect him to return around three, maybe sooner. Together we may be able to—"

"Do you like Chinese, Mr. Rauch?"

"Sure. Who doesn't?"

"I'll be there at noon."

The line went dead. So much for her being anxious. He glanced at the time on his phone. He had two hours to wait. His stomach gurgled. Hopefully she'd bring egg rolls.

****

No purple sports car. Bummer. Rauch couldn't blame Keira for not wanting to take a car like that out in such miserable weather, but still, it was disappointing. She arrived four minutes early in a hulking black SUV. He watched through the window as she removed two plastic grocery bags from the passenger side and strolled toward the door. He considered running down the stairs to lend her a hand but decided against it. Might appear too desperate. He needed to play it cool.

He cast a critical glance around the room. The apartment didn't look half bad for a bachelor-pad dump. He'd hidden the empty bottle of wine deep in the garbage can and cleaned the toilet for the first time ever, just in case. Usually, that was Frank's job.

Housework kept him busy, distracted him from worrying about how things were going for Frank. The guilt weighed heavily on his mind. When it threatened to intrude, he pushed it aside and focused on the future. This was the best way. Hopefully Frank's hysteria upon discovering Roy's corpse would solidify his innocence in the minds of the police. And now that Rauch believed the letter with the green lambda seal had been written by Keira, he didn't see any reason for Frank to know he'd been involved with Roy's death at all. The letter was on his list of things to discuss with Keira.

The enticing aroma of sweet-and-sour sauce wafted under the apartment's door, alerting him to her arrival on the floor. His stomach growled. God, how long had it been since he'd eaten a decent meal? It was gonna be tough to look chill while shoveling shrimp in his mouth by the forkful.

Rauch, knowing Keira's hands were full, opened the door without waiting for her to knock. They sized each other up across the threshold. She smelled amazing, and it wasn't the Chinese, although the food had an appeal of its own. Her perfume was clean and rich—a stark contrast to the cheap drugstore fragrances preferred by the local bar crawlers.

"Are you going to invite me in, or do we have to eat in the hall?"

He stepped aside and grabbed one of the bags as she sidled by.

Rauch and Frank didn't have a kitchen table. Hell, they didn't have much of a kitchen. Their "galley," as the landlord had called it when they'd first moved in, was basically a bumped-out wall lined by an ancient gas stove, a chipped sink, a fridge, and a half a foot of counter space. They ate on the sofa in front of the television. They never even bothered with the rickety TV trays they'd schlepped home from Goodwill. What a wasted effort.

Keira plopped the bag on the counter, unloaded the take-out cartons, and reached into the cupboard above the sink for paper plates.

"Make yourself at home." Rauch scowled. "Looks like you've been here before."

She responded with a cool, serene smile.

He assembled two of the trays and eyed them warily for signs of impending collapse. She carried her loaded plate to the scruffy brown recliner next to the sofa. After spreading a paper napkin over her thighs, she settled in, folded her hands in her lap, and waited for him to join her. Classy.

And that's how he knew he was out of his league. But at least she'd brought egg rolls and beer.

He filled two plates to overflowing and positioned himself at the end of the sofa farthest from the recliner. His carefully prepared speech vanished along with several mounds of steaming fried rice. She wanted to be in control? Fine. Her move. He was gonna eat while the food was hot.

Keira corralled her long strands of hair in an elastic band. "Jau's on Race and 11th. Best Chinese in the city." She stabbed a prawn with her plastic fork and dipped it in the glistening red sauce.

"It's good."

He skewered a bite-sized hunk of kung pao chicken and watched her as she ate. Everything about her reeked of old money, from the expensive bling on her perfectly manicured finger to the tips of her polished leather boots, high enough to conceal a decent weapon, if she was into that sort of thing. Yet here she was in his shitty apartment, sitting on his shitty furniture, and eating off paper plates. Rauch doubted he'd be as comfortable in her world as she appeared to be in his. She probably ordered Nebbiolo by the case and stored it in a climate-controlled wine cellar.

A few more bites of the spicy chicken and he was ready. He'd thought ahead and stashed the wax-sealed letter underneath the sofa cushions for easy access when the moment was right. Now seemed as good a time as any. Without a word, he slid it out and set it on the coffee table with the seal facing up.

Keira's eyes shifted, but her expression did not change. She pointed at the letter with her fork. "That was meant for Frank." Her eyes shifted back to his. "How'd you get a hold of it, I wonder?"

"Keep wondering. What does it say?"

She shrugged. "Nothing earth-shattering. It's an invitation to join Heroes2B, Inc. I patronized Baum's Books yesterday and gave it to the owner to pass along to Frank. I had my doubts he would do so and decided to pay Frank a visit and make the offer face-to-face instead. You can open it if you'd like. At this point, it's obsolete."

Rauch cracked the envelope's thick seal. As he withdrew the note, a business card identical to the one on the coffee table fluttered to the floor. The note read, "Heroes aren't born; they're made. Join us. Heroes2B, Inc." Below the text was a picture of Keira flanked by three grinning men in cheesy get-ups that made Frank's costume seem debonair by comparison.

"Who are the geeks?"

She smiled. "Pinball, Ruletka, and Deliverance, my previous recruits."

You actually talked someone into this shit? Rauch bit his tongue. He was job hunting, and the room and board sounded mighty nice. "Let's talk details."

He dumped his plates in the garbage and cracked open a beer, belatedly remembering to offer her one. They were hers anyway; she'd brought them. To his surprise, Keira accepted with a nod. He'd assumed the beer was a bribe for him and Frank. She definitely looked like the martini type.

He handed her the beer, and her ring flashed as her fingers curled around the can. He sat on the couch, nearer this time. "You run a school for wannabe superheroes."

"Correct."

"And you essentially pay these people with room and board?"

"And a small stipend."

"How small, and where exactly is Hero University located? Don't answer that. Let me guess: Northeast Philly, on the corner of K & A." The K&A gang was the city's branch of the Irish mob.

Her eyes narrowed. "At the moment but I plan to move the headquarters to Las Vegas after recruiting Frank."

Las Vegas. Now there was a town where he and Frank could disappear for a while. Rauch didn't know much about it beyond the obvious, but he'd heard it was a city of transplants—sun-seeking retirees, gambling addicts who ran out of money and decided to stay, and tourists. Two boys from Philly would blend in just fine. But he might not want to get stuck there permanently.

Rauch emptied his can of dark ale. "What happens to your recruits after they graduate?"

"My hope is that they'll stay with the business to help train others while performing missions for the greater good."

"For your greater good."

"For the good of everyone."

"Yeah, right. Who funds you?"

"My goodness, you are a cynical one, aren't you?"

"I prefer the term 'experienced.'"

Keira moved her TV tray to the side and stood. "I know who you are, Mr. Rauch, and I know what you've done. I did my research after you called. So why don't you just tell me what you want and be done with it."

Rauch crumpled the empty can in his hand. "I told you on the phone. I need a job and some cover. And here's a news flash for ya: I know who you are, too." He stepped forward and grabbed her hand in his, raising her ring to the light. "You advertise it on your goddamned finger. The only thing mysterious about you is your con."

She twisted her hand from his grasp, scraping the ring's faceted stone against his palm. "There is no—"

"Save it. I'll figure it out eventually. For now, whaddaya say we leave Frank out of it and keep our secrets to ourselves? Let him live the dream. I can persuade him to sign on the dotted line; I can also persuade him not to. We're a package deal. Guarantee us some safe new digs and a paycheck, and I'm in. But there's no way in hell I'm running around in a stupid cape and a pair of tights."

Keira crossed her arms and studied his face. Rauch held his breath and struggled not to waver. This had not gone the way he'd imagined. He'd planned to appear as suave and professional as a *consigliere*, a mafia don's advisor, mediator, and all-around right-hand man. He should've known it was too far of a stretch.

"Okay, Mr. Rauch—"

"It's Rauch. Just Rauch."

"Okay, Rauch. You've got yourself a deal." She held out her hand. "Welcome to Heroes2B, Inc."

Chapter Fourteen

The police cruiser whipped into the open parking space behind a gleaming black SUV and dropped Frank at the curb of his apartment building. "Yours?" One of the officers nodded at the hulking beast, shimmering in a coat of thin ice from the persistent sleet.

"I wish." Frank's voice lacked actual enthusiasm. "You don't usually see luxury cars around this hood."

The officers agreed. Frank shuffled into the building. When he looked back, they were running the plates. He thrust his frozen hands under his armpits and plodded up the unheated stairwell. The weather was brutal for November, but his numbness came from within.

He walked through the door and stopped short. Keira lounged in the recliner with her legs up and her shiny boots crossed at the ankles. Rauch, beer in hand, sprawled on the couch. An old '80's cartoon blared from the television, and the whole scene smelled like a Chinese kitchen. He'd traversed a portal in the space-time continuum and into an alternate reality. It was the only logical explanation.

Rauch struggled to rise from the couch without spilling his beer. He looked at Frank; Frank looked at Keira and back at Rauch.

When neither man spoke, Keira slammed the recliner to an upright position and rose with a smile.

"Hello, Frank. Nice to see you again."

The memory of Roy deferentially ushering Keira into his inner sanctum passed through Frank's mind. The image was quickly replaced by that of Roy lying in a pool of blood and gore. Frank flinched and avoided her outstretched hand. "You know what, lady? I've had a day from hell, and I'm not in the mood for your special kind of crazy right now." He stalked to the fridge and claimed the last can of beer.

Rauch shot her a conciliatory smile and tailed him to the kitchen, where they ducked behind the half wall. As soon as they were out of Keira's direct line of sight, Frank spun around, lowered his voice, and scowled. "What is she doing here?"

"She came to talk about her hero academy. It sounds like a real sweet deal, Frank. And get this—she offered me a job, too. In security."

Frank snorted. "Yippee ki-yay, mother—"

"Hey, she brought Chinese and beer, so she can't be that bad. I saved you some. Your favorite—kung pao chicken." Rauch balanced on one leg and chopped his hands through the air in a poor imitation of a karate master.

Frank leaned back against the fridge. "Rauch—"

"Just listen to her pitch. That's all I'm asking."

"Roy's dead."

Rauch swallowed and lowered his hands to his sides. He focused on a smudge on the floor. "Another heart attack?"

"Someone gutted him like a fish."

"Jesus, Frank. I'm sorry. Do they have a suspect?"

"Not yet. I spent the last four hours at the police station, answering questions."

"You're a suspect?"

"I don't think so, but who knows?" Frank fluttered his hands in the air. "I just want to get something to eat, go to bed, and not think about what comes next. I'm smoked." His voice trembled. "You should've seen him, Rauch. It was awful. Why would anyone want to hurt Roy?"

"I told you last night that the mob wanted him dead, but you didn't believe me. Roy wasn't the man you thought he was."

"But he treated me like a son. He was good to me, just like you."

Rauch cleared his tight throat and put a hand on Frank's shoulder. "Keira's been waiting here since noon, Frank. It'll be hard to get rid of her without at least pretending to listen to her pitch. Grab a plate. I'll ask her to keep it short, okay? You can zone out if you want. Just nod and smile. I'll fill you in on the details later."

Frank rubbed his bloodshot eyes. "Fine." He pulled the leftovers from the fridge and dumped them on a plate. "I'll be right in. Feel free to start without me."

Rauch ducked around the corner while Frank nuked his chicken. The microwave dinged, and Frank carried his plate and beer into the living room to join him. No more cartoons. The television was off, and Rauch and Keira were deep in conversation. From their solemn expressions, they appeared to be plotting the apocalypse.

He plopped on the sofa and raised fork-to-mouth in the habitual act of eating. He may as well have been eating dust.

Keira moved to sit on the sofa between the two

men at either end. She rested her slender fingers on Frank's thigh. "Rauch just told me what happened. I'm so sorry for your loss. Would it be better if I returned tomorrow?"

How about never? Frank bit back his angry retort. He wasn't good at being mean, and besides, she sounded sincere, though the hand on his thigh was a bit much. He suspected she deployed her feminine charm out of habit more than guile. Fortunately, he was immune. "Go ahead. Let's get it over with."

She launched into her spiel, periodically checking in with Rauch, who nodded his approval. When she finished, Frank tossed his fork on the empty plate. "Any questions?" She paused expectantly.

"Who provides your funding?"

"What is it with you guys and your funding questions?" Her arched brows rose, but she recovered quickly, and her demeanor returned to one of professional detachment.

"Rauch and I know the heart of every offer beats to a flashing neon dollar sign. I understand what's in it for us. I don't understand what's in it for you, and frankly, right now, I don't care," Frank muttered and guzzled the rest of his beer.

"The training academy is funded by the NIH. I received a grant."

"Who?"

"The NIH—the National Institutes of Health. I've got a master's degree in psychology, and I'm doing a doctoral study on heroism and empathy. Wannabe superheroes are the perfect subjects."

"So we're guinea pigs?"

"Absolutely not. There's no blood testing, no

scans, no super-secret soldier formula to drink. The study is observational only, designed to examine if heroism and empathy are inborn traits or learned behaviors. I proposed the latter in my master's thesis. Now I have to prove it."

Keira lifted the invitation off the coffee table and held it out to Frank. "Just like the card says. 'Heroes aren't born; they're made.' I can email you the links to my previously published studies and provide you with copies of my thesis and Ivy League diploma, if it would make you feel more comfortable."

"Another beer would make me more comfortable." Frank stared at the invitation's broken green seal stamped with his name: λ. A wave of exhaustion made his shoulders sag, and for reasons he could not define, his throat thickened with tears. He didn't feel like a hero. He felt like an unemployed loser whose entire future, once so well defined, was now in jeopardy.

He dropped the card on the sofa and shuffled toward his bedroom. "I'll think about it."

"I need to know by tomorrow. Otherwise, I'll be forced to offer the final open spot to another candidate or risk losing my funding." She fluttered her eyelashes. "But you're my preferred hero."

"Test subject, you mean. Lab rat, guinea pig—"

"No. I said hero, and I meant it." She gathered her coat and walked toward the door. "When I was a little girl, I was often afraid to try new things. My mother used to recite an old proverb, 'He who loses money, loses much. He who loses a friend, loses more. He who loses courage, loses all.'"

Keira paused on the threshold. Her lips curved into a sympathetic smile. "Today you lost your job and a friend. May you never lose the courage to continue your dream. I'll look forward to your call."

Chapter Fifteen

Rauch spent his first hour of the morning packing his essentials into a giant canvas duffel bag. He didn't have much he cared to take. Most of his possessions qualified as secondhand junk and could be left in the apartment for the next schlub to deal with. The only valuable thing he owned was his gaming system.

Frank didn't have much more—just an additional good-sized box of comic books and board games. Rauch gazed around his bare room. The baby boomers on TV talk shows yammered about upcycling and downsizing. If he and Frank downsized any more, they could both live in the same cardboard box on Derelict Row and still have enough room for a goldfish.

Rauch hadn't heard a peep out of Frank since last night, not that he could blame him. Frank had no reason to get out of bed. Baum's Books was shuttered for sure and most likely wrapped like a grisly package in a garish bow of bright yellow police tape. But Keira needed an answer, and Rauch was eager to supply it.

He paced the apartment, hoping old Mrs. Pagnotto would click on her television so the Bible thumpers would drive Frank from his bed. By the time eleven o'clock hit, Rauch was done cooling his heels. He couldn't contain himself any longer. He pounded on Frank's door. "Hey, buddy, you up?"

Frank, carrying a stack of neatly folded clothes,

opened the door. A baby blue vintage suitcase with old-fashioned flipper-style latches rested on the unmade bed. The case's lid, dented and scuffed to the point of disgrace, yawned open, waiting to accept the mounds of socks and underwear. Rauch peered over Frank's shoulder. "Going somewhere?"

"Yeah. Aren't you?"

"I've been packed and ready since eight."

"Do you have any of that money left?"

"Of course. All of it." Rauch corrected himself. "Minus a hundred bucks for the wine."

"You spent a C-note on one bottle of wine?"

"I told you it was expensive."

"I should've drunk slower." Frank looked at the piles of clothes on his bed. "Let's go get lunch—an honest-to-God sit-down lunch at a real restaurant—and say goodbye to our old selves. You're buying."

"What about Keira?"

"I've got twelve hours until the day is done. Let her sweat."

****

They passed by three delightfully aromatic Italian restaurants because Rauch knew from experience they were run by the Family and settled on Greek instead. The cheerful blue-and-white café had a second floor overlooking South Street, which in the bright light of a sunny afternoon appeared ordinary and calm. But come nightfall, the sidewalks teemed with hustlers and street performers of every wondrous and bizarre variety. They hawked their wares to dazed tourists drunk on revelry.

Frank shook his head. "I'm not sure I can do it, Rauch. I can't leave this all behind."

"Vegas won't be much different. Just add casinos,

an exploding volcano, and fountains that sing on the hour. You'll be fine."

"You realize Keira's a con artist, right? I'd bet Thor's hammer there's no grant money and no research study. She's lying, and if I can tell it, I know you can, too. You're smarter about those sorts of things."

"Not smarter, savvier. Less naïve."

Frank stared out the picture window and rearranged his silverware. "She's probably some sort of sicko serial killer or something. A female Hannibal Lecter."

Rauch laughed. "I know a killer when I see one and she's no killer. Come on—she's a college graduate."

"What does that have to do with anything? I can't think of a better training program for a con artist than a degree in psychology. It's not like they offer college courses in cannibalism or dismemberment."

The young couple to their left gaped at his words. Frank lowered his voice. "I'm not sure I'm allowed to skip town until the police are done investigating Roy's murder. That can be our out if things get weird, and I'm sure they will."

"If you're so worried, why accept?"

"Because you want me to and I'm out of a job, which means soon we'll be living on the streets. Besides, I kind of like the idea of getting paid to run around as Lambda Man. Not to mention that with the exception of flipping burgers, I don't have many other options."

"There's nothing wrong with flipping burgers. It's an honest job."

"Then why don't you do it? It's safer than running errands for the Family."

A waiter brought two plates of spanakopita, which

saved Rauch from answering. If he had to flip burgers, he'd probably end up killing someone with a spatula. It can be done.

Frank picked at his food. "I haven't seen you this enthusiastic about anything in a long time, and I don't want you, or me, for that matter, living off blood money for the rest of our lives. You're not mob material, Rauch. You're better than that. You just need a chance, and this might be it."

Rauch stared at his plate. "You give me too much credit, Frank. You always have."

They lapsed into silence. The cheerful strains of an accordion mingled with the clank of glassware and laughter from the street below. With a sigh, Frank abandoned his spanakopita and set his fork on the table. "If we can earn enough to stash some money away, or even if we manage to learn a marketable skill, then this whole acid trip will be worth it. We'll come back to the neighborhood as heroes. I can see it now: 'The Return of Lambda Man.'"

"I like 'Lambda Man Returns' better. Stronger. Manlier. More Batmanish."

"Whatever. In the meantime, we need to keep our eyes open and stay sharp while we wait for Keira's scam to play out." He signaled the waiter. "Can we have an order of hummus, please?"

Rauch rolled his eyes. "Hummus is so not manly."

"I don't care. I like it, and it's good for you. Lots of protein." He placed his order.

Rauch watched the waiter glide away. Frank was the only person on the planet who could manage to make him feel guilty while simultaneously spending his hard-earned money on something as nasty as hummus.

At least Frank understood Keira wasn't what she seemed. Skepticism was protective; with it, the truth was bound to hurt less in the end.

****

Yesterday's ice was gone, replaced by clear skies, bright sunshine, and warmer temps—a good omen, Rauch hoped, for the start of their new lives. The walk home was quiet until they reached the swankiest of the Italian restaurants they'd spurned on their stroll to South Street. A familiar black roadster idled at the curb.

Rauch's step faltered, and he tugged at Frank's shoulder. "Cross the street."

Without question, the two took off at a brisk pace, dodging traffic and melding into the thin crowd of pedestrians on the other side.

"Keep looking straight ahead." Rauch stuffed his hands in the pockets of his black leather jacket and puffed it out, trying to look intimidating. Frank did the same and tripped over a crack in the uneven sidewalk. He twisted just in time to avoid a face-plant, but his shoulder popped as he hit the pavement.

He rolled onto his back and clutched his left shoulder. "Ow!"

Across the street, the door to the restaurant opened, releasing a garlicky aroma and the lilting strains of an Italian classic folk song. With another whoosh of the door, the melody vanished, and Skinny stood on the curb in a sooty cloud of exhaust. He opened the passenger door for the don and walked around the polished hood to the driver's side.

Rauch turned his back, shielding his fallen friend from view. "Get up, Frankie. Get up." He grabbed Frank's right hand and yanked him to his feet.

Frank's olive complexion paled to a sickly shade of yellow, and his knees buckled. Rauch threw an arm around his waist for support. "We need to move." He cursed as a voice boomed over the traffic.

"Hey, Raunchy boy. Is that your boyfriend? He looks a little rough around the wing. Take it easy—you might break him."

If Skinny were anyone else—hell, even if Skinny was Skinny but the don wasn't sitting in the car's passenger seat watching—Rauch would've flipped him the bird. Instead, he nodded and lifted his palm in a half-hearted wave.

Skinny's raucous, high-pitched laughter followed them as they gimped down the sidewalk. The roadster tore away from the curb, and Skinny leered at them through the window. He laid on the horn as the vehicle zoomed past. Frank flinched, and Rauch once again pictured himself wrapping Skinny's ugly orange lanyard around his bull neck and pulling it until the mobster's eyes bulged from his head. He was a class A—A as in asshole—bully, and Rauch hated bullies more than he hated hummus, which was an awful lot of hate.

They made it into the apartment building where Rauch eased Frank onto the bottom step. While Frank took a breather, Rauch lit a smoke to calm his nerves. He'd met a lot of rotten people in his short rotten life, and he'd learned to ignore them. They weren't worth the bruised knuckles. But Skinny got under his skin.

He exhaled a perfect circle of smoke. "You picked a bad time to trip, Frank."

Frank coughed. "You're the one who told me to look straight ahead. Otherwise, I would've seen the crack."

"You think you can make it up the stairs?"

"I'm gonna try. Finish your cigarette first. No smoking in the apartment. Go outside. Shoo."

Rauch grinned, stepped into the crisp fall air, and made it quick. When he reentered the foyer, Frank had already struggled up the first flight. He bounded the steps two at a time to catch up. "Need a hand?"

"No. I've got this. I'm trying to think of it as practice for my upcoming training." Frank's forehead glistened with sweat, and he ground his teeth with each jarring step. "Who was the goon?"

"He goes by the name of Skinny. And he's bad news. The worst."

"I figured that much out on my own. Go ahead and unlock the door, will ya?"

Rauch ran ahead. He tossed his coat on the back of the sofa and flicked on the bathroom light.

Frank, pale and wheezing, stumbled behind. He gripped the chipped porcelain sink with his one good hand. "Good thing this is an old shirt."

"Why?"

"Because you're gonna have to cut it off me. No way is it going over my head."

Rauch pulled a pocket knife from his jeans and in one swift motion sliced Frank's shirt down the middle. They stared aghast at his left shoulder, which was situated somewhere south of its normal anatomic position.

"Jesus, Frank, why didn't you say it was dislocated?"

"I didn't know. I just knew the son of a bitch hurt."

"I'll call a cab to take you to Methodist Hospital."

Rauch turned to dash from the bathroom, but Frank grabbed him. "No." The effort caused Frank's knees to buckle again, and Rauch half-carried, half-dragged him to the sofa. "I don't have insurance. It'll cost a fortune. You've had these a couple of times before. Can't you pop it back in?"

Since the age of ten, Rauch's shoulder had been dislocated more times than he could remember. At this point, it slipped in and out at will. Someday he'd probably need surgery, but for now, it made for a cool party trick.

"Just because I can do it to myself doesn't make me qualified to try it on you. Besides, what if it's broken? We can use my money. I'm calling a cab."

"It'll cost twice that."

"Frank—"

A stare-down ensued. Frank won.

Rauch sighed. "Fine. But if I hear anything snap, we're going to Methodist, and I'll deny I ever touched you. Lie down."

Frank stretched flat on the sofa with his bad arm facing out. Rauch knelt next to him and straightened his arm to an outstretched position. "Grab the back corner of the sofa and hang on tight. I have to pull and twist at the same time, and you need to resist me. Otherwise, I'll just yank you off the couch, and it'll hurt like hell."

"It's gonna hurt like hell no matter what you do."

"You're probably right." Rauch pulled his tattered leather wallet from his rear pocket. "Here. Put this in your mouth."

"Ugh. I don't want that thing in my mouth. It's been sitting on your ass."

"Have it your way." Rauch dropped the wallet and

grabbed Frank's arm. "Hold on to the sofa."

"Wait a second. You're rushing me. At least turn on some tunes so Mrs. Pagnotto doesn't hear me scream and call the police. That'd be all we need. Do we have any more Guin—"

He screeched in agony as Rauch, knees braced against the sofa, leaned backward and yanked on his left arm, twisting it inward until it clunked into place.

Frank awoke with a cool dishrag on his forehead. "I was *not* ready."

"I was. You were stalling. How's it feel?"

Frank moved his arm delicately in every direction. "Better. It throbs, but the sharp pain is gone."

"I'll get you some aspirin." Rauch rooted through the medicine cabinet in the bathroom until he found an old bottle of expired aspirin. It would have to do. He had a few narcs stashed away for emergencies, but he didn't know if Keira was the type to drug screen new employees. Frank's bum arm was already going to be a problem. He didn't need to fail a drug screen, too.

Frank struggled upright and tossed back the aspirin. "How am I going to train with one arm?"

"It'll get better quick. Keep taking the aspirin. Maybe the first couple of weeks will be book work."

"I doubt it." Frank, his expression glum, stared at the business card on the coffee table. "You want to call Keira, or should I?"

"I'll call." Rauch clicked on the television and channel surfed until he found something Frank would enjoy—old Batman reruns. "You get some rest."

"Ooo, look—this one's got Julie Newmar. Best Catwoman ever. Turn it up, will ya?" Frank settled his shoulder into the cushions and propped his feet on the plastic bin.

"Sure, Frank. Sure."

Rauch lingered until Frank was absorbed in the show. Then he pulled out his phone, slipped into his bedroom, and shut the door. He dialed quickly.

"Hello, this is Keira."

"We're in."

Chapter Sixteen

By the time Frank returned from paying goodbye visits to Julia and other neighborhood pals, the hulking SUV had reappeared in front of his building. He'd slogged around the block with his arm in a makeshift sling but slid it off before entering the apartment. He didn't want to appear weak from the get-go.

As before, Keira and Rauch were huddled together in quiet conversation. Frank nodded as he entered, and Rauch grabbed both their bags. "Everything else is already in the car. You ready?"

Frank nodded again. "I'll sit in the back."

The SUV's high-tech dash looked like a cockpit. Keira clicked on the sound system as soon as they peeled away from the curb. She grinned at Frank in the rear view mirror. "This is my crime fighting mix. You're welcome to sing along." The speakers throbbed in time with Frank's shoulder.

They cruised up I-95 at a high rate of speed. Once they passed the exit for Fishtown, things stopped looking familiar. Frank had never been this far north. He frowned. "Where are we?"

"Almost there. As a matter of fact..." She rummaged in the center console and extracted two black ski masks. The holes for the eyes had been sewn shut with jagged stripes of bright green thread. She tossed one into the back. "Here. Put this on."

It landed in Frank's lap. "Whoa, lady. There's no frickin' way I'm going into this blind."

Rauch squirmed in his seat. "I don't like it either."

Keira frowned. "If you'd prefer, I can shoot you with my tranquilizer gun instead."

Neither man laughed.

"C'mon, guys, lighten up. The location's a secret only because I don't want the police shutting us down. You know how they feel about wannabe superheroes. As far as they're concerned, you're nothing more than a bunch of testosterone-poisoned vigilantes. The less you know about the campus's whereabouts the better. You only need to wear the masks for about fifteen minutes, which is the time it takes to get from the exit to the facility's front gate."

Rauch flipped the mask over in his hands and fingered the crude stitching. "Whaddaya say, Frank?"

Frank hemmed and hawed. Keira jerked the SUV's wheel and whipped out of the passing lane and in front of an eighteen-wheeler. The truck's horn blared its disapproval. She coasted the car to the side of the interstate and rotated in her seat to glare at Frank. "We're a quarter of a mile from the ramp. Make up your mind."

"Do I have a choice?"

"There's always a choice, Frank. You can wear the mask, or I can take the exit and zigzag around for the next two hours until you're carsick and thoroughly lost. This is my neck of the woods, not yours."

"Fine. But for the record, there are female heroes, you know."

Keira stepped on the gas and veered into traffic. "What?"

"Not all heroes are testosterone poisoned because some of them are girls."

"True, except they're women, Frank, not girls. I told you before—it's a respect thing. Every time you say the word 'girl' during training, you'll owe me twenty push-ups."

Frank's shoulder throbbed just thinking about it. He yanked the mask over his head, and Rauch followed suit. Frank grinned under the dark knit. He'd thought ahead and enabled his phone's GPS. Keira's subterfuge was for naught, though he still didn't appreciate not being able to see. He imagined Rauch, with his well-honed hyper-vigilance, felt especially vulnerable.

With the mask on and his eyes closed, the music seemed obnoxiously loud. Or perhaps Keira had cranked up the volume to purposely muffle the outside noise. Either way, Frank neither saw nor heard anything beyond the thumping of the bass. The only smell was that of her subtle perfume. His muscles tensed with each turn and change in velocity until finally the vehicle slowed to a stop, and he heard Keira's window drop. A blast of cold air hit him in the chest.

She clicked the sound system off. "You may remove your masks."

Static electricity crackled in his ears as he jerked the mask over his head and threw it aside. He peered through the gap between Rauch and Keira's shoulders. Outside the SUV's panoramic windshield, a huge metal gate topped with rolled razor wire glided open. Behind it, a dilapidated factory, its red brick scorched from a fire from days gone by, covered an acre or more of crumbling concrete.

Keira said, "Gentlemen, welcome to Heroes2B."

****

Whatever Rauch and Frank had vaguely anticipated, this campus was not it. They exchanged worried looks as Keira maneuvered the vehicle through the gate. As soon as its bumper cleared the opening, the gate slid shut. A huge metal latch clanked behind them, causing Frank's heart to flutter with what he hoped was anticipation but was more honestly fear.

They cruised over a black sea of macadam. Faded yellow lines indicated that at one time this had been a vast parking lot, long before years of weather had fissured and heaved the asphalt into irregular chunks the size of armadillos.

As they neared the factory, a faint odor infiltrated the vehicle's vents, tinging the air with the sulfurous smell of rotten eggs. Frank craned his neck. The building stood as tall as it was wide, at least three stories, but half the upper level windows were shattered or missing. The roar of the SUV's powerful engine sent jittery crows flitting around the jagged edges of glass with practiced ease. They congregated on the roof and followed the car's path with watchful eyes. In the distance, the city's skyscrapers gleamed in the waning light, a familiar warm beacon in the otherwise cold, desolate scene.

Keira drove around the corner of the factory where a smaller cinder block structure, sturdier in appearance, yet no more inviting, sat a short walk away. Its glass panes remained intact. A shadowy figure zipped across a backlit window on the second floor. Frank blinked. The light quickly extinguished; the room turned black.

"The dormitory." She cut the engine, and the vehicle slowed to a crawl. "I think Ruletka's prepared a welcoming party."

"Oh, goody," Frank muttered. Vanilla-scented candles, oatmeal raisin cookies, a crackling warm fire—nothing could make this God-forsaken place seem welcoming.

She parked in front of the entrance. "Stay here for a minute. I want to see if they're ready." She hopped from the driver's seat, strode through the door, and disappeared around the corner.

Frank unfastened his seat belt. "Rauch—"

"Don't say it, Frankie. I know."

"What the hell are we doing here?"

"I told you not to say it." Rauch swiped a hand over his face. "I don't know. It sounded like a good idea at the time." He paused. "I could probably hot-wire the ignition, and we—"

"Too late. Here she comes."

Keira, her face aglow, opened Frank's door. "They're ready for you, Frank. Grab your bags."

Rauch intervened. "I'll get them. You go ahead, Frank. You're the guest of honor at this party. I'm just the muscle." He opened the SUV's rear hatch, threw his duffel over his shoulder, and grabbed Frank's battered suitcase.

Frank said, "We'll go in together. We're a team."

Keira held the door and herded them inside. "Turn left. There's a central common area at the end of the hall. You can't miss it."

They plodded down the narrow hallway. The cinder blocks glowed a sunny shade of yellow, which reflected the glare from rows of overhead fluorescent tube lighting. Keira's boots clicked on the glossy laminate flooring, an obvious upgrade.

Rauch looked at her over his shoulder. "Reminds me of elementary school."

"I tried to spiff it up a notch, but since there's only the four of you right now, you'll find I left much of the building in its original condition. It was seriously dingy before. At one time, this property housed the workers for an old specialty steel mill. Made a super-strong type of steel for shovels and saws."

"You own the factory, too?"

"The entire campus. It was my father's." She paused. "He passed away, and now I co-own it along with my brother, Jack."

Frank remembered Keira mentioning Jack the day she'd visited Baum's Books. Maybe today he'd get to meet him. He'd love to see if lunacy runs in the family.

The hall widened into a large room decorated in a psychedelic '60's vibe. Colorful Chinese paper lanterns swayed from the popcorn ceiling. The galley kitchen, twice as large as that in Frank's apartment, featured vintage green appliances. A round table and chairs with space-age aluminum legs sat at one end. At the other, a huge sectional sofa faced a state-of-the-art wide-screen TV. Orange shag throw rugs softened the laminate floor, and the whole room smelled like patchouli—and vanilla candles.

A man in a black cable-knit sweater approached, carrying a tray of cookies. "Welcome, Frank and Rauch. Keira's told us so much about you. Please, have a cookie. I baked them myself. They're gluten and dairy-free." He thrust the tray under their noses. "And they're still warm."

Frank and Rauch exchanged glances. Rauch shrugged and dropped Frank's suitcase so he could grab a cookie. "Thanks. Mm—oatmeal raisin. My favorite."

Frank raised an eyebrow. Rauch hated raisins.

A young man with bushy red hair bounced on his feet with excitement. He grabbed Frank's suitcase from the floor. "You, too, Frank. Take a cookie. Take two cookies. But don't ruin your dinner. We've ordered pizza—three whole pies! I'll put this in your room."

"He has another box of stuff in the trunk. Do you mind, Deliverance?" Keira touched his arm, and he blushed until his freckles disappeared.

"No, no, no, I don't mind. I'll be right back. Don't start without me." He dashed down the hall, swinging Frank's suitcase like a yoyo.

"Wow. He's…hyper." Rauch mimed plucking a banjo. "Deliverance. Really? Like the movie?"

Keira's indulgent smile faded. "No, and he's very sensitive about it, so leave out the lewd references, okay? He's never seen the film, but he's endured enough teasing to get the gist."

"Then why doesn't he change his name? It's not like it's written in gold on his birth certificate." He grinned. "Not like Frank's is."

"Because it fits him. Before he joined Heroes2B, he delivered pizzas for a living."

"Plus, he's deeply religious." The man in the cable-knit sweater chimed in. "He says it stands for 'deliver us from evil.' I think it's lovely." He dropped the tray of cookies on the table and extended his hand. "I'm Ruletka. It's Russian for 'Roulette.' My real name's Toni, but like Deliverance, I can't imagine being called anything else. I'm sure you understand, right Frank? Or should I call you Lambda?"

"Frank's fine." He tried not to wince at Ruletka's

firm grip. "I take it you're a gambler."

"Of sorts, but not in the way you're imagining. Allow me to explain. I'm Russian-American." He removed a vintage revolver from beneath his sweater, flashing a well-honed pack of abs in the process. Rauch dropped the duffel from his shoulder and elbowed Frank aside.

"Relax, big guy." Ruletka chuckled. "For demonstration purposes only."

Aiming the revolver at the ceiling, he spun its cylinder with a flick of his slender finger and pulled the trigger. Frank flinched. The revolver clicked but didn't fire. Ruletka popped the cylinder open and displayed it to Frank and Rauch. Five of the chamber's slots were empty. The sixth contained a shiny copper bullet.

"Russian roulette. I played it often in my younger, angrier years. Fortunately, I never lost. I'm much better now." He waved his gun in a broad circle. "This has helped. I love it here, and I hope you will, too."

Deliverance zoomed into the commons and screeched to a halt in front of Keira. "Okay, everything's unloaded and upstairs."

He lifted the strap of Rauch's duffel off the floor, but before it reached his shoulder, Rauch seized his hand. "I'll get it myself, thanks."

Deliverance, eyes wide, released the strap and shuffled out of reach.

Keira glanced at her phone. "Time to pick up the pizza. Make yourselves at home and get to know each other. I won't be long." She spun on her heel and left.

An awkward silence followed.

Frank cleared his throat. "Would one of you mind showing us to our rooms? I'd like to unpack before dinner. Wouldn't want my shirts to get wrinkled. I hate ironing."

Ruletka laughed. "As do I. Follow me."

Deliverance grinned and grabbed another cookie. "What's ironing?"

Frank and Rauch followed Ruletka down the main hall. He passed the entrance and continued straight to the other half of the building, which contained an extensive assortment of gym equipment.

Rauch whistled. "Sweet."

Ruletka nodded. "We're encouraged to work out. You'll find me here most evenings after work."

"When you're not baking cookies."

Ruletka's eyes narrowed. "Today was a grand occasion. Consider yourselves special."

Outside the gym was a set of stairs. Ruletka jogged them to the second floor, followed by Rauch and Deliverance. Frank brought up the rear. Numbered doors lined the long upstairs corridor, where a hideous purple carpet in a swirled print, designed to hide wear and stains, replaced the laminate flooring. Ruletka led them past the yellow cinder block walls to doors five and six, directly across the hall from each other.

"Deliverance put your stuff in room five, Frank, but the dorms are all the same, so if for some reason you two want to switch, feel free. I'm in the first room if you should need anything, and Deliverance occupies room number two."

Frank peered down the hall. "Who's in three and four?"

"No one. The other rooms are empty. We skipped a room in between for privacy's sake. Though I have to say, not much sound penetrates these walls. They were built specifically to filter out the noise of the nearby factory. They block cell signals, too. If you want to use your phone, you'll have to do it outside. I don't know if you noticed, but we have a communal laptop in the commons. The Internet's sketchy, but it's good enough for ordering pizza."

Ruletka motioned for Deliverance to start down the hall. "Speaking of which, we'll let you know when it's here. Come along, Deliverance. Our new friends need time to unpack and adjust."

Deliverance's face fell, but he trotted toward the stairs as directed, glancing over his shoulder every so often as if to confirm Rauch and Frank were still there.

Frank waited for the echoes from the stairwell to fade. He grasped the knob to door number five and paused. "Do you care which one?"

"Nope. You?"

"Nope." Frank took a deep breath and swung the door wide.

Rauch did the same. "Here we go. Home sweet home."

****

Frank finished hanging the last of his clothes in the tiny closet. He left the box of board games and comic books packed in case he needed to make a quick getaway. His clothes, except for the autographed Stan Lee T-shirt he got a few years ago at a Philadelphia comic con, were replaceable. His comics were not. As an afterthought, he threw the T-shirt in the box as well. Better safe than sorry.

He sat on the edge of the twin bed and bounced up and down, testing the springs. No squeaking. Felt solid, like everything else in his new home. Truth be told, the spare but tidy room was nicer than the bedroom in his old apartment. It didn't house much, but the few items it did contain had been chosen with great care. He fingered the plush down comforter folded at the foot of the bed and ran his palm over the brushed flannel sheets. Keira had good taste—and deep pockets. He already knew the latter from her bling and her ride.

Someone pounded on his door, and he jumped to his feet. "Guys, guys, the pizza's here."

Frank opened the door to find Deliverance grinning from ear to ear. The deep dimples puckering his freckled cheeks combined with a shock of red hair made him resemble Howdy Doody. Or Chucky—if you put a butcher knife in his hand. Frank cocked his head and stared into Deliverance's blue eyes, which glowed with maniacal enthusiasm. Time would tell which doll he took after the most. Frank's money was on Chucky.

A yawning Rauch shuffled from his room and stretched. Frank shot him a quizzical look.

"You had time for a nap?"

"Sure. Didn't you?"

"I was unpacking."

"I tossed my stuff into a drawer. Took five minutes. How about that blanket, huh? Pretty swanky. It's like being in a five-star hotel."

"I wouldn't know, and neither would you." Frank shook his head and followed Deliverance down the stairs and back to the commons, where the tray of cookies had been shoved aside to make room for pizza boxes and beer.

Rauch sniffed the enticing aroma and exhaled with a sigh. "Pizza, beer, and cookies. It doesn't get any better than this."

Keira kept the conversation light, deflecting Frank's dogged questioning with a breezy, "It's the weekend, and we're celebrating your arrival. The work week starts tomorrow."

After his fourth beer, he gave up. He'd learned enough for one night. At two months, Ruletka had been at the company's Philadelphia campus the longest and was responsible for refurbishing the dorm. Deliverance joined him a month later and was something of a speed demon, boasting he could outrun, outrace, or outmaneuver the devil himself. Neither seemed to have any regrets—none they were willing to share in front of Keira, anyway—and both seemed quirky but genuinely friendly and pleased to have him and Rauch on board.

"It's normal," Ruletka said, after downing several beers of his own, "to have such doubts, but once the training starts, they'll soon disappear." He turned on the hockey game, because "every Russian loves hockey," and they settled on the comfy sofa to cheer on the Flyers. By the end of the second period, Ruletka was snoring, and Frank's eyes had begun to droop.

"Time for bed, I think. It's been an eventful day." Keira clicked off the TV and jingled her keys. "Breakfast is at seven here in the commons, and the workday starts at eight."

Rauch blinked. "*Seven a.m.?*" He looked at the others for concurrence. "She's kidding, right?"

Frank smothered a grin. Rauch rarely rose before nine and never before eight.

Keira was not amused. "Seven in the morning, buttercup. See you then." She strode down the hall. The SUV's headlights flashed before disappearing around the corner of the building.

"Where does she go?" Frank stood, and the room swayed. He grabbed the arm of the sofa for support. Too much beer and patchouli.

"I don't know." Deliverance tossed a fuzzy blanket over Ruletka's bare feet and switched off the light. "I never gave it much thought. She probably has a McMansion somewhere on the Main Line."

Frank and Rauch followed him down the hallway toward the stairs. Rauch snagged the last cookie from the table as he strolled past. "In case I need a midnight snack."

Frank snorted. "In case you miss breakfast is more like it."

"That, too."

They lingered in the upstairs corridor and waited until Deliverance disappeared behind door number two. Rauch followed Frank into his room. "What do you think so far?" He helped Frank out of his shirt, then examined his bruised shoulder. "Lookin' good. The swelling's gone down already."

"I think she's trying to buy our allegiance with food and beer. First the Chinese, then the pizza—"

"And it's totally working, at least for me." Rauch grinned. "Life is good."

"I'm withholding judgment until the actual job starts. Today was like the opening credits of a movie. The real action starts tomorrow. Let's just hope the movie isn't *Die Hard*." Frank yawned and fluffed his pillow.

Rauch ignored the hint. "What about the guys?"

"Deliverance is a little ADHD, but Ruletka seems nice. I think we'll get along fine."

"Did you see his neck?"

"Ruletka's? Duh, yeah. If I recall correctly, it was attached to the rest of his body. What about it?"

"No Adam's apple, no five o'clock shadow. I think he's a she."

"So?"

"I wonder if Keira knows, that's all."

"I'm sure she does. She seems sharper than a light saber and twice as bright. But even if she doesn't, it's none of our business."

"It kind of is. You might end up, you know, grappling with him—her, whatever—as part of the training."

Frank shrugged. "He says he's a he, and so that's what he is. It's that simple, Rauch. Let it go."

"I wonder if that's why he carries a gun and does the hero-thing. I bet he was bullied. He's probably over-compensating."

"Since when are you into touchy-feely psychoanalysis crap? Keira's the one with the degree. You can't learn that shit by osmosis, Rauch. Now go to bed." Frank flopped on the mattress and stretched his neck and arm, trying to find a comfortable position. "My shoulder's killing me. I thought I drank a medicinal dosage of beer, but I guess not. Tomorrow's gonna suck without any sleep."

"It'll be all right, Frank. I promise."

"I love you, Rauch, but I can't recall a single time when you've kept one of your promises."

"You're probably right." Rauch paused with his hand on the door. "But I'm starting right now." He flashed a lopsided grin. "I promise."

Chapter Seventeen

Rauch had never slept better, which made rising at seven in the morning more tolerable. Huge swathes of paved lots, inoperable street lights, and abandoned buildings insulated the campus, conferring a deep silence and darkness unfamiliar to someone who'd spent his entire life in the light-polluted inner city.

To some, it might have seemed eerie, but Rauch welcomed a night devoid of random gunfire, shrill sirens, and the night crawlers' raucous laughter. These were the songs which comprised the soundtrack of his turbulent youth. As his eyes drifted shut, he heard his first cricket. It took him a while to figure out what it was. He smiled and snuggled into his brand-new pillow. Life wasn't just good. It was awesome.

And now he smelled bacon. He threw on a rumpled shirt and a pair of faded sweatpants and pounded on Frank's door. No response. Knowing Frank, he was the one cooking the bacon. Rauch followed his nose to the kitchen. As predicted, Frank stood at the stove frying a glistening slab of marbled bacon while Ruletka manned the toaster. Deliverance sat at the table praying for grace over a fluffy mound of scrambled eggs.

"Good morning." Ruletka eyed Rauch's uncombed hair and sloppy outfit, and his lips tightened into a thin line. "White or wheat?"

"White." Rauch leaned over Frank's shoulder and

sniffed. "Mm, bacon. How'd you sleep?"

"Not so great." Frank's puffy eyelids and dark circles validated his assertion. "It was too quiet. I miss the neighborhood racket." He threw the bacon onto a communal platter and dropped it in the center of the table.

Ruletka finished the toast and poured them each a steaming mug of black coffee. "Guaranteed to put hair on your chest." He joined them at the table.

"Better make mine a double." Frank scooped himself some eggs. He waved his fork at Deliverance and Ruletka, who were dressed in matching black track suits. "Is that some kind of uniform?"

"Yes." Ruletka nodded. "Keira will issue you one after the morning weigh-in." He glanced at Rauch. "I don't know if you'll be required to wear a uniform since you're not in the hero program. However, this is your first day of a new job. You might want to consider sprucing up. Miss Keira appreciates punctuality and a professional appearance. At least comb your hair."

Rauch's fork halted midway to his mouth. "I was planning on it."

Ruletka dabbed at the corner of his mouth with a napkin. "Good."

Rauch was not planning on it. He'd dressed to impress when allying with Keira initially, and that was the extent of his wardrobe. If she wanted him to look like a man-in-black, she'd have to buy him new threads.

Deliverance chattered between mouthfuls of eggs, filling the void left by the others. Rauch watched as the faint tremor in Frank's right hand, probably triggered by a combo of fatigue and nerves, got progressively worse. Rauch loathed coffee, and he'd never known

Frank to enjoy it much either. But here he was, guzzling away. By his third cup, Frank was shaking like a hairless cat in a blizzard.

Keira arrived fifteen minutes early. Rauch jumped to his feet and ran a hand through his hair. "I was just heading back to the room to change." He sidled toward the stairs.

She held up her hand, signaling him to stop. "Never mind."

He grinned at Ruletka. Exactly what he'd hoped she'd say.

Ruletka glared. "You have bacon between your teeth." Deliverance tittered.

Keira pointed at Rauch. "Wait for me in the car." She tossed him the key fob. "Ruletka, you're in charge of weigh-in and initiation until I return. Deliverance, after your weigh-in, head to the target range. I want you in tip-top form before we head to Vegas."

"Yes, ma'am." He sprang to his feet so fast, his chair toppled over behind him.

Rauch noticed Frank's worried expression, and his own shoulders tensed. "Initiation? Is that, like, some sort of hazing?"

"Of course not." Ruletka belittled their concerns. "It's merely an assessment of a recruit's baseline skill level, as well as education on what's expected over the coming weeks."

"Then maybe you should call it an assessment and not an initiation."

Keira frowned. "You're supposed to be in the car."

Deliverance tittered again.

Rauch scowled and glanced at Frank, who nodded. "I'll catch you later, buddy, okay?" He strode to the exit, aware of four pairs of eyes following his progress with varying degrees of interest.

Fuming, he paced next to the SUV and watched the sun rise over the skyline. The way he saw it, he and Keira were partners in this venture. He understood if she needed to keep up appearances in front of the others, but she'd better not treat him like a valet in private. If he wanted to be disrespected, he'd work with Skinny.

With a toss of her purple pashmina, Keira strolled in through the exit. "It's cold out here. Why aren't you in the car?"

"Because I didn't know who was driving."

"I'm driving." She shot him a funny look as if he'd asked the stupidest question ever.

"Of course. Silly me." Rauch clenched his teeth and climbed in the passenger side.

Keira drove to the far end of the main building and parked by a loading dock. They labored up the steep ramp. A small sign marked "Security" hung to the left of the dock's huge overhead door. She unlocked the entrance and flipped a switch. The lights popped on in quick succession—two dozen rows of industrial, high-bay LEDs designed to bathe every square inch of the factory in their clear, white light.

He blinked. Repurposed equipment—gears and pulleys and presses of every mechanical sort—filled the vast space. Even in the bright light, the dusty warehouse felt vaguely sinister, as if one of the larger machines could, at any moment, rise up, shake off its layer of rust, and reveal itself to be a Terminator. With a bang and a hiss, a pair of overhead lights burst, releasing a shower of sparks.

"Shit. What was that?" Rauch flinched and reflexively raised his forearm to shield his face.

"Blew a bulb. Happens on occasion. Follow me."

She guided him to an open metal staircase along the right hand wall and bounded up its rickety treads. The stairs spiraled to a second-story catwalk, which spanned the length of the building, giving a birds-eye view of the entire space. From here, they were at eye level with an array of pulleys and levers as well as more modern hydraulic systems attached to the beams of the ceiling. The creaky catwalk swayed as Keira crossed toward the glass control room, which anchored the far end. Rauch clutched the thin handrail and tried not to look down.

The metal bridge groaned as Keira approached the end, and Rauch hesitated midway. She slowed her pace. "Come on. You're all right. It's sturdier than it looks. Although the factory was originally built in the 1800s, it was updated a bunch of times before it finally closed in the late 1950s."

"Which makes this bridge, like, sixty years old. Not helpful. Thanks for the history lesson, though."

"Do you want me to hold your hand? Or how about this?" She jumped up and down, causing the catwalk to shriek and shudder. Rauch paled. He lurched forward and sprinted the final few feet to join her at the end.

"You are so not cool." He exhaled as his foot touched the solid floor.

"It worked, didn't it?" She smirked and leaned over the railing so far Rauch was tempted to grab her by the waist. "I love this place, dirt and all. It has character. When the original owners had it updated, they didn't remove a lot of the older equipment, so there's a unique mix of vintage machinery and modern electronics. Gives it kind of a steampunk vibe, which is awesome. I've been tempted a couple of times to refurbish it and live here. I've had acquaintances who've turned old churches into homes, and they're incredible."

"Incredibly weird, maybe."

"Weird to you. I happen to like old things. Things with history attached to them. Makes me feel more adventurous and alive." She ushered him into the control room and flicked on the light.

Here the equipment was state-of-the-art. Monitors displayed views of the campus's four corners, the main gate, and three of the buildings: the factory, the dorm, and one he didn't recognize. Movement caught his eye, and he pointed to the high-resolution color display.

"Hey, there go Ruletka and Frank." Tiny images exited the dorm and walked away from the factory toward the unfamiliar building.

Keira nodded. "They're going to the training center. As head of security, you'll be working out of this building and mostly from this room where you can monitor the campus for intruders."

"What kind of intruders? Mice?" Rauch scoffed at the notion that anyone would be interested in such a dilapidated, depressing locale.

She shrugged. "We get the occasional group of intrepid teens looking for an out-of-the-way place to party. Sometimes if the police see activity at night, they do a drive-by. That's why I imposed a curfew. Lights out at nine."

"If you own the place, why worry about the cops?"

"I don't want to have to explain what I'm doing here. The official line, should someone ask, is that I'm planning to renovate and reopen the campus as a kind of extreme sports park. You know, trampolining, trapeze acts, skateboarding—that sort of thing."

"Actually, that sounds like a damned good idea."

"It would be fun, but not nearly as profitable as plan A. And if plan A fails, I won't be able to show my face in Philly again."

"True. Who else knows about plan A?"

"Just you and Pinball."

"Pinball?"

"Tico Harris, my original partner. He's been involved since the plan's inception. Pinball's a celebrity in the real-life superhero community. He rules the Vegas area, and that's not an easy thing to do given the sheer number of local cosplayers, not to mention the furries and plushies."

"And Elvis." Rauch swiveled his hips and grinned. "Don't forget about Elvis."

"Never. I met him at a Vegas comic con a few years ago, and—"

Rauch gaped. "You've met Elvis?"

"Pinball, you moron. Elvis has been dead since before you and I were born."

"So they say."

Keira sighed and rubbed her forehead. "As I was saying, Pinball's an electronics expert. Spent his youth fixing and rigging arcade games. Ran them out of his garage and collected the quarters for income. He's moved on to grander things. Wait 'til you meet his electronic bestie, Rictor. I know Frank did time at a tech school. I thought if Pinball needed help, Frank could assist him with some of the more technical aspects of the plan."

"Frank's version of Plan A is Hufflepuff; yours is Slytherin. Are you gonna clue him in on the not-so heroic details?"

She paused. "I don't know yet. We'll see what happens over the next few weeks. At this point, he seems too…moral to consider it."

"What's that make me?"

"You have your own moral code, as do I."

"I'm not sure that's a compliment."

"It wasn't meant to be. It's simply a fact. Show me your weapon."

"Huh?"

"Your gun. I know you carry one."

Rauch tugged his gun from his waistband and displayed it to Keira. Her lips twitched, and he shoved it back in his pants. "It may be small, but it gets the job done."

"You could use an upgrade."

Keira opened the door of a nondescript cabinet opposite the monitors to reveal a five-foot-tall wall safe. She pressed her finger against its touchscreen, and it unlocked with a click. The thick door swung open, and Rauch's eyes widened. "Wow."

Six velvet-lined shelves held an assortment of guns, ammo, knives, and mysterious high-tech equipment along with some decidedly low-tech staples such as zip ties and a lock picking kit. A long black whip, conspicuously displayed on the top shelf, coiled around a stun gun and a latex mask. Rauch reached to stroke the fine woven leather, but she smacked his hand. He raised an eyebrow in an implicit question.

"Pinball designed the high-tech stuff. The whip is mine. It's old. According to rumor, it once belonged to an original masked hero, the swashbuckling Douglas Fairbanks himself. I still carry it from time to time, mostly at cosplay conventions."

"Mostly?"

Keira's lips curved, but she ignored his question. "You require something easier to conceal." She browsed her selection and chose a German semi-automatic pistol before locking the safe and sliding the cabinet door shut. "You won't be able to carry this in the waistband of your sweats. It's too heavy." She tossed him a notepad and pen from the control desk. "Jot down your measurements so I can get you more appropriate attire. Do you prefer a shoulder or belt holster?"

"Belt." Rauch scribbled the requested information and handed her the pad. "I don't see why I need fancy duds to work in a dusty old warehouse like this."

"As the head of security, you may have to interact with the police, and they respond better to someone who is neatly dressed. It's a psychology-thing. Besides, once we get to Vegas, you'll function as my bodyguard, and you'll need to blend in. How are your fighting skills?"

He flexed his muscles. "Above average."

Keira threw a lightning fast jab at his nose, followed by a vicious right hook to the ribs. He bobbed and blocked the jab with ease, but the hook landed with a thud. A solid hit, but Rauch had experienced worse. He didn't so much as flinch. Then she surprised him. With a sweep of her boot, she knocked his ankles out of from under him, and he fell on his butt.

She stepped back. "You need to work on your reflexes, but otherwise—not bad."

He scrambled to his feet. "I was about to say the same thing." He lifted his ratty tee and inspected the red welt forming where her chunky emerald ring had impacted his ribcage. "That thing's more dangerous than a set of brass knuckles."

"You'll survive." Her fingers brushed over the mark, and his abs contracted at her unexpected touch. She bent to unlock a file cabinet and rifled through before extracting an unlabeled manila folder. "Take some time to get familiar with the surveillance system. Once you're comfortable with it, walk around campus and memorize the buildings. Then you can spend the rest of the day in the shooting range with Deliverance training with your new weapon." She handed him the file. "Leisure reading for later tonight. Any questions?"

Rauch grinned. "When's lunch?"

She did not return his smile. "Noon." She swept past him to the exit. "I suggest you take your new job seriously. We've got one shot at pulling this off, and you'd better be ready. If I fail, we all fail, and if I fail because of you…"

The metal catwalk clanked under her boots as she abruptly turned and stomped down the spiral staircase.

Rauch didn't need to hear the rest of her threat. He'd seen what her brother had done to Roy. But despite her tough talk, he doubted Keira was capable of Jack's level of brutality. Ordering someone else to do it—now that was a different matter altogether. That's why she'd hired him. He'd padded his oral resume with bold talk of mafia hits and other dramatic exploits. He had her fooled. At least, he thought he did.

He tossed the manila folder next to the gun, brushed the dust off the room's only chair, and plopped in front of the monitors. A dizzying array of buttons and knobs lay before him. He sighed. How hard could it be? Certainly no worse than learning the fight combinations for every video game ever made. He punched the biggest button and an ear-splitting siren blared throughout the building. He jumped to his feet and pounded the red button repeatedly with his palm in a desperate attempt to silence the alarm. Several switches and knobs later, the siren ceased, and Rauch, ears ringing, collapsed in the chair.

Shit. It was gonna be a long day.

Chapter Eighteen

Frank, wearing nothing but a thin pair of Squirrel Girl boxers, shivered in the frigid gym and wrapped his scrawny arms around his scrawnier chest. If he'd known he was going to have to strip, he'd have worn someone more intimidating. Ruletka guided him onto an old-fashioned scale, the kind with a lever that tilted and teetered every time Frank shifted his weight. It stabilized at one hundred-and-thirty-five pounds.

Ruletka clicked his tongue. "We need to put some meat on those bones." His fingers grazed the impressive purple-and-yellow bruises on Frank's shoulder. "What happened?"

Frank considered spinning a tale of heroic crime-fighting adventures but opted for the painful truth. "I tripped over a crack in the sidewalk." He inwardly cringed and braced for a shower of ridicule or at least a withering look.

"I see." Because Ruletka's demeanor remained unchanged, Frank decided he liked him for sure.

The Russian zipped through measuring Frank's waist, chest, and biceps and documented his findings on a spreadsheet. Next, he took Frank's pulse and blood pressure. "Good. We have our baseline measurements. Put your clothes back on, and hop on the treadmill."

Twenty minutes later, Frank wheezed off the treadmill and collapsed into a heap on the gym's padded floor. While Frank regained his breath, Ruletka scribbled complex graphs on a dry erase board mounted on the wall.

"Looks like we have a lot of work ahead of us. Your fitness level has something to be desired, especially for a hero. You're currently here." He drew a red dot with the marker. "And you need to be here." He plotted a second point on the graph and dragged the marker across the board to connect the dots. The resulting red line was steeper than most escalators.

Frank lifted his head from between his knees. "Tell me something I don't know. Too much beer and ramen, too many video games with Rauch, and not enough exercise."

"And probably a touch of asthma." Ruletka examined Frank's flushed cheeks. "Not to worry. I'll design you an individualized program, and I'll ask Miss Keira to get you an inhaler. We'll fix you right up. You'll be leaping tall buildings in no time. Speaking of which, let's assess your leg and core strength." He pointed to an evil-looking weight machine in the corner. "We'll skip the arms for now given your injury."

Frank slogged across the mat to the confusing array of bars and weights and sat on the machine's hard bench. "Are you some kind of coach?"

"Miss Keira recruited me specifically because I'm a certified personal trainer." Ruletka touched Frank's elbow. "You're facing the wrong direction."

After another twenty minutes of arduous strength testing, the ache in Frank's lungs convinced him he was going to die, and his training had not yet formally begun. Panting, he flopped on the sweat-slick floor, his oxygen-deprived brain struggling to find an escape clause from what was turning out to be a terrible decision. Plan A officially sucked.

"Why?" He coughed, paused to catch his breath, and tried again. "I must be insane. Why am I doing this to myself? Why do you do it?"

Ruletka chuckled. "I'm sure we have similar reasons. To be the best heroes we can be. To help the helpless. To give hope to the hopeless. Etcetera, etcetera, etcetera."

"There has to be more than that. There is for me."

The Russian lowered his gaze to log Frank's activity into the spreadsheet. "Then, there's the money issue."

"Truth. Now you're talking." Frank rolled to his knees and tried to stand but struggled to gain traction on the slippery mat.

Ruletka clasped his hand and hauled him upright. "And because I'm transgender."

"Okay. I'm missing the connection. How is that significant?"

He raised his brows. "You're okay with it?"

"Why wouldn't I be?"

"Because your friend Rauch is not."

"Nah. He's cool."

"Rauch is trying to be cool, but he's not. There's a world of difference between being and trying to be. But at least he's open-minded enough to make the effort. Many people aren't, even within the cosplaying community."

Ruletka rubbed the back of his neck. "The gun I showed you, the one I play Russian roulette with, belonged to my father. I inherited it when he died.

About once a week from the time I went through puberty and declared I was different, he'd point it at my head and threaten to blow my brains out. Homosexuality in any form is not 'cool' in the Russian culture. He raised me to believe I was damaged, unworthy to live."

Unsure what to say, Frank shifted his weight and stared at the floor.

Ruletka placed one hand on Frank's forearm. "To answer your question, I want to have sex reassignment surgery. I believe it's the only way for me to leave my past behind and permanently erase the damage. Hormone shots are expensive, and the surgery…let's just say thus far I could only afford the double mastectomy. Keira's promised to pay for the rest if I complete the entire training course. Afterward, once the wounds heal, I plan to throw my father's gun into the Delaware River and watch it sink." His somber expression lightened. "Unless we're in Vegas. Then I'll guess I'll have to bury it in the sand somewhere."

"Throw it into Lake Mead. No, I know—throw it into the fountains at Bellagio."

"There's a thought." Ruletka slapped him on the back. Frank winced. "I need to devise your training schedule. Why don't you join Deliverance at the shooting range? Have you ever shot a gun?"

"No."

"You're in for a real treat. Deliverance is so good, he's frightening."

****

Frank took his time wandering to the designated building, partly because his quivering calf muscles objected to anything more than a leisurely stroll and partly because he was in no hurry to bomb another aspect of his training. At this point, he wondered why Keira had chosen him to begin with. Maybe he was the control for her experiment, the never-gonna-make-it-as-a-superhero hero.

In retrospect, the whole concept seemed even more outrageous than when she'd first approached him. Yet, if he listened to Ruletka, he could almost believe it was real. He kicked a stone across the pavement and shook his head, angry at his own foolishness. It was a temporary job and nothing more. He'd accepted only for the food, housing, and Rauch's safety. His failure meant nothing to anyone except to Keira and her research. He was never going to see these people again once the training was over, except for Rauch. Hopefully he was faring better with Keira.

He stopped to pluck a weed that had somehow managed to sprout through a tiny crack in the asphalt. The recent frost had shriveled its brown leaves, and he crushed them in his fist, releasing the fine powder into the wind. It blew toward the city. He longed to follow.

Ruletka appeared to be thriving here, had found his own crack in the asphalt of life. But then again, the Russian had a concrete, long-term goal: he served as Keira's research subject; she paid for his surgery. Perhaps that was the secret to success—to have a goal which would render the physical suffering worthwhile. He'd quiz Deliverance about his objective when he arrived at the range.

A faint crack of gunfire, as innocuous as the popping of a child's balloon, indicated he was getting close. He'd learned to recognize the sound from an early age. "Life skills," his mother had called it, always with a sad smile on her face. With Rauch's aid and assistance, he'd completed a crash course in survival during his stint in juvie.

Frank followed the blasts to a whitewashed brick building laden with moss, thanks to the shade of the campus's solitary tree, a giant weeping willow. A faded sign revealed the building's original function: Sanatorium. Per Ruletka, the shooting range was in the basement, around the corner from the morgue. Convenient.

Given the building's age, Frank suspected its peeling white paint was heavy with lead and the floors rife with asbestos. As he heaved open the wooden door, a gust of wind sent paint chips swirling like drifting snow. He clamped a hand over his nose and mouth to avoid ingestion and hurried inside. The door slammed shut behind him.

Once inside, the noise of the gunfire became louder and more distinct. He located the stairs and descended to where Deliverance, wearing eye protection and noise-canceling headphones, stood blowing away the black silhouette of a man. Shreds of paper flew from the man's chest and head as Deliverance confidently released a round of shots, firing the bullets milliseconds apart. When he finished, he grinned and lowered his gun's smoking barrel. Light twinkled through two perfectly formed groupings in the tattered target.

Frank waited until he unloaded his clip before yelling his name. "Hey, Deliverance." He tapped him on the shoulder.

Deliverance jumped and swung around with his gun aimed straight at Frank's chest. Frank threw his hands in the air and stumbled backward. "Whoa there, buddy. It's just me. Frank. The new recruit. Remember?"

Frank held his breath as the seconds passed in slow motion. He watched as Deliverance's eyes, as wild and confused as those of the mumbling vagrants who roamed South Philadelphia's streets, slowly regained their focus. "Hey, hey there, Frank. Sorry about that. I was in the zone, you know?"

Frank nodded. He sort of knew. He'd stumbled away from many a gaming marathon looking just as confused and probably more than a little insane. Shooting zombies for twelve hours will do that to a man. But he hadn't been holding a real gun.

He cleared his throat and pointed to what remained of the paper target. "Nice job. Can you teach me how to do that?"

Frank never planned on owning a gun. First of all, he couldn't afford one. His Taser had been expensive enough. Secondly, he couldn't imagine himself shooting another human being, shredding a man's flesh to bloody bits with the same level of dispassionate efficiency as Deliverance. But a little knowledge never hurt anyone.

"Sure can." Deliverance slammed a fresh mag into the pistol's well. "Been shooting with my pop since I was seven years old. You're looking at a fifth-generation card-carrying member of the NRA."

What the hell was he supposed to say to something like that? "Um, congratulations."

Deliverance beamed. "That's why Keira chose me. I can outrace, outrun—"

"Or outmaneuver the devil himself. I remember."

"And as you just saw, I'm an excellent shot."

Deliverance pushed a button, and the target lurched into motion, riding the track until it was within arm's reach. He punched his fist through the grouping of holes in the silhouette's black chest before removing the target and replacing it with a new one.

"Vengeance is mine, sayeth the Lord. Sometimes I think I should've named myself Vengeance."

Deliverance talked with his hands, which under normal circumstances would constitute an innocent distraction. But in this case, his flailing right hand held a gun. The clean target slid down the track, squealing to a stop at half of its previous distance. Frank eyed the loaded weapon warily. "The name's already taken. *Ghost Rider*. From the comic books, not the movie. You'd better stick with what you've got."

Not that Frank had any idea what vengeance had to do with things, but offered a wan smile. Deliverance's frenetic brain operated on several channels at once, and Frank couldn't keep up. He wasn't sure he wanted to.

"As far as teaching me to shoot—you're gonna have to start at the beginning. Unless you count *Call of Duty* as experience, I'm a total newb."

"By the end of this morning, you won't be. You'll be good, good. Super good. Get it? Like a hero good." Deliverance placed his gun in Frank's hand. Frank stared at its ebony grip. Inlaid in mother-of-pearl in a fancy cursive script was a single word: *Vengeance*.

Chapter Nineteen

Rauch awoke to the incessant beeping of the motion-triggered gate alarm. He lowered his feet from the control desk and glanced at the clock. Noon. Damn. He rubbed his eyes. The seven-a.m. wake-up call, combined with the soothing hum of the room's electronics, had done him in.

He leaned forward in his chair and focused his bleary eyes on the monitor. An emerald-green sedan zoomed through the retracted gate, barely clearing the sides. The alarm stopped, only to retrigger when Keira's familiar black SUV raced to the open entrance. She leaned out the driver's window and with a punch of the keypad, aborted the gate's impending closure.

She tailed the foreign vehicle to the factory's cargo bay and screeched to a halt alongside, kicking up a plume of dust and pebbles from the decaying asphalt. Two men in dark suits and shades exited the sedan. They waited for Keira to do the same. She delayed, and he thought he saw her glance through the windshield at the camera mounted on the keystone above the factory's door. Maybe it was his imagination at play. But he wasn't taking any chances.

Rauch jumped from the chair and tucked his fancy new gun into the waistband of his sweats. He turned, and his pants fell to his ankles. The gun hit the floor with a clank. Shit. He was lucky it hadn't fired and shot him in the ass. At least he was wearing underwear. That wasn't always a given.

He pulled up his pants and grabbed his beat-up pistol. It might not impress, but it could still shoot yer eye out, kid. He hesitated at the catwalk, exhaled, and charged across. The metallic echo of his footsteps bounced off the factory's high ceilings. The entire building thundered as if the Mongol hoard were stampeding to Keira's rescue.

Rauch hurtled down the delivery ramp. The cold November air penetrated his thin tee, and he suppressed a shiver. He eyed his visitors' considerably warmer attire. Their fine wool overcoats, cozy enough to be left unbuttoned, covered collared shirts and silk ties. The shorter of the two sported a tartan scarf around his neck. A gold emerald ring similar to Keira's decorated his right hand. He scanned Rauch's disheveled appearance and grinned over his shoulder at the hulk of a man hovering a respectful distance behind.

"You must be Mr. Rauch, the man tasked with bringing my sister's crazy dream to life." He extended his bejeweled hand. "I'm Jack McConnell. I'm the man tasked with paying for it. All that schooling, and not one ounce of common business sense."

Rauch glanced at Keira's stormy expression before clasping Jack's hand in a firm grip. "It doesn't seem crazy to me, or else I wouldn't have accepted the job." *Sports park, right? Isn't that what she'd said?* He wished he'd paid better attention. It was her fault. She'd blown his mind with the whip.

Jack's grin broadened. "I hope she's paying you for that level of loyalty."

"Jack, enough." Kiera crossed her arms over her

chest. "What are you doing here?"

"Since you haven't bothered to return my calls, I thought I'd check the place out for myself."

"I've been otherwise occupied. Besides, you have no business here. I'm paying for this venture out of my inheritance. My progress or lack thereof is not your concern."

"But I own half the property."

"You signed it over to me."

"I may have changed my mind."

"You signed a legal document." Her fingers curled into tight fists. "Isn't it enough that you gypped me out of the family business and most of my inheritance? I'm the eldest. It all should've gone to me."

Jack feigned a yawn. "We've been through this a dozen times before. Dad, God rest his soul…" He directed his eyes to the heavens and made the sign of the cross. "…Didn't think so. And please, not in front of the help."

Jack's goon smirked at Rauch, who wondered if the muscle-bound bonehead realized he also qualified as "the help."

Jack grabbed Keira by the elbow and guided her inside. They ascended the stairs to the control room, where he shut the soundproof door. Rauch and Bonehead followed as far as the steps. Jockeying for position, they stood side by side at the foot of the stairs and watched the silent argument through the room's expansive glass window.

Bonehead grinned, revealing a pair of chipped front teeth. "Cailín talks with her hands like an Italian, don't she?"

"Cailín? Oh, you mean Keira."

"Who'd ya think I meant?"

"I didn't know. I was momentarily dazzled by your brilliant accent." Rauch had forgotten that when dealing with the Irish mob, one might encounter someone who spoke, like, Irish.

Bonehead cracked his knuckles. "Ya making fun of me, boy?"

"No, sir. Not today."

"Yer quite the rawny ponce, ain't ya?"

"Yes. No. Honestly, I don't know. I could be."

The control room door flew open, and with a flip of her purple hair, Keira stormed out and jogged down the steps. She jabbed her finger in Bonehead's broad chest. "Get out, and take that piece of shit with you."

Jack took his time meandering down the spiral staircase. He absently flicked a business card at Rauch. "Whatever she's paying you for this insane project, I'll pay you double to walk away." He cocked his head at his bodyguard, who fell in line behind him. "Think about it. As a savvy—and well-dressed, I might add—businessman, I'm sure you'll do the right thing."

Rauch snatched the card from Jack's fingers. Bonehead nodded and followed his boss out the door. Keira's glittering green eyes monitored their departure until the car cleared the gate. She spun on the heel of her black boots and paced the floor like a pent-up panther ready to pounce but lacking the necessary prey.

Rauch raised the card to the light. A tiny embossed jack of clubs leered at him from the right hand corner. He read the green text aloud. "Jack McConnell Imports." He flashed Keira a grin. "He seems like a cool dude."

She rushed to within inches of his face. "Jack is *not*

a cool dude. He's a psychopath. A maniac." Her voice, somewhere between a scream and howl, caused Rauch's ears to ring worse than the gate alarm. She grabbed a piece of rebar from the floor and whipped it across the factory. It clanged against a huge metal vat and skidded to the corner. "He's a reckless, dangerous man, Rauch. He's *not* a dude."

Rauch took a broad step back. "Okay, I get it. He's dangerous. I was kidding, actually. He's a total asshole." He stuffed the business card in the pocket of his sweats. "You seem a bit unhinged yourself at the moment."

"I only want what's rightfully mine, and if I can't have it, neither can Jack."

"Yeah, about that. I joined this little scam of yours because the Italian mafia was breathing down my neck. The last thing I want is to piss off the Irish mob. Your brother won't be happy when I refuse his offer."

"If we pull this off, you won't have to worry about it. You'll be paid enough to disappear. Plus the families in Boston and Chicago will have Jack replaced."

"Replaced, huh?" In Rauch's understanding, replaced was a mob euphemism for whacked. "And that doesn't bother you? I mean, he is your brother."

"Listen to me. When I was ten years old, my father decided I looked an awful lot like his lawyer and not in the least like him. When I turned eleven, said lawyer was found carved into little pieces and stuffed inside his cherry-red convertible. Six months later, my mother disappeared. After that, I was treated like a second-class citizen in my own family. I started working on this plan when my father was torched a year ago, after his new lawyer read the will."

Her father's grisly murder had caused a media frenzy up and down the East Coast, and Rauch recalled being surprised. The Irish mob rarely made the local, much less the national, news. They preferred stealth to flash and were happy to let the Italians corner the media's attention. Their network of businesses dealt with illegal imports, loan sharking, and now that Pennsylvania had legalized casinos, gambling. But when they did make the news, man, it was brutal.

Skinny once told him that of all the scum in Chicago, Al Capone feared only the Irish mob, and for good reason. When it came to retribution, those deceptively amicable, whiskey-swilling Catholics did not fuck around. Keira's father, the erstwhile boss, was a prime example. The authorities identified his pile of bones and ashes solely through dental records and the family crest on his emerald ring—the same ring, Rauch assumed, which now adorned Jack's finger.

Keira led him out to the car. "When my father's will named Jack the new head of operations, I admit I had mixed emotions. Part of me was relieved. Racketeering is not my jam. But when I found out he'd cut my inheritance to a flat million, I was jacked, no pun intended. I know it sounds like a lot to you, but trust me, my brother received much, much more. And a million doesn't go far these days."

Not for one who drives a Porsche. "Remember that when it comes time to pay me for my service."

She slammed the driver's door. "Get in."

"Where are we going?"

"Back to the dorm."

"We could've just walked."

"Not unless you want to carry the new wardrobe I

bought you."

They drove the rest of the short distance in silence. Keira parked in front of the dorm and opened the back hatch. "Take your luggage upstairs and unpack. I'll see you in the lunchroom." She stormed inside and disappeared around the corner.

Rauch shook his head and whistled. Lady needed a 'lude. He lugged the heavy bag up the stairs and tossed it on his bed, which groaned in protest. The suitcase's main compartment flipped open with a tug of its shiny brass zipper. A new holster, its stiff leather pleasantly aromatic, rested atop a pin-striped suit with tissue paper tucked beneath the pristine collar and its perfectly creased lapels. A stack of polos and khakis peeked from below, and in the very bottom, a new pair of men's dress shoes nestled in a pile of socks with gold-stitched toes.

He unfolded a shirt from the top of the stack. The baby blue polo had an embroidered green alligator over its breast pocket. Rauch grimaced and tossed it in the back of the closet. He'd never worn a polo in his life, and he wasn't about to start now. Why anyone would want to wear an alligator on his titty was beyond him.

Now the suit—the suit was all right. He tried on the pants first, which fit as if they'd been tailored to his specifications. He shrugged on the jacket and modeled in front of the bathroom mirror. Man, he looked dope. Respectable even. He had to give it to her. Keira liked quality shit, which is why to her, a million seemed like lunch money. This suit alone had to cost two grand.

The mirror reflected his stupid grin. He tugged on the suit's starched lapels and ran a hand over his hair. What kind of dude would a girl—sorry, woman—like her find attractive? Not someone like him, for sure. But any boyfriend of hers would be set for life. Maybe when the con was done, he'd consider applying for the job. If she weren't so damned bossy, they might get along fine.

Everyone was gathered over heaping plates of spaghetti when Rauch strutted into the commons. While Deliverance chattered about nothing and everything, Keira picked the polish off her manicured nails and zoned out, nodding just often enough to appear interested. Frank, he was pleased to note, was still alive and appeared to have survived his initiation unscathed. Rauch winked at him and ran his hands down the jacket's glossy fabric. Frank choked on a meatball, and Keira awoke from her rumination in time to stop Rauch from serving himself a pile of pasta marinara.

"Oh no you don't. Not while wearing the suit," she said. "Either go and change, or you're wearing a bib."

Rauch twirled on one fashionable heel. "Whaddaya think? I clean up real nice, huh?"

"You're welcome. Now go change."

"I'll choose option number two, thanks." He removed his jacket and draped it carefully over the back of the sofa before tucking a cloth napkin into his shirt collar.

Ruletka tossed him a second napkin. "Just in case. My meatballs tend to be juicy."

Rauch shot Frank a look, and they dissolved into giggles.

Keira rolled her eyes. "Now that Rauch has decided to grace us with his dapper presence, I have an important announcement to make. Due to unforeseen circumstances, I've decided to transfer our base of operations to Nevada sooner than previously planned. Will that be a problem for anyone?"

Ruletka prepared Rauch a plate, then neatly wiped away any drips of marinara from its rim with a clean dishtowel. "How soon?"

"This week."

Ruletka's hand jerked; the plate bobbled. Rauch pushed away from the table as if expecting a lapful of spaghetti. The room fell silent.

Deliverance was the first to speak. "Is there a problem, Miss Keira?"

"I received a threat to cut my funding, and if it happens, I can't afford to operate both campuses. I think it's best to consolidate now on our own terms rather than wait until we're forced to do so. I'd rather not be evicted. You'll receive equivalent training in Vegas, I promise. Can I count on you to join me?" She clasped her hands and waited with an expectant smile.

"Hells, ya." Deliverance bounced in his seat. "Vegas, here I come. Sin City could use a man of faith like me."

Ruletka nodded. "I told you from the beginning I was in this for the long haul, no matter what."

"Thank you, gentlemen." Keira's clenched fingers relaxed. "What about you, Frank?"

"But I....I...we just got here. Like, yesterday."

"I know." She sighed and rubbed her temples. "This is not how I wanted it to play out either. Fortunately, Rauch pledged his commitment earlier, so I'm hoping you can be as flexible as he."

"Oh, he did, did he?" Frank scowled at Rauch, who crammed a meatball in his mouth to avoid giving a response. His ploy failed. Frank waited.

Rauch speared another meatball. "Come on, Frank. It'll be fun. Keira told me there's a huge cosplay convention the week before Thanksgiving for people who can't make Vegas' official comic con in June. When will we ever get another chance at an all-expenses-paid trip out West? Never. That's when."

Ruletka dropped his fork with a clatter. "Oh my God—really? A cosplay convention? We could all go. It'd be like a team-bonding thing. I love it." He placed a hand over his heart and swooned.

"See?" Rauch shot Ruletka a grateful look, and he smiled. "Everyone's excited except you. Just think about it—it could be Lambda Man's big-time debut. What bigger stage than Vegas?"

Deliverance tossed a stack of napkins in the air. They fluttered to the ground like giant confetti. "Cosplay convention! Cosplay convention!" He jumped from his seat and moon walked around the table. "I get to be Sandman. I'm Sandman, I'm Sandman."

Keira laughed. "Looks like you're outnumbered, Frank. I'll contact Pinball at the Vegas campus and start working out the travel itinerary. We'll meet tomorrow after breakfast at the obstacle course. I should have more info then." She breezed out the door.

Ruletka glanced at Frank's apoplectic expression and blithely strolled to the stove. He returned carrying a replenished platter of steaming pasta with sauce. "Now, who wants more of my juicy meatballs?"

****

Rauch avoided Frank for the rest of the day. He gulped down the rest of his lunch and escaped to the factory to retrieve his new gun and the manila folder he'd left behind after Jack's unexpected visit. He spent the rest of the afternoon at the sanatorium with Deliverance in target practice. When the waning sun shrouded the dormitory in shadows, he hid in his bedroom to change clothes and used the hour before dinner to study the file's contents.

The folder contained a mishmash of newspaper clippings, copies of Jack's purloined emails, and pictures. The black-and-white photos were standard fare: aerial views of the campuses and their buildings, headshots of Jack and his team of thugs, and so on. Rauch flipped through quickly until he reached the final photo. Stuck in the folder as if by afterthought, the image was compelling enough for him to remove it from the folder and hold it closer to the light.

The McConnell family portrait featured the boss, his wife—a gorgeous woman with long, flowing hair— and their two young children. Jack, wearing a vest and knickers, sat on his father's knee. Despite his tender age, the boy somehow still managed to look like an arrogant prick. Keira stood beside her mother, squeezing her hand.

Rauch's throat tightened, and a familiar, bitter taste formed in the back of his mouth. This one photo told him everything he needed to know about Keira's childhood. Behind the women's wide eyes and artificial smiles lurked terror.

Their rigid postures stood in stark contrast to the relaxed poses of Jack and his father. Keira's torso was slightly turned as if she were shielding her mother with her tiny body, and in a flash, Rauch understood. He'd tried to shield his mother once, too, before he realized how little she cared about anything but heroin. Frank had shielded his mother and baby brother dozens of times, offering up his body in place of theirs, until the day they died—a day he'd escaped to the movies and wasn't home to take their beatings for them.

Keira had escaped to college instead. But now, her father was dead, and she was back. This con was about money, yes, and hopefully lots of it, but it meant so much more. It was about payment for a childhood lost to grief and abuse, and for a murdered mother who'd never been put to rest. It was about revenge.

In that way, Keira wasn't so different from Frank, and Frank was everything Rauch strived to be. Minus the green hockey pants. He liked his new threads better. And although Keira was bossy, she was a hell of a lot better than taking orders from Skinny. Easier on the eyes, too. He found himself looking forward to Vegas, if nothing more than to see Keira dressed for the con. With that purple hair of hers, she'd make a mighty fine X-Man.

Chapter Twenty

After lunch, when the other team members bolted, Frank helped Ruletka clear the table and load the dirty plates into the sink. Frank washed; Ruletka dried. The Russian hummed while stealing glances at Frank's stormy expression. "You don't like Las Vegas?"

"Don't know. Never been there."

"You don't want to go?"

"Vegas is not the problem. The problem is Rauch." Frank tossed the last of the silverware into the sudsy water. "He's been cramming Keira's wild ideas down my gullet since she first showed up at our apartment. He and I both know this is some kind of scam—we agree on that much—yet he's acting like he'd jump off a cliff at her command. It's not like him. I swear he has the hots for her."

"And the fact that he likes her bothers you?"

"Of course it bothers me. I don't trust her, and I certainly don't want to follow someone I don't trust to a city like Vegas when I've never even left my own little neighborhood. It's foolish."

Ruletka nodded. "You're feeling insecure; I don't blame you. It's truly a leap of faith. But what's the worst that can happen?"

"When this con hits the skids, we could get stuck out there and end up living on the streets. That's one scenario. As far as the rest...I don't know. I guess I...I haven't thought that far ahead." Frank threw the dishcloth on the counter and shook his head. "Since Roy was killed and I lost my job, my life has been total weirdsville. Things have changed so fast, I haven't had time to think. And now I'm moving to Vegas."

"Give us a fair shake. I've been with Heroes2B for over two months now, and I've never known Keira to be anything but forthright and kind. You want to be a real hero, don't you?"

Frank blushed and nodded. "It sounds silly when you say it out loud. Do you truly believe this whole deal is genuine and not some kind of crazy scam?"

"I choose to believe. You and I are in this together, Frank, just like you and Rauch are. If you end up on the streets, I'm likely to be right behind you, and I won't allow that to happen. Now, let's get back to work. Come. You can digest your lunch on the way."

They left the dorm and strolled across the chilly campus to the training center's main gymnasium. A gust of wind blew the door out of Ruletka's hand, and it flew backward on its hinges, slamming against the brick wall. Frank rushed over the threshold. Ruletka shoved the door shut behind them.

Frank shivered. "On the plus side, Vegas will be warmer."

"There's always a plus side, if you choose to embrace it."

"Why do I get the feeling this workout is about to suck?"

Ruletka laughed. He lowered himself to the floor, bent his legs to sit in a cross-legged position, and gestured for Frank to follow. Frank struggled to appear nonchalant as he matched his mentor's posture, tugging and twisting his knobby knees into compliance. His tight hip flexors spasmed in protest. He shifted his stiff legs, and the mat released the pungent smell of sweat and body odor. He grimaced and tried, as Ruletka has advised, to focus on the plus side. The stagnant air stunk, but at least the gym was warm.

Ruletka slid a folder bearing a colorful graph across the mat. "I charted out your fitness plan. We'll review it while we're processing the carbs we ate for lunch. Then I'll teach you the cardinal rules of being a hero, and we'll end the day with light stretching and relaxation techniques."

"There are cardinal rules to being a hero?"

"Of course." Ruletka grinned. "Every occupation has them. The real-life superhero community is no exception. The old indoctrinate the young. To begin—"

"Wait. Let me guess. The first rule of Heroes2B is you don't talk about Heroes2B."

Ruletka scratched his head. "No, but that's a good rule, Frank. I like it."

"You've never seen *Fight Club*, have you?"

"No. Enlighten me."

"It's Rauch's favorite movie of all time."

"Then I doubt I'd like it. Rule number one is: A hero must be physically strong."

Frank scoffed. "That's a dumb rule. First of all, it's obvious. Secondly, it means I failed already. What's number two?"

"A hero must be mentally strong."

His shoulders sagged farther. "Crap. I'm down two for two."

"You're stronger than you think. Trust me—I train people for a living. I can tell. You're eager to succeed, and for now, that's enough."

"And numero three?"

"A hero must always follow the code."

"ASCII or binary?" Frank groaned at Ruletka's blank expression. "Man, you're a tough audience. Okay, I'll bite. What's the code?"

"The ethical canon behind your actions. Your personal moral principles, whatever form they take."

"But everyone's code is different. What if my moral standards are like—I don't know—Deadpool's? That would suck. Even Batman's are iffy. They don't call him the Dark Knight because he wears black."

"Batman is morally ambiguous. In the real world, that would put you on the wrong side of the law." Ruletka sighed. "You're missing the bigger picture, Frank. The point is to stay true to yourself and to the reasons you first donned the mask declaring yourself a superhero. If you find yourself bending the code to fit the circumstances, you need to relinquish your cape. The first step is to spend quality time contemplating your beliefs. If you don't know what you stand for, how can you defend it with your life?"

Ruletka handed him a pen. "The folder contains a blank piece of paper. I want you to meditate for the next twenty minutes. Afterward, write down three things you exemplify and would protect with your life. By that time, our lunch should be digested, and we'll lift for arms, chest, and back."

Frank coughed. "Did you say meditate?"

"Yes."

"Um, how exactly does one do that? My hips can't take another twenty minutes of sitting like this. Now you want me to—what—rock and chant, too?"

"Sit however you like. You can even lie down, if you find that most comfortable. You don't need to rock. Just relax and breath." Ruletka closed his eyes and led by example, inhaling deeply through his nose and exhaling through pursed lips. His lids fluttered open, and he smiled. "Chanting is optional."

****

How did the hallway grow to such a titanic length? Frank stared with dismay at the second-floor corridor leading to his room. He'd barely made it up the steps after Ruletka's afternoon of beginner exercises, which included old-school calisthenics and isotonic stretches designed to turn a neophyte into a yogi. And Ruletka even took it easy on him because of his shoulder.

"Don't worry," the Russian had said with a smile. "You'll be fine—until tomorrow."

He was wrong. Frank already felt like he'd been trampled by a rampaging Hulk.

A sliver of light winked from beneath door number six. Frank took a deep breath and, grunting and groaning with each step, hobbled down the hall to tap on Rauch's door. His best friend answered wearing his usual scruffy sweats, which made Frank happy. He hardly recognized Rauch in that swanky suit.

Frank shuffled into the room without waiting for an invitation, and Rauch hurried to gather a host of photos and other papers he had scattered across his bed. He stuffed them in an unmarked manila folder and threw the whole thing on the dresser.

"What was that?" Frank cast a curious eye at the folder. If it hadn't been the entire way across the room, which in his current state seemed very far indeed, he might've grabbed it for a peek. Instead, he flopped on

Rauch's bed and moaned.

"Nothing. Just security stuff Keira asked me to review. It does have aerial photos of the Vegas campus, which is pretty cool. Looks like it's in the northeast corner of the city not far from the convention center."

"Makes it easy to crash the cosplay convention."

"Yep. My thoughts exactly."

Frank rolled on his side and winced. Rauch furrowed his forehead. "You okay?"

Frank rubbed his aching neck. "Ruletka is determined to pump me up. He assures me I'll feel worse tomorrow."

"You will. The second day is always the worst. That's why you're never supposed to exercise the same muscle groups two days in a row."

"Great. Tomorrow's obstacle course should be a blast, then."

"I'm kind of looking forward to it, actually."

"I'm not surprised. Just like you're looking forward to Vegas." Frank's tone sounded sharper than he intended. He covered by changing the subject. "What did you do this afternoon while Ruletka destroyed my self-worth?"

"Shooting range with Deliverance." Rauch twirled a finger next to his ear. "Dude's a little touched in the head, if you ask me."

"More than a little. I think he's totally mental. I bet he's got that bipolar disease. Whatever his official diagnosis, he doesn't seem like hero material to me. You have to wonder why Keira hired him. Did you see his gun?"

"You mean 'Vengeance?' Duh, Frank. That's why she hired him. He's an expert shot."

"An expert shot who's seeking vengeance against God-knows who for Lord-knows what. Keira's a psychologist. She has to know he's unstable. She's taking advantage of his mental illness. I'm not even sure he's with it enough to understand what he signed up for."

"Don't underestimate him. Trust me. Deliverance may be loony, but he's not dumb. He understands exactly what Keira wants from him. He's been freed. No more delivering pizzas for a living. He's probably thrilled someone hired him to shoot off his gun instead." Rauch grinned. "Either that, or she's paying him in Prozac."

"Sometimes you can be such a dick."

"I know, but you gotta admit it was funny."

"It's never funny to mock the mentally ill."

"Who crammed the stick up your butt? The old Frank—"

"There is no old Frank. I haven't changed. You're the one strutting around in fancy threads with a new girlfriend hanging off your arm."

"Girlfriend?" Rauch raised an eyebrow. "You think Keira likes me?"

"No, I think Keira's playing you. You, me, Ruletka—we're her patsies."

"We're not patsies; we're partners."

"Gimme a break, will ya?" Frank pushed himself off the bed. "And you call me naïve. I'm this close to not going to Vegas, Rauch. All I need is one more thing to push me over the edge, and I'm outta here."

"Frankie—"

"If you were thinking with your head and not your dick, you'd be right behind me."

"I am thinking with my head. Where would you go with no money and no apartment? We've got a chance here—a chance to score big for a change. Keira—"

"Keira sells snake oil. Just because she's pretty doesn't mean she's not dangerous. In fact, the opposite is true." Frank trudged out the door. "I'm sure Julia would let me crash at her place until I found a job. You're chasing a dream, Rauch. You and I were never meant for anything big."

"That's your father talking."

"Maybe. You told me you know who you are. But I know where I came from and where I belong. And it sure as hell ain't Vegas."

Chapter Twenty-One

Rauch, Frank, and the others stood shivering on the loading dock as they waited for Keira to unlock the factory's door. She flipped the light switches and deactivated the alarm before allowing them to enter the unheated space.

"I think it was warmer out there." Rauch pulled his hands into his coat sleeves. "I can see my breath."

"Piss and moan, piss and moan." She jeered at his complaints. "Take him to the basement, Ruletka, and give him something to moan about. You know what to do. Go ahead and start without me. I'll be there shortly." Her phone buzzed, and she jogged up the spiral steps to the control room. The door slammed, kicking up a cloud of dust and filth which sank through the air to rain upon their heads.

Ruletka led the team down a serpentine flight of steep concrete steps enclosed in a passage so narrow they were forced to walk single file. Scales of industrial green paint shed from the crumbling walls crunched underfoot. Rauch reached out to touch the damp cinder block with his left hand. He didn't have to reach far. His elbow remained bent. Good thing he wasn't claustrophobic.

He sniffed his fingers and gagged. His hand smelled like a sewer. It took every ounce of self-control he had not to wipe his fingers on the back of Ruletka's shirt. The thought made him grin. Frank was right—sometimes he could be such a dick. But then again, he wasn't the one wearing a cape. Clean living was for heroes.

The twisting stairwell ended at a windowless steel door slick with mildew. Ruletka cranked the levered handle. The door creaked but didn't budge.

"It sticks sometimes from the moisture." He threw his shoulder against the cold steel, and the door flung open, smacking against the wall behind it with a resounding bang. A blast of cold, dank air rushed from the darkness. Ruletka fumbled for the light.

Rauch peered over the Russian's shoulder into the black void. "You sure you want to do that?"

"Of course. Why not?" Ruletka shrugged Rauch's chin away from his neck.

"You might awaken the vampires."

Deliverance giggled from the back of the line. "Vampires. That'd be awesome."

Ruletka's fingers found the switch. The overhead light roused from its sleep, sputtering and popping like a creaky old man awakening from a long winter's nap.

Deliverance bounced up and down, sending mini-avalanches of paint chips, grit and all manner of crud down the pockmarked walls. He clapped his hands. "Fun, fun, fun."

Ruletka stepped into the maze. "Depends on your definition of fun. I ran this course for the first time two months ago. I recall feeling pretty intimidated, and I came to campus in prime physical condition. It's more enjoyable to watch someone else do it." He shuffled aside to allow the others to enter and waved his arm in a grand motion. "Behold Pinball's greatest creation, designed to separate true heroes from mere men."

The obstacle course crisscrossed the basement's open space, making optimal use of the entire square footage. Structural features such as the wide support beams and deep pits used to hold mega amounts of molten steel were cleverly incorporated into its fiendish design. An assortment of rejects—discarded industrial debris, misfit machinery, and other found items—had been pounded, twisted, and molded into objects of torture. Anything not rusted through had been polished to a high sheen, enhancing the maze's disorienting hall-of-mirrors effect.

Rauch wandered forward to examine the first chunk of twisted metal, a catwalk similar to the one upstairs, which had been refashioned into a crude set of monkey bars. In the middle of the room, a metal chute had been converted into a sliding board which ran through a giant fan with widely spaced blades. On either side of the chute, a series of support beams had been padded with bald tires.

"This is seriously awesome." He bounced himself off a rubber-clad beam and into a metal drum. "It's a life-sized pinball machine."

Ruletka nodded. "Except you're the ball. If you like it already, wait until I fire up the light effects. Guaranteed to blow your mind."

"I'm holding out for the soundtrack. I bet I can guess who. Get it? Guess *who*?"

"Your intuition serves you well, young Padawan." Ruletka moved toward a plain metal desk sitting a few feet inside the door and booted up the laptop incorporated into its surface. Multi-colored overhead lights strobed through a test pattern before freezing into their starting positions to await the trigger. A projector beamed a seven-foot-tall image of Roger Daltrey's face onto the far wall, and a fierce guitar riff exploded through speakers mounted on the beams.

Frank's olive complexion blanched. "I think I'm gonna have a seizure."

Deliverance grinned and shut the door. "Run, run as fast as you can. You can't catch me, I'm the delivery man." He yanked his T-shirt over his head and tossed it aside, revealing a lean, but well-muscled torso replete with colorful tattoos. "I get to go first."

A pair of angelic wings adorned his shoulder blades. The word "Deliverance," inked in an elaborate cursive script, linked the two wings. The rest of his back displayed standard Christian imagery: Jesus's face dripping with blood from his crown of thorns, an intricate Celtic crucifix, praying hands intertwined with rosary beads.

But Deliverance faced the world with a different attitude. The ink that covered his chest and abs bore illustrations ripped from Dante's version of hell. Demonic entities leered from each pec. Jagged red and black slashes formed the word "Vengeance." Tortured souls engulfed in flames and a montage of bizarre creatures, which Rauch recognized from video games such as *Silent Hill*, covered the rest. Exposed and awash in multi-colored light, the red-headed pizza delivery boy was terrifying. Rauch took a step back. Frank, too green to notice, stared at the floor.

Deliverance shadowboxed and shuffled on his feet like a bantamweight limbering up for the big fight. Ruletka typed a command on the laptop. Daltrey's face morphed into a giant, glowing LED stopwatch.

"The reigning champion has the option of going first or last. Deliverance holds the record for the fastest time, and as you can see, he's opted to go first." Ruletka hit the start button.

The distant sound of machinery grinding into motion added to the sinister vibe. The massive fan began to turn, its blades chopping the air with increasing speed. Deliverance leaned forward and tensed his muscles. Ruletka's finger hovered over the electronic stopwatch. "On your mark, get set…"

The wings on Deliverance's back rippled.

"Go!"

The basement erupted in an explosion of sparkling lights and throbbing music. Deliverance, guided by white flashing arrows which directed him to each subsequent hurdle, dashed through the maze without hesitation. He dropped out of sight several times, having plummeted into or crawled through an obstacle designed to impede or outright injure the participant. Never sure what to expect, Rauch held his breath, his own adrenaline surging, until Deliverance finally reappeared.

Rauch's head was pounding by the time Deliverance rounded the final bumper and sprinted down the home stretch, which was interrupted by a dark pit with a ladder on each side. From where Rauch stood, he couldn't discern the pit's depth or the exact distance across its gaping mouth, but it looked pretty damned wide.

Deliverance ducked his head and dug in his heels, vaulting himself over the pit. His jump fell short. Arms flailing, he disappeared into the cavernous depths.

Frank's sallow complexion paled farther, and he

lurched forward. "Oh my God." Ruletka flung out an arm to hold him back. "Just watch. No one is allowed to help unless help is requested."

Rauch grabbed Ruletka's wrist and twisted it away from Frank's chest. "I'm sure that rule doesn't apply if someone's sitting at the bottom of a hole in a couple of pieces."

While Rauch ran interference, Frank sidestepped Ruletka's restraint. He paused when one freckled hand and then the other slowly appeared on the ladder. Deliverance popped out of the hole like a red-headed gopher, and he finished his climb to the surface looking no worse for the wear. Arms waving overhead, he stumbled to the finish line.

Ruletka sent Rauch an "I-told-you-so" glare and powered down the lights and music.

"Aw, man." Deliverance pouted at the time flashing on the wall. "Five minutes flat. I would've broken my record if I'd made that final jump."

Rauch shook his head. "Have you ever made that jump?" He and Frank exchanged incredulous looks.

"Hells, ya," he said, between gulps of air. "Twice, as a matter of fact. I'm the only one who has."

"And you're humble about it, too. Isn't pride a sin?" Rauch stepped toward the pit.

Ruletka blocked him with his body. "No. Not until you've run the course. No pre-planning allowed."

Rauch clenched his fists at his side. "Dude, you're taking this stuff way too seriously, don't ya think?"

"Or you're not taking it seriously enough. This is nothing compared to what happens in the streets. Today is preparation, not a game. What happens here could save your life someday."

"Now I know you're taking it too seriously, and you're pissing me off to boot."

Deliverance circled the two men, stoking their tempers. "Fight, fight, fight."

Rauch tugged off his shirt. "I don't need to fight. I'll let my performance speak for itself. Why? Because I'm a professional, that's why. I'm chief of security." He cracked his neck and swung his arms in frenzied circles, warming up.

"Frank goes next. He's the hero-in-training." The Russian lowered his voice. "You're just Keira's pet, a twofer."

"Okay, that's it, jackass. Enough—" A snarling Rauch lunged forward, fists raised.

Ruletka dodged, positioning himself behind the metal desk. Before Rauch could pursue, the door behind them flung open with a clang, and Keira strode over the threshold. She raised an arched brow. Rauch forced his hands and face to relax, but it didn't matter. As the only true professional in the room, she'd already assessed the situation with cool efficiency.

Her green eyes flicked over Rauch's bare chest. As she bent to retrieve his shirt, he caught a whiff of her perfume. She no longer smelled like the ocean. The musky fragrance was as intoxicating as the spicy haze of an incense-laden opium den. He decided he liked it, not that she cared.

She handed him his shirt. "Cold?"

He snatched it from her hand. "No. I was getting ready to run the course."

"How did Frank do?"

Ruletka stepped from behind the desk. "He hasn't run yet."

"Good. I wanted to watch. Frank, you're up." Keira turned to Rauch and smiled. "I'm afraid you'll have to stay cold a little while longer."

"I said I wasn't cold." Rauch pulled his shirt over his head to avoid Ruletka's smirk. "Frank has a bad shoulder. There's no way he can safely—"

She cut him off with a wave of her hand. "Frank's a big boy. He can speak for himself. Isn't that right, Frank?"

Frank flushed. "I do have a bruised shoulder—Ruletka can vouch for that—which means the monkey bars are out."

"So skip them." Keira shrugged. "I'm more interested in how you handle the rest. This course isn't just about strength and agility. It tests ingenuity, too. The ability to think on your feet. Pinball's a genius of design. I can't wait for you to meet him. Now go on. Show me what Lambda Man can do." She gave him a gentle nudge on the small of his back.

Frank shuffled to the starting line. Ruletka reset the system, and the same guitar riff blared from the speakers. Frank frowned. "Does the music have to be so loud? It's distracting."

"I'm afraid so, Frank. It's designed to simulate the noise, confusion, and chaos of an urban street fight. Clear your mind, and remember rule number two: A hero must be mentally strong. You can do this, even with your shoulder. I'm not expecting you to match Deliverance's record. You only need to prove that you can finish."

Rauch leaned close to Frank's ear. "It's just an oversized video game, buddy. You heard Keira. Show the bastard what you can do."

The stopwatch projected on the wall, and Ruletka began the countdown. "Three, two, one—go!"

Frank took off and tripped a few yards from the starting line. He got up, flashed a sheepish grin over his shoulder, and carried on. Deliverance snickered, and Ruletka shot him a disapproving look.

The first time Frank disappeared from sight, Rauch's stomach clenched. "What's happening back there? What's taking him so long?"

Deliverance's maniacal grin widened. He spread both arms wide and twirled in irregular circles. "The wheels of the bus go round and round."

Rauch exhaled when Frank chugged into view. No blood, which was a good sign, but he sure didn't look perky. He searched Ruletka's impassive face for any sign of concern. "You know he has asthma, right?"

Ruletka crossed his arms. "I know."

Frank disappeared again, and this time, the wait was excruciatingly long. "Something's wrong." Rauch rushed the desk. "Turn this thing off. I'm going in."

Ruletka placed his palm over the controls. "Step away from the desk."

"Listen, fuckface—"

"Rauch, look." Keira intervened as Frank reappeared in the distance. Rauch squinted, assessing for damage, but the strobing lights and churning machinery cast too many shadows. The only thing Rauch knew for certain was that Frank was alive and moving. And maybe, just maybe, he saw blood.

Chapter Twenty-Two

Frank bounced into the first bumper, a tire-padded support beam, and imagined his virtual score increasing by a hundred points. Ahead lay three tombstone-shaped sheets of metal coated with fluorescent orange paint. Drop targets. They had to be. Flashing yellow arrows projected on the floor, guiding him in their direction.

He stopped in front of the first target, unsure what to do next. He pushed it, and it wobbled. He pushed it harder, and it flipped backward on hidden hinges and landed on the ground. A loud ding sounded. Another hundred points. He shoved the others, and they dropped in quick succession. Ding. Ding. On to the next.

A metal stepladder led to the tallest sliding board he'd ever seen. As he put his foot on each step, the tread illuminated with a different color in the order of the rainbow.

Red, orange, yellow…Cool. His admiration faded when he reached the top and assessed not only the long drop, but the dastardly twist at the bottom. An industrial fan churned over the end of the slide, its shiny steel blades generating a loud whoop with each slow rotation. To clear the blades, he'd have to time his descent carefully and hope his ass didn't stick on the way down.

His courage waned. Totally not worth it. He preferred to keep his arms and legs intact. He placed his foot on the violet tread to descend the stairs. An obnoxious horn blared until he thought his eardrums would burst. He jerked his foot off the step, and the squawking stopped. He'd be deaf by the time he reached the bottom.

Heart pounding, Frank plopped on the slide and waited for the right moment. *Whoop, whoop…*Go! He pushed off with both hands and careened down the slippery surface, lying flat on his back with his fists clenched by his sides like an Olympic luger. The fan loomed larger, the whooping blades louder, and he screwed his eyes shut and prayed for a quick death. A breeze ruffled his hair, convincing him he'd cleared the razor-sharp blades with only millimeters to spare.

He opened his eyes when his ass hit the ground. Worried his wobbly legs wouldn't hold him, he wasted a few precious seconds gathering his wits. When he finally managed to stand, the fan had stopped. Huh. Wonder when that happened. Maybe he'd imagined the breeze on his face. Now that he thought about it, he couldn't imagine Keira allowing her employees to suffer traumatic amputations during their training.

The stopwatch on the wall flashed a reminder that now was not the appropriate time for reflection. The insistent arrows nudged him on, directing him over sawhorses wrapped in razor wire and into an eight-foot-wide drainage pipe.

A thin layer of moisture pooled in the bottom of the dank passage, which was just long enough for its midpoint to darken with menacing shadows.

Frank splashed through the blackness toward the strobing lights at the opposite end. When he reached the murky middle, his arms began to tingle and burn. An unseen tendril stroked his cheek. Its wispy touch left a trail of fiery pain, and he gasped, arms flailing as he frantically tried to brush the feathery attacker from his skin. His step faltered. *Don't fall. Whatever you do, don't fall.* He wasn't sure he'd get up. He fixed his gaze on the beacon of light and charged forward.

With a final burst of speed, he cleared the pipe and chanced a look over one shoulder. Sparks danced in the central portion of the tube, illuminating the darkness with fireworks of electricity. Shock wires. Holy Mother of God. There was no going back now. No way would he subject himself to that a second time. He lowered his chin, ignored the burn on his cheek, forcing his feet to pick up the pace.

After another tire-padded bumper and a set of spinners made from broken shovels, the only obstacle separating Frank from the finish line was the pit. He'd never make that jump. Not in a million years of trying. But if his experience on the slide was any indication, going around was not an option.

Frank slowed his pace to a jog as he approached the abyss. He peered into the darkness and wheezed out a sigh at what he saw lurking in the bottom. He knew one thing for certain. If he survived, he was never touching another pinball machine again.

Chapter Twenty-Three

Rauch watched helplessly from afar as Frank jogged to the home stretch and stopped to peer over the pit's ominous edge. He gritted his teeth. "Walk around it, Frank. Don't be a hero. You can't make that jump. Just walk around."

"That would be cheating." Deliverance wagged his finger at Rauch. "No cheating allowed. No, no, no."

"I don't give a rat's ass, wacko, and get your goddamned finger out of my face." Rauch's snarl dissolved when Frank hurled himself into the pit feet-first. "What the hell? Frankie!"

Deliverance chortled at his horrified expression. "Bouncy, bouncy."

Frank rose into the air as if levitated by an invisible force. He grabbed the ladder with his good arm and clung to it until stable. Then he hoisted himself out of the pit and belly flopped on the hard ground.

"Frank?" Rauch yelled over the earsplitting whine of the electric guitars.

Frank gave a thumbs up. He staggered to his feet, limped to the finish line, and collapsed on his ass in front of Rauch and Keira.

"Seventeen minutes." Ruletka halted the stopwatch and announced the time. "Seventeen long minutes, but you did it, Frank. I knew you could."

Frank's lips twitched in a failed attempt at a smile.

"I feel terrible." Lips pursed, he wheezed with each laborious breath.

Rauch crouched beside him. "Did you bring your inhaler?"

Frank shook his head, too short of breath to speak.

Keira waved her hand dismissively. "Give him some time. He'll be fine."

"What—you think you're a medical doctor now? Sorry to break the news, but your psychology degree isn't worth squat right now."

Ruletka eyed the rapid rise and fall of Frank's chest. "Let's get him back to the dorm where it's warm, and I'll make him a nice, strong cup of tea. The caffeine will help open his airways. It's an old training trick."

They helped drag him up the stairs and into the SUV. During the short drive to the dorm, Frank's breathing slowed to normal. He accepted Ruletka's tea, opting for a solitary recovery in the quiet of his room.

Rauch waited until Frank's door clicked shut before letting loose on Keira and Ruletka. "You're pushing him too hard. He was close to quitting before this happened. I wouldn't be surprised if this doesn't tip him over the edge."

Ruletka raised his eyebrows. "I can't see why. He did great. He finished the maze on his first try, which is a huge accomplishment. Those shock wires in the last tunnel—"

"Shock wires? Jesus Christ." Rauch ran a hand through his hair. "You people are insane. You could've killed him."

"You're exaggerating. Shock wires are a common feature in mud runs and military obstacle courses." Keira placed her hand on Rauch's arm and, with an amused smile, chided him gently. "You're such a mother hen."

Rauch clenched his fist. "Listen, sweetheart, I've been protecting Frank since we shared time in juvie, and I'm not about to stop now. I'm the one who talked him into this crazy scheme of yours, which makes me responsible if anything goes wrong."

Ruletka sniffed. "Funny. I thought you only looked out for yourself."

"You would think that, you self-righteous bitch, but I know how the world works. Frank doesn't. I'm doing this for him, so he doesn't have to spend the rest of his life eating ramen in a shelter."

"Keep deluding yourself, my friend."

"Gentlemen, I grow tired of saying it, but enough." Keira squeezed Rauch's tense forearm, a reminder, he assumed, to keep the details of her con a secret from Deliverance and Ruletka. He shook her off, and she scowled. "Get packed. We're leaving for Vegas the day after tomorrow. Maybe a change of venue will improve your outlook. And don't you ever, ever call me sweetheart again."

Rauch spun on his heel and headed for the stairs. "It's not my outlook you need to worry about. It's Frank's. I'm done convincing him to stay. It's your turn. If you fail and he leaves, I'm going with him." He glared at Ruletka and Deliverance. "And if that happens, *sayonara*, suckers, and good luck with your plan. You're in for a wild ride."

Chapter Twenty-Four

Frank huddled on the bed, contemplating a future without Roy and minus Rauch as well. He couldn't stay here, not after his humiliating performance in front of the team. Once upon a time when life was normal, he'd have assumed Rauch would be right there beside him. But that was before Keira.

The tea, black but with a touch of lavender honey, warmed his chest and calmed his wheezing. His eyes drifted shut as he sniffed the sweetly fragrant steam. His hands tightened around the ceramic mug. His mother used to give him something similar whenever he stayed home from school, sick with another cold. He stared into the dark liquid, lost in the kind of bittersweet melancholy generated when warm memories clashed with cold reality.

He wasn't surprised by the knock on the door. He was, however, surprised when it was Keira who entered instead of Rauch.

She shut the door behind her and motioned a request to sit next to him on the bed. "How are you feeling?"

He shifted aside. "If you're here to fire me, save your breath. I quit. I never should've agreed."

"Fire?" She appeared genuinely surprised. "Why would I? You're doing fine; Ruletka speaks highly of you. Says you've got a huge heart. The physical conditioning will come with time. That's why you're here—to train your body to do what your heart desires."

"Is that truly why I'm here?" Frank placed his mug on the nightstand and turned to face her straight on.

She avoided his gaze, and for the first time since they'd met, he sensed a hint of doubt in her demeanor. Her expression wavered as he watched an internal battle march across her face. Finally, she raised her eyes to his. "No. You're here for revenge."

"Mine or yours?"

"Mine and yours, if you seize the chance."

"I have no idea what you're talking about. Revenge is hardly a noble goal for a hero."

"Maybe not, but you know as well as I that most heroes are seeking revenge or redemption of some kind. I mean, hello—Batman."

"Ruletka and I have already debated this. Batman is the exception."

"I think not. You need to dig deeper, Frank. For example, would it make a difference if I told you I know who killed your boss?"

Keira kept talking, but he heard nothing. The blood rushing to his ears deafened him to everything except the hammering of his pulse. As the surge slowly abated and his hearing returned, he focused on her moving lips and wondered what he'd missed.

"...Ironic, isn't it, that we both seek revenge against the same man?"

"What did you say?" Frank grabbed his mug and downed the last tepid gulp. His mother used to put a shot of whiskey in his tea, and he longed for her fortifying remedy. Given Keira's bombshell, it might take more than one shot to steady his frayed nerves.

She arched her brows. "Which part?"

"All of it."

"My brother Jack, the head of Philly's Irish mob, had Roy Baum killed for siphoning profits from the Family's import business. I tried to warn him the day I came to the shop—"

"Why?"

The bluntness of his question must have caught Keira by surprise because for the first time since he'd met her, she stammered. "I, um, I actually offered him a trade. I told him I'd intervene on his behalf if he'd let me have you for my project."

"If he'd 'let me have you?' What am I—some sort of prized poodle?"

She had the decency to blush. "He said no. He didn't want you following in your father's footsteps. He didn't want you exposed to the mob. Said you were a good boy, and I, by nature of my pedigree, was a bad influence." She plucked at a loose thread on the comforter. "He was right."

"And because he said no, you let your brother gut him. You let him die." Frank's chest tightened all over again, as if his heart and lungs were being squeezed by a giant vise grip.

"I didn't 'let' my brother do anything. That's the problem with Jack. He's an impetuous, pig-headed narcissist. In short, I can't control him, as evidenced by the fact that he robbed me out of my inheritance. You want to know the worst part?"

"There's something worse than slaughtering Roy?"

"Think about it, Frank. That immature boob now has my father's vast wealth and a network of brutal thugs at his disposal. Roy Baum was just the beginning.

South Philly's in for some nasty weather once Jack gets a better handle on the day-to-day operations of my father's businesses. My father flew under the radar by choice; with Jack's conceit, I know he will not. That's not his style. It'll be all-out war with the Italians before long."

"Then how did you expect to intervene?"

"I'd hoped I could delay Jack long enough for you and the others to finish your training." Keira leaned forward. "That's what this is about, Frank. Together we can save your neighborhood from the Irish mob. I can feed you intel, and you and the team can hamper, harass, and otherwise derail Jack until he's either replaced by the Family or relocates to Vegas permanently. That's my revenge. Get rid of Jack, and his local resources become mine and mine alone."

"Why Vegas?"

"Jack has this hare-brained idea that Vegas has been lacking a decent mob presence since the '80s when the large casino groups sold out to foreign investors. He sees an opportunity to expand his territory and make a name for himself with the families in Boston and Chicago. It's grandiose and reckless—classic Jack McConnell—but it gives us a chance to practice against a smaller group of thugs. He'll only have a few loyal bodyguards and some local hired help, who aren't known for sticking their necks out when the going gets tough. Jack's been boasting about this venture for months up and down the East Coast; this is a perfect way to embarrass him in front of the Family.

The silence stretched, broken only by the sound of Frank's whistling breath as he digested the load of information. "And the research project?"

"Doesn't exist, but don't tell Ruletka and Deliverance." Keira wrinkled her nose. "Rauch knows the truth. I had to tell him so he could keep an eye out for Jack. I do actually have a psychology degree, if you care. I guess you could call it a half-truth."

"Of which there've been a whole lot."

"I apologize for misleading you, Frank. I truly do." She clasped one of his hands in hers, and he twitched in surprise. "We have a flight scheduled in two days. I'll understand if you decide not to join us. But if you do, keep what I've told you to yourself. Ruletka and Deliverance don't need to be dragged into my family's sordid underworld. As far as they know, they're training to kick criminal ass, and kick ass they shall. It's safer for them that way."

Keira dropped his hand and strode to the door. "Take the rest of the day off. You've got some thinking to do." As she opened the door, a murmur of conversation echoed from down the hall. She exited, and another door opened and shut a few seconds later. The murmuring disappeared.

He stretched out on the bed and willed his quivering muscles to relax. The tea calmed his breathing but did nothing for his jumbled thoughts and feelings. They strobed through his brain in piercing pulses of emotion more disturbing than the gauntlet's sinister machines. Ruletka, were he present, would tell him to meditate. Frank closed his eyes and tried to focus on something positive.

He'd finished the course—not like a boss, but he'd finished. He didn't give up, and truth be told, he'd found the adrenaline rush thrilling, like the time he'd faced down the thugs who'd killed Carmine. The experience was more intense than the holographic danger rooms in any of the virtual reality video games he'd ever played. Next time, if he took a puff of his inhaler prior to running the course, he might improve. He could do better, maybe even smoke Deliverance's record.

He shook his head. What was he thinking? A few minutes ago, he was prepared to pack up and leave. But that was before Keira implied he was responsible for Roy's death. The insinuation was subtle, but it was there. Roy had died trying to protect him from the mob; ergo Frank was indirectly responsible. Frank had a debt to repay.

Knuckles rapped on his door. *Shave and a haircut.* Rauch. Frank knocked his response on the bed frame. *Two bits.* Hopefully, Keira hadn't locked the door. He hurt too much to get up.

The door cracked open, and Rauch stuck his head through the gap. "Okay if I come in?"

"Sure. Just don't expect me to move."

Rauch sat in the same spot Keira had vacated a short time prior. "You had me worried there for a while, but you look much better now."

"Ruletka's super tea."

"Yeah, whatever. Commie's riding my last nerve."

"Show some respect. The Russians gave us Tetris."

"Ruletka's more like Omega Red."

Omega Red was a notorious comic book villain originating from Russia. Frank sighed. "Ruletka's an American, Rauch. He's not a Commie or a villain."

"It's nicer than calling him an asshole. I can, if you'd rather."

Frank closed his eyes and let it go. He was too

physically and emotionally exhausted to fight. "What do you want?"

Rauch squirmed in his seat. "I want to know if you're coming to Vegas with me."

"You mean now that I know who killed Roy? That this whole damned setup is to destroy Jack McConnell, a man I've never even met?"

Rauch's squirming stopped. "What did she tell you, Frank?"

"Enough to know you've been lying to me this entire time."

"I haven't—"

"Stop it, Rauch. Just stop. You've picked your position, chosen your side. It's all about her, isn't it?"

"No, it's not about her." Rauch jumped to his feet. "It's about you, Frank. About keeping you safe and providing for our future. I told you before—she's given us a golden opportunity. I knew you wouldn't budge from the neighborhood for something as dishonorable as revenge."

Frank shook his head. "Unbelievable. All this time, and you still don't get it. Being broke, homeless—they don't bother me. I don't like them, for sure, but I don't need much to survive. I can deal with hunger. As for the rest..." He struggled to sit upright. "You're wrong. I am going to Vegas. I am going to destroy Jack McConnell for what he did to Roy. I'm all about revenge, Rauch. My father went to jail before I could make him pay for what he did to Mom and Joey. They will remain forever unavenged, and that's on me. But as for my boss—Roy Baum will have his revenge."

Chapter Twenty-Five

They arrived in Vegas under the gloom of a pre-dawn sky. Faint twinkles of white light stretched across the flat landscape, indicating lonely outposts of humanity in an otherwise desolate terrain. Rauch blinked, and everything changed. A city appeared out of the darkness, as if the hand of God had pulled a cord and lit a lamp twelve miles across.

The plane descended in a wide arc. Its final approach took it straight over Las Vegas Boulevard, giving the appearance it was about to land on the storied Strip itself. The Great Pyramid of Luxor loomed on the left, and Rauch stared, rapt and amazed by the glittering lights and astonishing structures zooming into view on both sides of the plane.

He jostled Frank's elbow with his own. "Frank, Frank—look at that, will ya?"

Frank kept his eyes screwed shut and clutched the armrests of his luxe leather seat. The barf bag, with its absurdly narrow opening, rocked on his lap as the aircraft shuddered and touched down. With a final shriek of rubber on tarmac, the plane slowed to a crawl and taxied toward the gate.

Rauch pressed his nose against the pressure-resistant glass. "Dude, you're missing everything."

Frank opened one eye. "I don't think I like to fly."

"You'd make a piss-poor Superman, then. Better

surrender your cape."

Keira ignored the illuminated "Fasten Seat Belt" sign and stood in the aisle. "Listen up. Pinball's waiting. Look for the white stretch SUV. Grab your gear." She wrapped a green pashmina around the bottom half of her face. "And keep your heads down. Let's be discreet until we get to our facility."

They descended the steps and claimed their plane-side baggage. A gust of cold, dry air whipped Rauch's face and stung his eyes. He shivered, wishing he hadn't packed his leather coat. "It's freezing out here." He blew on his hands. "And we're in the desert."

Keira shot him a look. "It's November. What did you expect?"

"Palm trees and sunburn."

"The desert gets cold at night, but it'll warm up as soon as the sun rises." She adjusted the scarf to cover her nose.

A long, sleek vehicle glided their direction. Rauch whistled. "Sweet."

The SUV limousine parked next to the luggage cart. The driver, as tall and sturdy as the vehicle, exited, and Keira's eyes brightened. "Pinball."

"Hey there, Miss Keira. Nice to see you again."

After a quick embrace, she tugged him by the hand to where the others stood dawdling with uncertainty. "Come meet the newest members of our team. Frank, Rauch, this is Pinball, tech wizard extraordinaire. Pinball, Frank is otherwise known as 'Lambda Man.' Rauch is our new head of security."

"Pleased to meet you." Pinball extended his hand, which Frank, mouth agape, limply accepted.

Rauch wore an equally dumfounded expression.

"You…you…"

Keira rolled her eyes. "Sorry, Pinball. I forgot to warn them."

"You look just like a young Samuel L. Jackson." Rauch blurted out the words in a mad rush. He grabbed Pinball's hand and shook it vigorously. "I mean, dude, just like him. You could be our very own Nick Fury."

Frank's eyes grew wider. "Ooo—do you wear an eye patch?"

"Do you see an eye patch?" Pinball scoffed at Frank's spellbound expression and cocked a thumb in his direction. "Skinny man knows I'm not really Samuel L. Jackson, right?" His broad smile held a hint of concern. "Right?"

"Of course." Keira's throaty laughter was that of someone enjoying great fun at another's expense. She wrapped an arm around Frank's shoulders. "He's just super impressionable. Come along, Frank." She guided him to the car.

Pinball chuckled and slapped Ruletka on the back. "How ya doin', Toni? Been a while. Training going good?" They chatted while hefting the bags through the limo's rear hatch.

The sun crested on the horizon, dimming the dazzle of the Strip's luminous lights. Rauch entered the vehicle last and sat next to Frank in the back row of seats. As he had in the plane, he pressed his nose against the window. "Will we take the Strip?"

Pinball scowled in the rear view mirror. "Wasn't planning on it. Less traffic and fewer drunken tourists on the side roads."

Keira flashed an indulgent smile. "It's early yet, Pinball. Give them a thrill."

Pinball's frown deepened, but he eased the vehicle into the appropriate lane and slowed to rubbernecker speed.

"I knew it. I knew there'd be palm trees." Rauch craned his neck to stare up at the trees lining the Strip's median. They swayed in the desert wind, and he dropped the tinted window to hear the green fronds rustle, the sound as gentle as fine-grit sandpaper sweeping over a freshly buffed surface.

Rauch, too excited to play it cool, closed his eyes and allowed the soothing sound to set his mind adrift. No matter what happened going forward, no matter if Keira's con left them broken and lost, at least he'd experienced something more magnificent than Mama Vittone's bakery. Crickets and palm trees and stars in the night sky. His life was complete and hopefully far from over.

He reopened his eyes to marvel at the parade of structures. The golden pyramid gave way to a medieval castle on the left and the Eiffel Tower on the right. The gentle strains of classical music wafted through his open window. The vehicle stopped at a red light on Flamingo Avenue, and Keira pointed. "Good timing. Look left. First show of the day."

As music swelled, the glassy surface of Bellagio's lake rippled and exploded into a choreographed burst of water cannons. The majestic plumes, accompanied by a dazzling light display, swayed and pranced in sync with the music. Even Pinball was transfixed—so much so that he missed the green light. The shiny black limo idling at his bumper blared its horn.

"Asshole." Despite the tinted windows, Pinball flipped the driver the bird. He pulled a cell phone from his pocket and focused its lens on the limo's front passenger window. Then he tapped away at the screen, typing faster than Rauch could do with both hands.

"Gotcha." The light at the next intersection changed to red. Pinball pulled into the right-hand turn lane and stopped next to the limo. "Watch through the window, and get a listen to this." He put the phone on speaker and dialed.

The limo driver fumbled with his phone. "Hello?"

Assuming a faux British accent, Pinball said, "Your mother was a gerbil, and your father smelt of boysenberries." Click. He disconnected the call.

The team roared with laughter as the limo driver stared at his phone in confusion. The light changed, and Pinball floored it, leaving the limo in a gritty cloud of sand and exhaust.

Rauch hiccupped and wiped a tear from the corner of his eye. "Any dude who riffs off Monty Python is okay by me. How'd you do that? Wait—don't tell me. You pinged his phone, right?"

"Nope. Pinging individual phone numbers is the stuff of overwrought action flicks. Pure fantasy."

Rauch's face fell. "You mean you can't do that?"

"No one can. To answer your question, I zoomed my camera on the dash and got the driver's name and company info from the posted identification. It's mandatory in Nevada. I used the info to find his cell number. Easy-peasy, no wizardry required. Fortunately, his front windows weren't as darkly tinted as the rear. The police have been cracking down on that recently. We're fortunate we don't get pulled over ourselves."

"Don't jinx us." Keira scanned the streets with an uneasy eye. "We're almost there."

They drove past Venetian canals, signs for the convention center, and the giant tower of the Stratosphere. Pinball slowed the vehicle to a crawl so the newcomers could stare at the impressively tall structure.

"They've got a roller coaster up top called the X-Scream, and you can bungee jump from the observation deck. Eight hundred feet of sheer exhilaration. Proud to say Miss Keira and I did both when we set up shop here in Vegas. I almost pissed my pants, but she was as cool as Dino's martini." He glanced in the rear view mirror. "Who's next in line?"

Frank snorted. "Eight hundred feet of sheer terror is more like it. No way in hell. I wouldn't even ride the elevator in that thing. Not without a parachute."

Deliverance snickered and waved one hand in the air. "Pick me, pick me. I'm next. I scream, you scream, we all scream for X-Scream."

"Settle down, Deliverance." Keira squeezed Pinball's arm. "Don't get distracted. You're approaching your turn. Take the next right."

He nodded and resumed the stuffy accent. "We just passed Fremont Street, which is considered the heart of downtown Las Vegas and is home to the Neon Museum and the Fremont Street Experience. The lovely building to your left is the Mob Museum, which recounts the glory days of organized crime, not only in Vegas, but in the United States a whole." He turned onto Bonanza Road. "Say goodbye to the Strip—for now."

Rauch stared out the rear view window until the lights faded. Away from the Strip and the neon of downtown, Vegas's glitz dwindled and died, a man-made mirage shaped by money but built on a shifting foundation of sand and dust. The strip malls along Bonanza Road were brown and drab. A fine layer of sepia-colored grit coated the windows, giving the buildings the appearance of being one sandstorm away from being swallowed and reclaimed by the ravenous desert.

They headed east until the neighborhood buildings thinned. Within one city block, the structures disappeared altogether, yielding to the flat desert plain, which stretched to the mountains looming on the horizon. Scraggy shrubs pockmarked the rough terrain. The SUV bounced toward a tiny building, which grew larger and more intimidating as they approached, thanks to its massive square footage and miles of razor wire fence.

Pinball drove to the gate and swiped an ID card, allowing them access. He steered toward the main entrance, and Keira twisted in her seat to address the team. "This facility used to belong to the Unites States Air Force. Nellis Air Force Base is a little farther north. The military sold this location when they moved their operations there. It's changed hands a few times since. The current owners rent it out, mostly to wealthy snowbirds with private aircraft. I was fortunate to secure a six-month lease."

A runway appeared to the right, and Rauch shook his head. "Would've made a helluva lot of sense to land here instead, don't you think? Not that I minded the grand tour. Pinball's an excellent guide."

"Thank you. Thank you very much." Pinball did his best Elvis and pretended to preen in the side mirror. He parked the vehicle in front of the hangar.

Keira removed a remote from the glove box. She

pressed a button, and the hangar door lurched into motion. "I would've loved to have flown directly here, but I didn't want the pilot or crew to know our exact final destination. Plus, the space is filled. We couldn't have parked a plane in here anyway. You'll see."

The overhead door shuddered to a stop, and Pinball drove through the hangar's yawning mouth. He followed a series of yellow reflectors imbedded in the concrete floor to a parking area near the rear of the building. Frank and Rauch scrambled from the vehicle. With their heads tipped and mouths agape, they spun in slow circles and took it in.

Pinball had manufactured the obstacle course in Philly from repurposed rejects, molding the factory's gloomy basement into a steampunk gauntlet of tarnished goods. In contrast, the Vegas design was sleek and futuristic, a gleaming maze of high-tech objects a circuit shy of sentience. Partially formed robots blinked from nests of wires and burbled in a language of their own. Long tables overflowed with bizarrely shaped gizmos ranging from the cute and quirky to the ominously strange.

The hangar itself was enormous. Despite Keira's assertions that the space was full, Rauch guessed from its span and the height of the vaulted ceiling, it could've fit three planes with enough room left for a TIE fighter.

"I've spent the last six months customizing the place," Pinball said, with a wicked grin. "As you can see, I made it my own."

"Yeah, just a bit. I feel like we were tractor-beamed into the Death Star's landing bay. Where are the Storm Troopers?" Rauch eyed a sliding door at the back of the building as if expecting a squadron of the white armored soldiers to file through with their blasters at the ready.

"No Troopers." Pinball's grin widened, obviously pleased by the newcomers' awe. "Though I did build a sweet droid. Rictor's my sidekick when I patrol the streets at night. He's saved my tush more times than I can count." He whistled, and the shrill sound echoed off the walls and around the room. "Here, Rictor. Code yellow."

A cheerful chirp sounded from behind a stack of metal crates. The high-pitched burble faded, and a deep, resonant boom shook the hangar. A second boom, louder than the first, vibrated Rauch's breastbone. He held his breath, expecting a colossal robot the size of a Transformer to come stomping across the hangar, crushing everything in its path.

Instead, a small black device zipped across the floor and stopped next to Pinball's feet. It whirred, and Pinball smiled. "Good boy. Standby."

"This? This thing saved your life?" Rauch crouched for a closer examination of the strange object. "Looks like a subwoofer on wheels." He extended a hand, and Rictor scooted out of reach.

"Or a shoebox," Ruletka said.

Frank added his pithy assessment. "Nah, definitely a toaster. An ugly toaster. An ugly, tiny toaster with a loud mouth."

"He's quite the little con, isn't he?" Pinball glowed with pride and affection. "He may not look like much, but he's got voice and facial recognition, a speaker, a remote control, and a few other surprises I'll keep to myself. Plus, he's made of adamantium."

Frank raised an eyebrow. "Adamantium is not a

real metal. It exists only in comics and the movies."

"Don't tell him that. You'll hurt his feelings."

Keira's phone rang, and she stepped away to answer the call. She returned glowering. "Another change in the time line. Pinball and Rauch, we need to discuss the facility's security system ASAP. I want the rest of you to unload your bags and head through the door in the back. It leads to the employee kitchen and rest area. Claim a room, and we'll join you shortly."

Rauch watched as Frank, still sore from his efforts in the maze, lagged behind. He cast a curious look over his shoulder before following Ruletka and Deliverance through the thick metal door. Keira waited until she was sure they were out of earshot.

"I planted a mole in my brother's inner circle. She called to say Jack's transferring the money sooner than planned. He wants to throw a big shindig over the holidays to woo the local crime lords into helping him, and he needs the funds to do so. The vehicle is scheduled to leave Philadelphia tomorrow evening. We have three days to get everything in place."

"Three days." Pinball pursed his lips. "My tech is ready, but something tells me your team is not."

Rauch scowled. "In our defense, Frank and I have been Heroes2B employees for six whole days."

Pinball, his expression contemplative, ignored him. "And Vegas's comic con starts in three days. As you know, I'm a legend among the local cosplayer community—"

Rauch snorted, and Pinball shook his head. "You can laugh, man, but it's true. My presence will be seriously missed. I've got no problem skipping it for this level of coinage, but for me, the con is an annual gig. For you guys, it's a once-in-a-lifetime opportunity. There's no way you're going to talk your team out of going. Not unless you tell them about the mother lode."

"About that. The boss…" He cocked his thumb at Keira. "…Has been sketchy with the details. I could use some hard numbers. How much money are we talking about here?"

Pinball looked at Keira as if to say this was her baby to spank. She twirled her gold ring and cleared her throat with a delicate cough. "Thirty million."

"*Thirty million*—" Rauch's voice rang off the sheet metal roof. He lowered the volume after Keira made a shushing gesture. "Thirty million dollars? That's five million apiece."

"No, that's ten million apiece." Keira's green eyes glinted brighter than the emerald on her acrylic-tipped finger. "For Pinball, you, and me. The heroes are getting paid by other means."

"Oh, yeah, I forgot. Ruletka's sex change." Rauch's lips curled into a sneer. He didn't give a rat's ass about the Russian, but Frank—Frank deserved a piece of the action, if for no other reason than as reparation for what Jack did to Roy.

Keira crossed her arms. "That was the deal, yes."

"You mean the con. You've been conning them all along. I don't know how you keep your stories straight."

"Call it whatever you like; it makes no difference to me. Feel free to share your cut with Frank, but the money gets split into three chunks and three chunks only." She tilted her head. "You want out?"

Pinball tensed his muscular shoulders at her softly spoken threat, causing Rauch to wonder about their definition of the word "out." His own muscles twitched in response, and he flashed back to his meeting with the Italian don. Frank was right. Keira was prettier, but no less dangerous. He swallowed. "I didn't say that."

"Good. Just checking. Now let's get back to business. We have a heist to plan, and we're at three days and counting."

Chapter Twenty-Six

Frank purposely left the door to his room ajar so he could hear when Rauch arrived in the rest area. He unpacked his bag and surveyed his bland new digs. Gray scale predominant without an ounce of warmth. Perfect. Matched his mood.

He stuck his head out the door at the sound of approaching footsteps. "I saved you the room next door." Rauch responded with a strained smile. Frank glanced down the hall. "Where's Pinball?"

Frank hovered in the doorway as Rauch entered his room and threw his luggage on the bed. "Keira didn't want to tool around Vegas in a stretch, so Pinball took her to rent something more suitable."

"Like what—a dune buggy?"

Rauch snickered. "Your guess is as good as mine. They said they'll be back soon. With food."

"She and Pinball certainly seem—thick as thieves."

Rauch whipped around, his expression guarded. "What do you mean by that?"

"Just what I said." The scar above Rauch's left eye twitched, proving he was on edge. Frank guessed at the cause. "Not to worry, pal. I still think she's got the hots for you."

Rauch flopped on the bed. "I wouldn't be so sure."

Frank shrugged. "Her loss. Did you get the security issues ironed out?"

"Yes. Yes, we did." Rauch ran a hand through his hair and rolled to sit on the edge of the mattress. "Three days until the comic con, Frankie. Three days to train hard and make a good impression."

"Am I embarrassing you?"

"Of course not. Just do your best for me, okay?"

Frank's shoulders drooped. With his lousy performance on the obstacle course fresh in his mind, his best friend's hasty response was hardly reassuring. "I am doing my best, but not for you. This is for Roy, Mom, and Joey. For our neighborhood. For Carmine and Julia. I'm doing it for them. What about you?"

****

Dinner was take-out Mexican provided by Keira. She dropped it off, mumbled something about an important meeting, and with a quick "see you at breakfast," zoomed away again in a silver four-seater convertible.

Frank speared the corner of an unidentified green object peeking from beneath a slop of refried beans. Using his fork, he eased it into a bare spot on his plate and poked at it as if it were a worm squirming on a mound of mud. "What fresh hell is this?"

"It's a *chile relleno*. Stuffed with cheesy goodness and one hundred percent dee-lish." Pinball chuckled at Frank's doubtful expression. "Man, you never ate Mexican before?"

"Sure I have. There was a fast food taco place a few blocks from our apartment, right, Rauch?"

Rauch's mouth was too full of Spanish rice to allow him to respond. He nodded instead.

Pinball clucked his tongue. "Those joints are about as Mexican as you are, Frank. The *chile relleno* on your plate—that, my man, is quality Mexican. Stop mangling it, and give it a try."

Frank sliced a fine sliver off the chile, then popped it on his tongue. "It's spicy."

The heat from the chile intensified from a pleasant tingle to a five-alarm fire. He gasped and dashed to the sink to stick his mouth under the running faucet. "You could've warned me." Still sputtering, he splashed his watery eyes.

Rauch choked on his Spanish rice, spewing a mouthful of the fluffy yellow grains across the table. Everyone laughed except Ruletka. The Russian gave the team the evil stink eye and fussed over Frank, patting him soothingly on the back.

Pinball dabbed a tear from the corner of his eye. "You know what we should do? We should get dressed in our costumes and patrol the Strip. If we start at the convention center, you guys can learn the lay of the land for the comic con. We'll work our way south from there. It'll be fun. Call it a team bonding exercise."

Frank, cheeks still flushed from the hot chile, frowned. "I don't know. Keira didn't say anything about us being allowed to leave."

"I come and go as I please." Pinball scowled. "We're not prisoners; we're employees. Besides, your buddy here's head of security. Keira will never know we were gone unless he tells her. You can keep a secret, can't you, my man?"

Rauch slid the forsaken *chile relleno* onto his plate and chowed down. "Only if I get to come with you."

"Deal." Pinball slammed his hand on the table. "Rictor will guard the base. Finish up, boys, Pinball's going to town."

****

The convention center's vast parking lot was vacant save a few stragglers. Pinball parked the stretch SUV and eased his huge frame out the driver's door. "Good thing Keira took the convertible. It would've been a tight squeeze with all of our gear."

They stood in the middle of the empty lot and stared toward the flashing neon of the Strip.

"Where is everybody?" Frank asked. "It's only seven o'clock."

"Most business-type conventions end early so people can support the local economy by drinking and gambling. Comic cons are the exception. Once they start, this place hops past midnight with activities. If you poke around the dark corners, you might even catch a couple of furries yiffing."

"Yiffing?"

"Having sex in their furry animal costumes. A yiff is the sound a fox makes when aroused."

Frank turned as green as his costume. "Yuck. That's just sick, Pinball. I could've lived my whole life without knowing that fact, thank you very much."

"You're welcome. Viva Las Vegas, Lambda Man. And by the way—for future adventures, lose the cape. I'm sure Keira's told you that at least once already. It's a pet peeve of hers. They're not a practical fashion accessory for any crime-fighting hero, and they're especially bad here with the high desert winds. You'll find yourself being dragged down the street by your neck someday. Leave it in the car next time. You, too, Ruletka. We've talked about this before."

The Russian nodded. Tonight was the first Frank had seen the rest of the team in costume, and Ruletka's was nothing short of awesome. His flowing black cape bore two images: a gun with a single bullet in its chamber and a roulette wheel with the winning number "00." The suit was stitched from squares of red and black leather. Overall, he resembled a lean, mean hybrid of Harley Quinn and Deadpool, and Frank couldn't give a better compliment than that. Cape or no cape, Ruletka looked fierce, and in the real-life superhero community, attitude and appearance were everything.

Poor Deliverance, on the other hand, was as far from fierce as Malta is from Maine. Dressed in a hooded brown bathrobe sashed at the waist and sporting a black plastic eye mask, he appeared to be striving for the warrior-monk look. Instead, between his short stature, the wooden staff he carried, and the nubby cheap chenille of his robe, he looked like an Ewok with mange.

Pinball, followed by Ruletka, Frank, and Deliverance, led the parade down the Strip. Rauch, in his new tailored suit, brought up the rear. With a wicked grin, he waddled behind Deliverance and shook an imaginary spear, leaving no doubt that he, too, noted Deliverance's resemblance to a certain furry creature from the forests of Endor.

"Yub, yub," he whispered in Frank's ear.

Frank suppressed a grin. It was ignoble to mock another hero's attire. Cosplay was expensive, and not everyone could afford a kick-ass costume. Deliverance obviously fell into that category and was likely as penniless as the monk he portrayed. Or else he'd spent all his money on tats and guns.

As they approached the first of the major casinos,

Pinball stopped to address the team. "You can tell the locals because they'll ignore you. They've seen it all a thousand times before; the only reason they come to the Strip is for work and the occasional show. Otherwise, they avoid it like the plague. The tourists, on the other hand, will gawk, and some will ask you to pose for pictures. On a busy weekend, you can make good money that way. That's how I funded Rictor."

"Oh my God, look. There's fat Elvis." Frank pointed down the street, where a throng had formed around a dude in a too-tight white sequined pantsuit.

"Forget Elvis," Rauch said. "Get a load of Marilyn Monroe."

Marilyn and Elvis preened and posed for five bucks a pop. By the time the crowd dispersed, Marilyn had stuffed a wad of bills in her white satin purse.

"See what I mean?" Pinball shook his head. "Easy money."

They continued down the Strip and stopped outside a mega-casino, where Pinball dispensed them each a roll of pennies. "Time for a drink—on the house."

He led them inside to the nearest bank of penny slots, and they each claimed a machine. "Just bet a few coins at a time until the cocktail waitress comes. If you play it right, you can get a nice shot of cheap tequila for less than a quarter."

Deliverance fingered his roll of pennies and stared at the flashing lights. His lips moved, and Frank watched him warily, trying to discern if he was praying or conversing with a ghost in the machine. Without warning, the mangy monk lurched out of his seat and thrust the roll of pennies back in Pinball's hand. "I don't drink. I don't gamble. Neither should you."

Pinball slipped the pennies into his pocket. "We gamble every time we step outside in our costumes." He grinned.

Deliverance did not smile but his right hand curled into a fist.

Pinball's grin evaporated. "Relax, man. You can order a soda. You don't have to shoot tequila."

"I don't gamble, and neither should you."

"You said that already." Pinball's eyes narrowed. "How about you sit there quietly and pretend to gamble while the rest of us enjoy our drinks?"

A pair of security guards strutted past, eying the team's masks and hoods. The burlier of the two made eye contact with Pinball; his face flickered with recognition. "You know you're not supposed to be in here, Tico," he said. "Take it outside."

Pinball raised his hands in mock surrender. "Okay, okay. Don't get your jingle in a jangle. I was just giving some rookies the grand tour." He cocked his head toward the exit. "C'mon, guys. Time to blow this joint."

"But I've got a hot one." Rauch pouted and gave his machine one final spin of the reels.

Frank leaned over his shoulder. "Rauch, you've won a whole twenty-five cents."

"At least I'm winning." He tore his eyes from the spinning reels, appraised the security guard's stony expression, and sighed. "Fine."

The guards escorted them to the exit and watched them leave. Frank glanced over his shoulder to where they stood with their beefy arms crossed, monitoring the team's progress down the street and away from the casino. "What was that all about?"

"I told you I'm famous around these parts." Pinball

flashed a sheepish grin. "Unfortunately, my fame extends beyond the cosplayer community."

"Are you gonna tell us why, or do we have to guess?" Rauch dropped his unspent pennies into his pocket. "I'm not giving those back, by the way."

Pinball shrugged. "I may have figured out how to rig certain electronic devices, resulting in a winning streak. A beauteous winning streak, if I may say so myself. Casinos are such sore losers."

They reversed their tracks and headed back to the convention center. Deliverance suddenly faltered, then stopped in the middle of the crowded sidewalk outside a luxury multiplex theater. A bald man with a babe on his arm shoved him in the back and muttered a spate of unintelligible words.

Rauch snickered. "I'm pretty sure he just called you an Ewok."

Pinball pulled Deliverance into the dirt alongside the pavement. "What the hell is wrong with you, boy?"

Transfixed, Deliverance pointed at the ticket line. A long queue of excited tourists, eager to view the latest cinematic adventure on a giant screen with a state-of-the-art sound system, shuffled toward the entrance. He focused his attention on one young man who appeared different than the others. Unsmiling and alone, the man wore camo pants and had a black backpack strapped over his green flak jacket.

Pinball followed his line of sight. "You think there's a problem?"

"I know there is. He's a bad man. A bad, bad man."

Frank squinted. "How can you tell?"

Deliverance's gaze shifted to Frank's face. He grasped his hood with both hands and lowered it around his neck. Frank backed out of arm's reach. Deliverance's cheeks were flushed, his forehead sweaty, and his eyes smoldered with the same crazed glow Frank had witnessed at the sanatorium's shooting range in Philly.

"I just know." He directed his gaze back to the theater, where his person of interest had succeeded in purchasing a ticket. "See how he glances over his shoulder every few seconds? See his stance and how his backpack strains at its straps indicating a heavy load? And then there's his aura. His is as dark as a demon's and reeks of blood."

Frank and Ruletka exchanged worried looks. Frank cleared his throat. "You can…you can smell him?"

Deliverance nodded his head vigorously, causing his fuzzy brown hood to bob around his neck. He tucked his staff under his arm. "The devil has his soul. He must not succeed."

"Okay, that's it. Enough about stinky auras. We're heading back to the car. Move it, bro." Pinball grabbed Deliverance's elbow and attempted to steer him onto the sidewalk. With a lightning burst of speed, Deliverance tore free and, robe flapping behind his legs, sprinted toward the theater's entrance.

A shriek, loud and shrill, rose above the usual cacophony of the Strip, followed by the rat-a-tat of semi-automatic gunfire.

"Jesus." Rauch ducked and snatched his gun from its holster. "The wacko was right."

The doors to the theater flew open and a herd of hysterical people, some carrying wailing children, flooded the sidewalk.,

"Come on." Ruletka fought his way through the

195

screaming horde, Pinball at his heels. "We have to help him. That wooden stick of his won't hold up long against an AR-15."

"Shit." Rauch rocked back and forth on his feet. "Frankie, are we doing this?"

A movie theater. Why did it have to be a movie theater?

Frank gritted his teeth and lurched forward, keeping his eyes fixed on Ruletka's black cape. He stumbled into the lobby, which had evacuated except for the half-dozen glassy-eyed wounded, who lay bleeding on the ugly purple carpet. The sickening scent of butter, salt, and blood assaulted his nose. His ears began to ring; his head spun.

On either side of the concession stand, long dark corridors led to the individual screens. Another burst of gunfire exploded from the end of the hallway to their right. The Russian's black cape fluttered and disappeared into the darkness. Frank followed but only made it as far as the first theater before the dizziness overwhelmed him. With both hands clasped over his ringing ears, he crumpled to his knees.

The smell of the popcorn triggered a flood of memories, long-suppressed by his self-imposed exile from the cinema. They flickered through his brain like a stop action movie, reel after horrific reel taunting him with the gory details of the worst day of his life, the day that gave birth to his fifth of November curse.

He'd saved some popcorn for Joey, knowing how much his little brother loved it—the gooier, the better. The movie reel spun again, and grainy images projected onto his mental screen. Popcorn scattered across the bloody linoleum of their kitchen floor. Joey's broken three-year-old body. His mother's face, swollen and bruised beyond recognition. His father's drunken leer as he spat at the officers escorting him to jail in handcuffs. The social worker at the hospital telling him everything would be all right. But it never was.

Never once. Never again.

The graphic images, painfully vivid despite the years passed, commanded his sole attention. They rewound, playing over and over as he gagged on his knees in a theater as far removed from his Philadelphia neighborhood as he'd ever imagined he'd be.

"Frank."

An insistent voice penetrated the psychedelic haze of memories. Frank blinked until the misty film coating his eyes cleared and his tunnel vision abated. A firm hand gripped his shoulder, and the voice bellowed again. "Frank, are you okay?" Rauch's stubbly chin swam into view, his face inches from Frank's eyes.

"I…I can't be here."

"I know, buddy. I know."

Rauch hoisted Frank to his feet by one arm and steadied him while he swayed. His vision sharpened, and his hearing returned. The shooting had stopped. Inside the theater, the lobby was eerily quiet, the silence broken only by the soft moans and gentle weeping of the wounded. Outside, sirens screamed as they raced toward the theater, their combined volume drowning out the clamor of the crowd still foolishly gathered outside the doors.

Frank waved a limp hand at a blood-spattered blonde propped against the wall. She'd wrapped the strap of her designer purse around her lower leg as a tourniquet. From the expansive stain on the carpet and the pallor of her skin, her improvisation, while innovative, had not been highly successful. "We should help her."

Rauch dragged him across the lobby. "Help is on the way, Frank. I hear them coming now."

The doors blasted open and a SWAT team rushed through, weapons raised. "On the ground. Hands above your head. Move."

Frank dropped back to his knees. This time, Rauch joined him. "To the right," Frank said, although he wasn't sure they'd pay him any attention. "The last room on the right. Our friends are in there."

Chapter Twenty-Seven

The next few hours passed in a blur of chaos as the police secured the scene and interviewed the witnesses. Frank and Rauch, huddled against the ticket booth, answered questions until they were hoarse. Frank surveyed the victims as they were ferried from the theater on gurneys and loaded into individual ambulances. None wore costumes.

When the witnesses were finally allowed to vacate the premises, Frank and Rauch headed north toward the convention center. Frank checked his phone. He had three text messages, separated by a half hour each.

—R you guys, okay? We'll meet at the car—
—We're at the car now—
—We're still at the car—

He and Rauch quickened their pace, pushing against the cold, dry wind which parched their lips and sent Frank's cape flying stiffly behind him.

—We're coming— Frank texted. *—Don't leave without us—*

They covered the blocks in half the time it'd taken them to meander down the Strip, thanks to their sense of urgency and thinner crowds. News of the shooting traveled fast, and the gawkers vacated the Strip in favor of the ubiquitous TV screens mounted above the gaming tables and bars.

Rauch cleared the sand from his throat. "You do

realize if we have to call a cab, we have no idea where to tell it to go?"

"They're waiting for us." Frank's voice quivered. "Pinball said they'd wait."

"Let's hope so." Rauch paused. "Feeling better?"

"I don't want to talk about it."

"No problemo. I just want you to know that I…um, I understand, and if you want to keep this to ourselves, I'm fine with that, okay?"

Frank stopped next to an ornate musical fountain. Its fantastical orbs of light reflected off the water to highlight the anguish on his face. "Keep what to ourselves, Rauch? My epic failure? Is that what you're referring to?"

Rauch stammered. "I'm just saying the guys don't need to know anything beyond the fact that we didn't make it past the lobby before the cops showed up, that's all. A team is just a team, but you and I, we're like family, Frank. And every family has its secrets."

A strong squall lifted the trash from the sidewalk, sending a toxic flurry of pornographic playing cards, cigarette butts, and spent monorail passes swirling around them. A fine mist from the fountain soothed Frank's chapped lips, and he sighed. "Sometimes you're more Italian than an Italian, Rauch."

"Is that a compliment?"

"I guess it is."

They continued to the convention center where the SUV, its headlights off, idled in the center of the lot. As soon as the pole lights illuminated their presence, the vehicle roared to life and sped across the asphalt to intercept their slow progress.

Pinball lowered the driver's window. "Get in."

They scrambled into the back; Pinball stomped the accelerator. With a squeal of the tires, they careened onto Paradise Road, and the lights of the Strip faded like an early morning dream as Pinball slowed the car to a legal speed. "The last thing I need after a cluster fuck like tonight is a speeding ticket." He gripped the leather wheel with an excessive amount of force, but physically, he appeared unharmed.

Ruletka, sans mask and cape, rested in the passenger seat. Aside from the grim set of his mouth, he also appeared unscathed.

Rauch nudged Frank's elbow and pointed to the vehicle's spacious third row where a wooden staff lay stretched across the length of the seat.

Frank's chest tightened. "Where's Deliverance?"

"He's fine. We took him back to the hangar to settle down. He was bouncing off the walls. Totally out of control." Ruletka's tone was as hard as his expression, and Frank knew there had to be more to the story. Something was terribly wrong.

Ruletka twisted in his seat to better scrutinize Frank's appearance. "Besides, we needed to discuss the situation without him present." A faint smile relaxed his stern expression. "Glad to see you're not hurt, Frank."

"What am I?" Rauch muttered. "Chopped liver?"

"Of course not. You're the one—the only one of us—who was packing a gun. The one who somehow didn't make it into the theater."

Rauch spoke through clenched teeth. "I was protecting Frank. Also, fuck you."

Frank wheezed and put a hand on Rauch's balled fist in an attempt to stifle any further outbursts. Keira was the boss, but Ruletka was both godfather and matriarch, their moral leader in every sense of the word. Upsetting him would disrupt the dynamics of the entire team. "What happened, Ruletka?"

"The shooter climbed the theater stairs and shot at anyone who hadn't escaped or crawled under the seats. Deliverance sneaked up behind him and cracked him over the neck with his staff."

"That's a good thing, right? Go, Deliverance." Frank felt Rauch's fist relax, and he removed his hand.

"I knew the Ewok would come through." Rauch grinned. "I knew it."

"And then, while the shooter was flat on his back and helpless, Deliverance picked up the guy's gun, stared him straight in the eyes, and shot him in the goddamned face. Three times."

Rauch's smile froze on his face. Pinball uttered something under his breath which may have been a curse or a prayer—Frank couldn't tell which. He knew one thing for certain—he was suddenly grateful to have collapsed on his knees in the lobby.

Rauch recovered first. "I'm not sure we should feel sorry for a guy who blew away a group of innocent people."

"This isn't about him. It's about Deliverance. The boy is unstable." Ruletka rubbed his forehead. "You should've seen the look on his face. He stood over the shooter waving his staff and gun like some kind of crazed jihad soldier. Tico and I essentially had to mug him to force him to drop the gun. We grabbed him by the bathrobe and shoved him out the rear exit."

"His prints are on that gun." Rauch shook his head. "You should've brought it with you."

Pinball scowled. "No way in hell was I carrying a

murder weapon out of that theater. Not with SWAT closing in. The question at this point is whether his prints are in any of the national databases. If he hadn't been babbling like a maniac, I would've asked him. Either way, the prints are his problem. I'm not taking the fall for a dude I've known for twelve hours."

"Did anyone see his face?" Frank pictured Deliverance's red hair and freckles. He'd be easy to identify in a police lineup.

Ruletka shrugged. "The theater was pitch-black, and any potential witnesses were either ducked under seats or running toward exits. Hopefully no one saw him or us. If they did—"

"You're up shit creek," Rauch said.

"Not just me. The entire real-life superhero community. Pinball's local reputation. Miss Keira's plans for a hero university. The ripple effect extends far and wide, but you get the idea. She needs to know what happened before Deliverance hurts someone else. He should be fired, forbidden from representing a hero. He's not worthy, and more importantly he needs help."

They drove in gloomy silence to where human development yielded to the desert. Pinball flexed his stiff fingers before easing the car onto the barren stretch of road leading to the hangar.

Again, Rauch was first to break the uncomfortable hush. "Keira may not agree to fire him. I remember her telling me once that everyone has his or her own code, an individual moral line to be crossed—or not."

Ruletka's jaw tightened. "He's a danger and a liability. He must be purged from the collective and referred to a mental health treatment program."

Pinball hit the brakes and threw the vehicle in park.

"We need him. End of story."

"For what?" Ruletka exploded in a startling burst of rage. Frank and Rauch flinched in their seats. "For what, Tico? You've worked too hard on your reputation to let one mentally ill recruit ruin everything. You're already a hero to so many. If this hits, you'll be labeled a vigilante by the police and dragged through the muck by the press. You're over. Done. Keira must be told about tonight."

Away from the city in the desert flats, the stars shone bright in the night sky. Pinball sat still and quiet as if contemplating a future only he could perceive. Finally, he shifted the car back into gear and zoomed toward the hangar.

"I'll talk to her. But unless the police start sniffing too close to home, it'll wait until after the con. Deliverance deserves that much before he's fired. Tonight's our secret until then. Agreed?"

Frank held his breath, awaiting Ruletka's response. The Russian smoothed the scowl from his face. "Thank you, Tico."

The hangar door lurched open, and Pinball guided the car to its designated space. Rictor burbled a greeting as they exited the vehicle.

"C'mon, Rictor. Time for bed." With Rictor by his side, Pinball strode straight to his room and slammed the door.

Ruletka exhaled. "At least Miss Keira isn't here to see us crawling in so late."

"She doesn't sleep here?" Frank wasn't sure why he asked. He couldn't imagine Keira slumming it with the staff.

"Hell, no." Ruletka's derisive response seemed to

surprise even himself. He took another deep breath as if trying to force himself back to his usual serene demeanor. He placed a hand on Frank's shoulder. "It'll be all right in the morning, Frank. Tomorrow, this'll seem like a bad dream, and we can return to our training." With a final pat, he, too, retired to his room.

Frank waited for him to disappear behind his bedroom door. "He asked a good question, Rauch. Why do we need—not want, but need—a mentally unstable, cold-blooded murderer on our team? Pinball didn't answer, in case you didn't notice. Totally dodged it."

"I didn't notice. It's been kind of a crazy night."

Frank stared at his best friend, who looked everywhere but at his face. "Why do I get the feeling Ruletka and I are the only two team members who don't know the whole truth behind Heroes2B? And I have an even stronger feeling what I don't know is about to bite me in the ass."

Rauch shifted on his feet. "You do know. You know about Keira's revenge."

"Yeah, but I think it's high time I learned the actual plan."

Chapter Twenty-Eight

Breakfast started off a miserable affair, with Pinball's brooding, Frank's moping from last night's failure, and Deliverance's unrelenting chatter about things the others would rather forget.

Ruletka did his best to gloss over the tension, stifling Deliverance's sustained and macabre adrenaline high with a few well-placed words before turning to fawn over Frank. He spooned an extra helping of Pinball's special *huevos rancheros* onto a tortilla and set it next to Frank's fork. Frank pushed the plate away, and Rauch whisked it out from under his friend's nose, claiming the dish as his own.

"Christmas on a plate." He shoveled a spoonful of salsa and egg yolk in his mouth.

"What's that supposed to mean?" Pinball plopped his own plate, covered by an overflowing tortilla, on the table.

"It means they're Christmas-morning good. It's a compliment, Pinball. You know, a compliment, where you say nice things to other people?"

"This from a guy whose favorite Christmas movie was *Die Hard*." Frank perked up after his second cup of Ruletka's special tea.

Ruletka raised an eyebrow. "I thought you told me his favorite movie was *Fight Club*."

"I said favorite Christmas movie. Big difference."

Rauch scraped his dish clean. "You'd have to be a grinch not to like these eggs."

"Holy Mother of Kal-El, Rauch." Frank shook his head at his friend's empty plate. "What are you, a human vacuum cleaner?"

The door to the employee rest area hurled open, and the moment of levity died.

Ruletka lowered his voice. "Remember what we decided last night, Pinball."

"I said I'd talk to her *after* the con."

Keira stormed into the kitchen, waving a newspaper in one hand. "What the hell is this?" She tossed the paper on the table in front of Frank.

Rauch smirked. "I think it's called a newspaper. I saw one at a convenience store once. In the wild."

Ruletka leaned closer to take a look. "Oh, dear."

The headlines screamed of the shooting, but it was the largest of the grainy black-and-white photos, with its caption centered and in bold print, which first caught the eye. Keira read it aloud. "Not-So-Super Hero. Look familiar, Frank?" She jabbed her finger on the page, smearing the cheap black ink.

It was a wide-angle shot of the lobby and its carnage. He was on one knee with his hands clasped over his ears and his eyes screwed shut. Rauch, looking every bit the polished businessman in his suit, knelt beside him with a consoling hand on his shoulder. Despite the poor quality of the print, the anguish on Frank's face was palpable. He uttered a noise from somewhere deep in his throat and pushed away from the table.

Rauch grabbed him before he could bolt and jumped to his friend's defense. "We went out for a beer and ended up in the wrong place at the wrong time. Frank was unarmed and unprepared. We have nothing to be ashamed of. The lead started flying, and we hit the deck like any sane person would do."

Deliverance snatched the paper from the table. "Except we're not just any people. We're heroes." His eyes scanned across the page. He stuck out his lower lip and pouted like a toddler. "No one knows what happened. No one saw—"

Keira cut him off. "I don't care that the team didn't intervene. But I asked you to keep a low profile, not pose for a front-page picture in the *Las Vegas Sun*."

"They were hardly posing, Miss Keira." Ruletka's soft voice held an unfamiliar edge. He nodded at Pinball, who pried the newspaper from Deliverance's white-knuckled grip and pushed him back in his seat by both shoulders.

Pinball ignored Deliverance's squirmy attempts to shrug off his grip. "It was my fault, Miss Keira. I thought it would be fun to don our costumes and hit the Strip as a team. Like Rauch said, I never expected something like this to blow up around us."

"You're good at accepting responsibility, Pinball, but you suck at apologies. I don't believe I heard you say 'I'm sorry.'" She tucked her hair behind her ear. "I think this program needs fewer mazes and more real-life training scenarios. Meet me at the station at ten. Wear your suits, and bring your weapons of choice. I expect nothing less than your best efforts. You can make amends with a good performance." She skewered Pinball with a vicious glare and stomped out of the hangar.

"Get off me, man." Deliverance finally succeeded

in breaking free of Pinball's grip. He struggled to his feet and scowled at the team.

"You almost blew it." Pinball tightened his fist. "We talked about this when we dropped you off last night. About what we were going to say if she asked."

Deliverance repeated his words in a mocking, sing-song falsetto. "We talked about this, me, me, me—"

Pinball's fist flew, but Deliverance, as quick-footed as a boxer, ducked to avoid the blow. Rauch nonchalantly extended his foot behind Deliverance's knees and sent him crashing to the ground. With a slick move of his own, Rauch flipped Deliverance onto his belly and pressed a knee into the small of his back, pinning him to the ground. "Don't make me break out the banjo jokes, asshole. I've got a bucketful, and I've been dying to use them."

"Enough." Ruletka's voice thundered around the enclosed eatery. "Let him up, Rauch."

"In a minute." Rauch removed the ebony gun stashed in Deliverance's belt holster and stripped it of its bullets. In one fluid motion, he removed his knee and stepped out of the flailing man's reach.

Deliverance, his face twisted with rage, scrambled to his feet. "You touched my gun. You touched Vengeance."

"You bet your sweet ass I did. And I'm sure the dude from last night felt the same way about *his* gun—right before you used it to blow him away, that is."

Deliverance spat. "You're no hero."

"No news flash there, brilliance and sunshine. Who told you—the voices in your head?"

Deliverance's face flushed a deep shade of red. The purple tinge hid his freckles, making him appear older and a thousand times less congenial. He snatched his gun off the floor and stormed out of the kitchen. Ruletka glared at Rauch and hurried after Deliverance's receding figure.

Pinball smacked his palm on the table. "Shit, man. This team's going to hell in a hurry."

"You ain't kiddin'." Rauch eyed Frank, who sat at the table, head buried in his arms. "You okay?"

Frank's hunched shoulders twitched in a barely perceptible shrug. "I want to go back to Philly."

"I'm with you. As soon as the comic con is over, we'll figure something out, okay? Another day and a half. You can survive that long, can't you?"

"Depends on if Deliverance has more ammo."

"Is that a joke?"

Frank's shoulders twitched again. "How are we gonna get home, anyhow? We've got no money, Rauch. Keira's got us by the balls."

The opening was perfect. It would've been so easy to tell Frank about the impending heist, the money—all the details of a con he suspected to exist but lacked confirmation.

Rauch glanced at Pinball, seeking permission. With a furrowed brow and slight shake of his head, Pinball communicated his concern. *It's not our decision*, his eyes seemed to say. *It's not our story to tell.*

Rauch sighed and plopped in the chair next to Frank. "I told you. We'll figure something out. We always do, one crisis at a time. Speaking of which, give us a hint, Pinball, about this 'station' scenario. What are we in for, and more importantly, who's singing the tunes?"

Pinball chuckled. "Liked the soundtrack to my

human pinball machine, did you? The station, alas, is as it sounds—an old abandoned way station in the desert which Keira had me wire for training purposes. Nothing sexy about it. There's sound, but it ain't classic rock, so be prepared."

"And the scenario?" Rauch had a sneaking suspicion the only thing the heroes would be rescuing was thirty million dollars. This "real-life training scenario" had to be a dry run. The heist was to unfold during the insanity of the comic con, that much he knew. Keira had choreographed every detail; she wouldn't let her plan fail from an unanticipated glitch. This afternoon was a dress rehearsal, a time for the heroes to hone their reflexes and quash their nerves, especially given last night's disaster at the theater.

"You'll find out soon enough." Pinball assessed Frank's defeated posture. "The station itself might be nothing to look at, but it requires some really cool tech to run the scenario. Miss Keira told me you have some electronics training, Frank. If you're interested, I can show you the basics before the simulation starts."

Frank raised his head from the table. "Like what?"

"Like my HackRF board and the drone I use for GPS spoofing attacks."

"No way." Frank's eyes brightened. He pulled his cell phone from his back pocket and waved it in the air. "Can you—"

"I sure can. But smart phones were too easy, so I set my sights on the holy grail—hacking into a vehicle's operation systems."

"They say it's impossible."

"They tell you that so you won't try. Don't believe them. I've found not one, but three different methods, and they all use equipment which costs less than a thousand bucks. I even built a GPS-guided drone to follow a car and transmit false data, effectively hijacking not only the vehicle's GPS, but control systems like braking, the radio, and even the ignition."

"Cool. Did you name it?"

"Of course I did. Rictor needed a girlfriend. I call her Sin."

"Sin. I like it. Deliverance wouldn't approve, but I might be in love. Can I meet her?"

"Whoa, guys—am I the only one who's a little freaked out about this?" Rauch stared in amazement. Pinball and Frank bonding over drones. Who would've figured?

Pinball smirked. "Freaked out about what—that I can control your car with you in it, or that I name my drones?"

"Both."

"Welcome to the future. Get used to it now. There are things on the horizon that would make George Orwell shit his pants." Pinball slapped Frank on the back. "Come with me, Lambda Man. I've got a collection of gadgets to show you that'll fry your fragile circuits, my friend."

Chapter Twenty-Nine

The team left the hangar at nine o'clock and drove east through the desert. The SUV's tinted windshield did little to reduce the blinding glare from the sun, which hovered in the mid-morning sky at the worst possible angle for driving. Pinball squinted as he steered the vehicle around tumbleweeds and the occasional lizard sunning itself on the heated expanse of road.

Frank tugged at his collar. He felt naked without his cape. Mindful of Pinball's veteran advice, he'd left it in his room and noted Ruletka had done the same. Deliverance's fuzzy bathrobe had been replaced by head-to-toe camo, making Frank wonder if the bathrobe had been a costume at all.

Between the camouflage, the weapons, and the large crucifix dangling from his neck, Deliverance looked more like a redneck soldier from an extremist militia than a superhero. Ruletka was right; Deliverance needed help, not training. Frank hoped Keira's choreographed exercise kept him as far away as possible and out of the range of any potential friendly fire. He'd never been shot, and he preferred to keep it that way.

The outpost was a desolate hunk of pockmarked sheet metal with a '70's era gas pump standing sentry. They arrived before Keira, and Pinball parked the SUV in a sliver of shade in front of the garage. Frank and Rauch climbed from the vehicle and were met by the sting of hot sand swirling in the desert breeze. The howl of the wind, combined with the crunch of their boots on the gritty baked ground, registered preternaturally loud in the silence of the abandoned station.

Frank wandered to the main structure, which listed dangerously to the left on its rotten foundation. He swiped a palm over the filthy window, then peered inside. "Where are we?"

The building looked like it once housed a diner and sundries shop. A cherry-red counter separated the rear of the space from its kitchen, and cheap vinyl booths circled the perimeter. Cola advertisements featuring sexy blonde models with feathered-back hair plastered the walls.

Thanks to a partially collapsed roof, much of the diner had been reclaimed by the desert. Its attached garage, however, was clear of drifted sand and tumbleweeds, and the shiny padlock hanging on its door was conspicuously free of rust.

Pinball pulled a hefty chain from his pants pocket and sorted through the keys. "Nowhere. We're nowhere, at least according to satellite-based mapping systems, and that's how Miss Keira and I like it."

"Not true." Rauch ran to pose against a rustic signpost, which bore hand-painted metal strips pounded into various shapes. The uppermost rectangle read, "Welcome to Tatooine." Below it, an arrow bearing the words, "25 miles to Mos Eisley" pointed to the right. Rauch's face stretched into a dopey grin. "Whoever ran this wretched hive is all right by me."

"You *Star Wars* geeks are the worst. Seriously,

were you always such a dork, or are you ramping it up for my benefit? Feel free to stop anytime." Pinball found the correct key and grabbed the padlock, burning his hand on the hot steel. He dropped the lock to the ground and spewed a spate of colorful expletives in both English and Spanish.

"Says the king of the Vegas cosplay underground. Besides, you've got it all wrong. Frank is the geek. I'm the tough guy." Rauch slipped Frank his phone and whispered, "You gotta get a picture of me next to this sign."

Pinball stuck his burnt fingers in his mouth and cursed again. "Put the phone away. No pictures." He hoisted the overhead garage door open by one hand and ushered the team over the threshold's peeling blue paint. "Watch your step. It's bigger on the inside."

Cool air caressed Frank's cheeks—a pleasant surprise given the space was essentially a windowless box resting in the unforgiving desert. "Air conditioning, Pinball? Out here?"

"The garage is solar powered and has a portable air conditioning unit." Pinball switched on the lights, illuminating the unexpected.

The garage, like the old steel mill in Philadelphia, had been given a modern facelift, with banks of laptops, headphones, antennas, and other assorted tech lining the walls. A central workbench contained scattered blueprints and reports. It covered a gaping, rectangular hole in the floor, which Frank assumed had been the garage's oil pit.

A glint of metal caught his eye, and he crouched under the table for a closer look. A small pot, the size and shape of a pressure cooker, sat in the center of the pit's dirt floor. The overlying table blocked the light and cast muddying shadows, but Frank thought he detected a tangle of wires protruding from under the pot's duct-taped lid.

"What's that?" Frank stood and banged his head on the underside of the table, jostling the papers covering its smooth surface.

"Hey, careful. You'll mess up my system." Pinball straightened and smoothed the blueprints into their previous positions. "What's what?"

"The thing in the pit. Another one of your drones?"

Pinball laughed. "That, my friend, is a bomb."

A gust of wind rattled the sheet metal roof, disturbing the sudden silence. Pinball, busy fussing with his papers, failed to notice the team's reaction until Ruletka cleared his throat with a subtle "ahem."

"Tico, maybe you should explain. I think you're freaking them—us—out."

"Huh?" Pinball looked up from the table. Four somber faces stared back. He flashed a devilish grin. "Relax, guys. You think I'm stupid? It's not armed. Not today, anyway. It's for emergency use only. I've got some exceedingly proprietary tech here, and I don't want anyone stealing my goods. I'd blow the place clear to Asgard before I'd let that happen."

"By proprietary, do you happen to mean illegal?" Ruletka reached for one of the blueprints. "Stolen perhaps?"

Pinball grabbed his hand. "By proprietary, I mean *proprietary*."

A proximity monitor bleeped a warning. A sporty convertible roared outside. Pinball released Ruletka's hand and opened the door for Keira. Rauch peeped under the table at the bomb and pursed his lips in a silent whistle.

Judging by the smile on her lips and the spring in her step, Keira was in a much cheerier mood than this morning. She strolled into the center of the room. "Gentlemen, welcome to Heroes2B's off-campus training facility."

Rauch looked over both shoulders. "I thought it was a garage."

Deliverance snickered, and Frank elbowed Rauch in the ribs. He, for one, was happy Keira's foul mood had passed. Rauch didn't need to kindle her wrath.

Her smile never wavered. "At this humble gas station, we can simulate a variety of crime scenarios, including robberies, abductions, gang assaults, and murders."

"You forgot bombings," Rauch added, with a helpful nod toward the pit.

"Okay, and bombings." Keira shot him a quizzical look. "Today you'll be rescuing a van full of abductees—human trafficking victims. Pinball will run the simulation from here, giving him the opportunity to demonstrate the scope of his amazing techno-wizardry, lest the obstacle course in Philly left you with any residual doubts. Rauch, since you're not a trainee, you'll play the role of the bad guy and drive the van. I'll judge everyone's performances. Let's blow away the memory of last night's debacle with your dazzling teamwork. This should be fun." She clapped her bejeweled hands.

Rauch mocked her enthusiasm. "My, aren't we full of confetti and rainbows this morning?"

"You do seem upbeat, Miss Keira." Ruletka

smiled. "It's nice."

"Thank you, Ruletka. I'm excited. I've waited to see this set-up in action for a long time. And let's not forget the comic convention starts in two short days. I put the finishing touches on my costume late last night, and it turned out fab, if I may say so myself."

"Who are you going as?" Frank was genuinely curious. He had an inkling based on her lustrous purple-tinted hair and her purchase of the rare *Captain Britain* comic book. He sighed at the memory. That felt like a lifetime ago. But if his guess was correct, Rauch was about to fall and fall hard, if he hadn't done so already.

"Psylocke, of course." Her cheeks dimpled. "But you already knew that, didn't you, Frank?"

Frank stared at Rauch's gaping mouth. *And there he goes.*

In the not-so distant past, in the grips of adolescent horniness, Frank and Rauch had ranked which of X-Men's mutants they most longed to bang. Frank's pick—the shape-shifting Mystique. Rauch's choice was Betsy Braddock, the buxom, leather-clad knife-fighter with purple hair otherwise known as Psylocke.

"Am I—are we—going to get to see your costume?" Rauch asked, in one rushed breath.

"Of course, silly. You'll be accompanying me to the comic con as my bodyguard, remember? Hence the swanky suit. No bodyguard of mine dresses in sweats."

"With all due respect, Miss Keira, you don't seem the type to need a bodyguard." Ruletka frowned at Rauch's goofy expression. "And if circumstances required one, I'm not sure he's your man."

"I am so her man," Rauch said, "and I have the big gun to prove it."

"I've got a big gun, too." Deliverance chimed in. "I even replaced the bullets Rauch stole. Wanna see?"

Ruletka cringed. "No, thank you, Deliverance. We've all seen your gun. We don't need to see it again."

Deliverance stomped his feet. "But mine's bigger than his."

Keira covered her face with her hands. "Guys, please. Shut up. Seriously, it's like trying to herd an alliance of overactive chipmunks."

"I reject that analogy." Rauch crossed his arms over his muscular chest. "I am not a chipmunk."

Frank shook his head. "I think you mean 'resent.' You resent that analogy."

"No, I reject that analogy, and I'd like to insert my own—one with manlier creatures, like lions or banthas."

"I don't think Miss Keira approves of you inserting your analogies." Pinball jumped into the mix. "She's liable to whoop your lily-white ass." He wrinkled his forehead. "What the hell's a bantha?"

"Gah." Keira threw her hands in the air. "I give up." She grabbed a pile of headsets off the table and passed them around. "Let's roll."

****

Rauch sat behind the wheel of the SUV and waited for his earpiece to signal that the simulation had gone live. His job was simple compared to Frank's and the others'—unless you happen to like running around in spandex in the hot desert sun. All he had to do was stay put and pay attention. Pinball needed to know, in minute detail, everything that happened inside the air-conditioned vehicle during the exercise. Rauch was happy to oblige.

"We're ready. Pull into position." Pinball's disembodied voice crackled in Rauch's ear.

He drove to the gas pump and parked in front as though he intended to fill the tank. The silence stretched. He squirmed in his leather seat and peered outside the windshield at the blue sky. "Where's Sin?"

"Flying overhead and out of sight. A lone drone in the desert would be a sure tip-off that something's about to go down. Tell me about the vehicle."

"The low-fuel light is on. The gauge says we're almost empty, which is weird. It was at three-quarters when I got in. Everything else seems okay."

"Excellent. How about now?"

The locks clicked, and Rauch reflexively reached for the handle. No go. The door refused to budge. He pressed the lock button repeatedly without effect. With a sigh of exasperation, he leaned over the center console to try the passenger door. As if sensing his proximity and finding it loathsome, the radio shrieked to life, blaring an unearthly blur of voices as it scanned up and down the frequencies with inhuman speed. Rauch gasped and bolted upright, smacking his head on the sunroof.

The radio, though still pegged at max volume, stopped scanning and settled on a soft pop station. Rauch rubbed the growing bump on his head and sagged in his seat. Jesus Christ. Barry Manilow. His cupcake job just got harder. He pressed his headphone against his ear, partially to block out the noise and partially to ensure he could be heard over the syrupy strains of the '70's pop ballad.

"Dude, is that really necessary?"

Pinball chuckled. "Sorry. Too loud?" The volume diminished but not by much.

"Too obnoxious."

"That's what we're going for—distraction. Glad to hear it's working. Try to stay focused."

"Sure. No problem."

Seconds after Rauch muttered his response, movement in the side mirror caught his attention. The garage door opened, and Keira, wearing a headset identical to his own, stepped out. Her index finger hovered over the screen of her smartphone as she waited for Pinball to give the final signal.

"Are we ready to release the hounds?" Pinball asked. She replied with a silent thumbs-up. "All righty, then. Ready, set…go!"

The convertible zoomed forward, kicking up a cloud of sand and dust. It covered the short distance from garage to gas pump in a flash and screeched to a halt behind the SUV.

Both doors popped open, as did the trunk. Deliverance jumped from behind the wheel. Frank and Ruletka tumbled from their respective seats and rounded the rear of the vehicle. As Rauch watched, they hefted a giant, overstuffed duffel from the shallow trunk. They each grabbed an end and, grimacing under the strain, shuffled toward the SUV, where they disappeared in the vehicle's blind spot.

Rauch twisted in his seat, but the rear window was too darkly tinted for him to get a bead on their intentions. The SUV lurched on its frame; his stomach lurched with it. A tap on the glass inches from his head prompted him to spin around. He found himself staring down the barrel of a gun named "Vengeance."

Deliverance leered through the driver's window and rattled the door handle.

Pinball shouted his disapproval. "Deliverance, stop. I told you—the doors on most armored vehicles are wired with enough juice to knock you flat on your bony ass. It's a common upgrade. Do not touch. Same goes for you guys in the back."

"While you're at it, can you tell him to get his fucking gun out of my face?" Rauch pounded on the glass with his palm. Deliverance's maniacal grin grew wider.

"Relax." Keira's warm voice soothed Rauch's jangled nerves. "And watch your language. You're a professional now. The SUV may not be a true armored vehicle, but it does have bulletproof glass. That said, if you so much as scratch the surface, Deliverance, you owe me a new window. I'll take it out of your salary."

Deliverance sulked. "But Frank and Ruletka—"

"They have my permission. They need the practice." She glanced at her phone. "Speaking of which, it's been six minutes, gentlemen. I suggest you hurry the hell up. Lives are on the line here."

The SUV jolted again, and Frank and Ruletka reappeared in the side mirror. They lugged the duffel back to the convertible and hoisted it into the trunk. Deliverance joined them and assumed his position behind the wheel. As soon as the others were in, he threw the car in reverse and gunned the engine. With a skid of the tires, they returned to the garage, and Keira punched the stopwatch on her phone.

Inside the SUV, the radio silenced, the locks clicked, and Rauch exhaled with relief. Easy-peasy his ass. Next time, he was the one pointing the gun.

He reached for the door. "Can I get out now?"

"Yep." Pinball resumed control of the airwaves. "Watch the shock handle."

Rauch jerked his fingertips from the door. The team's hysterical laughter boomed through the headset. "Very funny. You guys are a real riot."

"It's not just us guys. Miss Keira's laughing, too."

Rauch ripped off his headset and tossed it in the back seat. "I'm sure she is." He huffed from the car, rounded the bumper, and jerked to a stop. Deep, serrated gouges marred the SUV's hatch. He ran his fingertip over one of the marks and drew a slit of blood. He stuck his finger in his mouth and joined the others in the garage. "What the hell was in that duffel—an alligator?"

"A hydraulic rescue apparatus, otherwise known as the 'jaws of life,' capable of peeling a door off its hinges as easily as you and I would pop open a can of tuna." Pinball swaggered to the convertible's trunk and removed the duffel. "With modifications, natch."

"It's so wicked." Frank, babbling with excitement, bounded to where the duffel lay on the floor. "I've always wanted to play with one. I can take it out if you want to see it." Wide-eyed, he gazed expectantly at Rauch.

"I'll pass, thanks." Rauch looked at Keira. "Did you see what that thing did to your stretch?"

"Technically, it's not mine. The SUV's a rental, and it happens to be in Jack's name. I anticipated some damage as part of the learning process and acted accordingly." She strode to a dry erase board hanging on the wall and wrote the time in bold letters. "Nine minutes, forty-seven seconds. Not bad for a first attempt at a rescue. Goal is five minutes or less, though."

She nodded at Pinball. "Get everything reset. Let's do it again."

Chapter Thirty

And again. Seven simulated rescue attempts later, they met Keira's goal. By that time, the sun had taken its toll. Frank was wheezing. Sin had overheated, adding to Pinball's crankiness, and even Deliverance looked as limp as a dead snake. They shared the final bottle of warm water and rode back to the hangar with the dinged-up SUV's air conditioning cranked to max.

Once inside the hangar, Ruletka mumbled a general reminder to continue hydrating and disappeared into his room. Deliverance followed suit. Frank, wheezy but too pumped to take an afternoon nap, grabbed his inhaler and returned to the kitchen for a cold drink and a snack. To his surprise, he found himself alone.

From somewhere deep in the bowels of the hangar, he heard Pinball talking to and tinkering with Rictor, who, based on the droid's flurry of electronic burbles, enjoyed the extra attention. Rauch never missed an opportunity to take a nice long nap, so Frank assumed he was already snoring. Keira had followed them to the hangar in the convertible, which remained parked behind the stretch, but she'd disappeared while he was retrieving his inhaler. He listened for the familiar click of her boots on the concrete floor. Nothing.

Frank frowned. She had to be here somewhere. They needed to have another heart-to-heart. He might be naïve, but he wasn't stupid. Her revenge scenario, so nebulous at first, was starting to take shape, and he doubted it involved rescuing hostages.

But what did it involve, and more importantly, once she had her revenge, who would take the fall? His gut told him the answer. As much as he longed to see Roy's killer receive his due, it wasn't worth time in jail for grand theft, or worse, a painful demise at the hands of a sadistic Irishman. He knew what Roy would tell him, probably while sipping single-malt whiskey. "A life well-lived is the best revenge." It'd be tough to live well in prison.

He rolled his aching shoulders and was surprised to feel the ripple of burgeoning muscles. Ruletka's training regimen was showing early results. It helped that Frank wasn't reading comics all day and playing video games half the night. No matter what happened over the coming weeks, he had to admit that expanding his world beyond a few Philadelphia blocks had been good for him. He felt stronger not just physically, but in ways he couldn't define, and that was despite his failure in the theater. He'd faced his biggest fear. Next time, he would do better.

He searched the facility without success, completing a full circle before returning to his starting point in the kitchen. Still too wired to rest and now slightly uneasy, he grabbed two beers from the fridge and headed down the hall to the bedrooms. Rauch would forgive him for interrupting his nap as long as Frank brought him a cold one.

Frank gave a quick rap on the door and entered without waiting for a response, figuring he'd have to shake Rauch awake. He stopped mid-stride, a beer in each hand. He'd found Keira.

They sat side by side on the bed with their thighs touching and heads bent over her phone. The expression on Rauch's face, somewhere between that of a lovesick schoolboy and a stoner, implied whatever he was viewing involved a lack of clothing. Or maybe a surfing cat. It was up to Frank to determine which.

Keira looked up as Frank entered. Rauch remained transfixed by the screen. She clicked it off and smiled at the beer bottles in Frank's outstretched hands. "Aw, you shouldn't have."

"I didn't. These are for Rauch and me."

She arched her perfectly tweezed brows, and he sighed. "Fine. You can have mine if you want."

She accepted the cold bottle with gracious aplomb. "Such a gentleman."

He gestured at her phone. "Whatcha lookin' at?"

"Pictures from last year's comic convention. Since Rauch will accompany me to the opening festivities, I wanted him to have at least a general idea of the event's magnitude and layout. It can be overwhelming for a first-timer."

That explained Rauch's dazed expression. The image of Keira in her costume must've overloaded his adolescent-grade circuits. "Did you go as Psylocke?"

"I always do. She is my doppelgänger, after all."

"Because you were born with purple hair."

She ignored his snark and sipped her beer.

Rauch shook his head as if awakening from a trance. "What do you want, Frank?" His brusque tone took Frank aback.

"Actually, I was looking for Keira, but when I couldn't find her, I thought I'd bring my best friend a beer. That's what best friends do, right?"

Rauch flushed and snatched the bottle from Frank's hand. "Thanks." He twisted the cap, releasing a fizzy rush of carbonation. For more than a few minutes, it was the only sound in the room.

Frank inhaled the heady aroma of malt and hops and wished he'd brought three. Next time he needed Keira, he'd know to search Rauch's room first. Rauch chugged from the sweaty, long-necked bottle and smacked his lips in appreciation.

Frank's testiness surged. He turned on Keira. "You're supposed to be taking the entire team to the comic convention, not just him. He won't even be in costume. The con was the dangling carrot to get me to Vegas, if I recall."

Keira's eyes narrowed. "I am, and you will. The events run for a full week. Day one is registration and set-up—nothing exciting. Rauch and I will get everyone checked in; we'll attend as a team on subsequent days."

"And what are the rest of us supposed to do while you're running around in black leather brandishing your psychic knife?"

Rauch snorted beer up his nose and coughed until tears coursed down his cheeks. "That hurt." He blotted his runny nose with his shirtsleeve. "You can't brandish a psychic knife, Frank, because, well, it's psychic. You can't see it."

"Thank you, Captain Obvious." Frank grabbed a tissue off the nightstand and handed it to Rauch. "She knows what I mean."

Keira assessed Frank's irritability with the steely composure of a trained psychologist. "What did you really want to talk to me about, Frank?"

"When is it going down?"

"When is what going down?"

"Will you knock it off already? Both of you. Stop lying to me. I'm not a moron." Frank rushed the bed, his hands balled into fists by his side. "Don't you see what she's doing to you?"

Rauch's eyes widened at the unexpected outburst. His expression hardened, and Keira jumped to her feet. She stretched her hand toward Frank like a trainer attempting to soothe a frantic puppy. He shuffled out of reach.

She set her beer on the bedside table. "No one's calling you a moron, Frank."

"Just tell him." Rauch stared into his bottle's amber mouth. His breath echoed off the hollow bottom of the empty glass. "Tell him so he can make his decision now. It's safer that way. If he leaves, Ruletka and Deliverance can handle the heist without him. It'll just take them longer, that's all."

Frank knew Rauch had been holding back, suppressing and parceling out information on a need-to-know basis, just like Keira. But the confirmation still hurt. He willed Rauch to raise his eyes so he could judge the depths of his best friend's remorse or resolve…or ongoing deception. But Rauch's gaze stayed fixed on his bottle, which told Frank everything he needed to know. He relaxed his tight fists and waited for Keira to stop scowling and start talking.

She matched his posture. "I've worked on this plan for a year, Frank. I can't have you running to the police." Her tone was cooler than her icy glare.

"He won't." Rauch's gaze flew from his empty bottle to Keira's taut face. The scar on his forehead throbbed in response to her implied threat.

"I can speak for myself." Frank, aware he was mentally jousting with an elite professional, paused to gather his thoughts. He had no intentions of running to the police, not when, as far as he knew, he remained under suspicion for Roy's murder. But Keira didn't know that. On the other hand, he didn't want to test the limits of Keira's criminal tendencies with an empty bluff. She did spring from a family of homicidal maniacs and had both motive and means to make him disappear.

He calculated his next move, ultimately succumbing to the easiest option—the truth. "I won't. Not as long as you tell me the truth, the whole truth, and nothing but the truth. You have my word, and my word…" He shot Rauch a withering look. "…Is good. Doesn't mean I'll go along with it, though."

"Fair enough." Keira paced the narrow room. "You already know this is about revenge. I want to hurt Jack; you want to hurt Jack. But neither of us wants to go to jail for murder. The next best option is to whack him in the wallet. A big enough hit will disgrace him in the eyes of the Family. Then it's their choice whether to demote or bury him. And since none of us wants to be hunted by the Irish mob for the rest of our lives, our plan has to be deployed discreetly and anonymously. He thinks I'm in Vegas for the comic con. I come every year. And once the convention begins, Vegas will be crawling with cosplayers. None of you will stand out in the crowd."

Frank interrupted her spiel. "And you'll have a solid alibi."

"Precisely. After the heist, my presence in Vegas

will seem more suspicious. Rauch and I have been studying the layout to insure I get my face on as many security cameras as possible. I'm sure Jack will still assume I was behind it, but he won't be able to prove a thing."

"And he's never met any of us."

"He's met Rauch, which is why he needs to accompany me on camera."

Frank nodded. The plan was coming together in his mind, and he had to hand it to her—it sounded good. "I take it we'll be robbing an armored car loaded with cash."

"Not just any car. A custom armored SUV."

"The same one you drove at the steel factory?"

Keira nodded. "My family has used it for years to transfer money around the Philadelphia area. Jack has a trusted corps of drivers, so I've no doubt he'll send them. I flew Pinball to Philly a year ago and hired him to masquerade as a mechanic. He now controls the vehicle inside and out. He says there are three ways to hack a car, and he's covered all of them in case one method fails. You saw how he deployed his drone to hack into the rental's telematics during the garage simulation."

"Sin. You should call her by her name. Pinball would want you to."

Keira stopped pacing long enough to flash Frank a look he'd come to recognize. It roughly translated to "don't be such a dipshit."

"Please continue." Frank smothered a grin. He should be appalled. But instead he felt the same slow burn of mounting anticipation he experienced each time he donned his costume. The thrill was in the prep, prowl, and hunt. The execution itself was often painful.

"He also planted malware in the car's computer via a tainted MP3."

"Probably Barry freakin' Manilow." Rauch, jolted from his brooding silence by the memory, grimaced and shook his head as if the saccharine tune still echoed in his ears.

She grinned. "I happen to adore Barry Manilow. Anyhow, Frank, here's the plan as it stands: Pinball and Sin commandeer the car, Deliverance distracts and guards, you and Ruletka break in the hatch and transfer the money, and everyone gets the hell out. No one gets hurt. The thugs in the car see three dudes in costumes and a generic getaway car with no plates."

"I wouldn't exactly call the convertible generic." Frank frowned.

"Pinball and I are returning both the stretch and the convertible tomorrow. I'll rent something more appropriate using a fake ID. Any requests?"

"Something with a big trunk." Frank pictured the jaws of life resting atop piles of money. "A ginormous trunk."

"I'm thinking a small cargo van. One with no back-seat windows."

"That'll work."

Frank paced a tight circle. Though he and Jack had never met, he'd pictured the young man in his mind based on Keira's pithy descriptions. The scrawny, red-haired Irishman of his imagination stood trembling and apoplectic with rage upon discovering his family's custom armored SUV desecrated and bare of cash. The aftermath could be brutal.

He stopped abruptly. "You do realize you'll never

be able to set foot in Philadelphia again. You'll be done with the Irish mob, with the only family you've ever known. Jack will turn them against you—if they don't kill him first."

"They're not my family. Jack can embrace the scum. I'm breaking the bank and heading somewhere with an island breeze and Jimmy Buffet playing twenty-four seven." She fluttered her dark eyelashes. "But thank you for your concern, Frank. It's quite touching."

"I like Jimmy Buffet." Rauch blurted out the words like a confession.

Frank stared askance at his best friend's rapt expression. Keira truly had him in her psychic grip. He shook his head. "Rauch, have you ever even heard a Buffet song? I doubt you can name a single one."

"Sure I can. 'It's Five O'Clock Somewhere'." Rauch beamed as if he'd been crowned a *Jeopardy* champion.

"Technically, that's not a Jimmy Buffet song. It's an Alan Jackson song."

"Says who?"

"I don't know. Says the people who make records."

"No one makes records anymore, Frank. Jesus Christ, how old are you? Get with the times. Music's digital now. Even I know that."

"It was a figure of speech. Besides, people collect vinyl."

"Yeah, people like you who collect comics and dusty old books. People who can't let go of the past." The darkness returned to briefly diminish his mood. He waved his hand in the air. "It doesn't matter. The Parrotheads who run the PhilaBama Bar and Grill on 19th say it's a Jimmy Buffet song, which is good enough for me. You don't ever want to piss off the Parrotheads. Those people are freaking nuts. The whole block is crawling with them." Rauch leaned forward and lowered his voice. "The men wear coconuts on their titties."

They giggled, and for a second, it felt like old times. Then Keira opened her mouth.

"Um, guys? I hate to interrupt, but we have a con to plan."

Frank shrugged. "Who's planning? You've already got it all figured out. We just need to show up and play our roles."

Keira retrieved her beer from the table and held it in the air in a mock toast. "I have to say, Frank, I never expected you to be this gung-ho about the plan or else I would've let you in from the beginning."

"I can think of nothing I'd like more than to steal a fortune from the man who killed Roy Baum and use it to buy his store. It's very Robin Hood-esque, don't you think? Rob from the rich, and give to the poor."

"What poor?" Keira's good humor vanished. "If you think for one instant I'm giving Jack's money to charity—"

"Relax." Frank brushed her protests aside with a wave of his hand. "Rauch, Ruletka, and I—we're charity. We're as poor as they come, and like I said, I can think of a lot of good deeds we can do with Jack's money." He paused at Rauch's stony expression. "We are getting paid, right?"

Rauch looked at Keira. She drained her bottle in one toss and thrust it in his hand. "Of course you are, Frank." She headed out the door. "One way or the other, you'll get paid."

Chapter Thirty-One

Rauch tucked his fancy new gun into the fancy holster of his fancy new suit and stared at his freshly shaven self in the bathroom mirror. Today was the big day. If everything went right, he'd be ten million dollars richer by sunset. Problem was, he couldn't remember a time in his life when every single thing had gone right. Maybe it never had.

He tugged at the red silk tie encircling his throat, the sensation as unfamiliar as it was unpleasant. He never understood why businessmen chose to wear nooses. Skinny once told him it made them easier to strangle. The mobster boasted he'd never worn one in his life. Wouldn't have matched his track suit anyhow. Or that ugly orange lanyard.

After a final glance in the mirror, he left his room and strolled down the long hall toward the kitchen where he was to meet Keira. After they left for the con, the plan was for Pinball to ferry the team back to the abandoned gas station for another live simulation, this time with paid actors driving the car. Only they weren't. The armored SUV's occupants would be Jack's most trusted—heavily armed men whose only goal was to protect their boss's money, even if it meant whacking a couple of masked dweebs in the process.

It didn't seem proper, him galivanting away and leaving Frank to do the dirty work, especially since no

matter what Keira had told him to his face, he wasn't
getting paid. In private, she'd made that abundantly
clear. Rauch would have to split his share, which he
planned to do. At least with Frank. Deliverance and
Ruletka were shit out of luck.

The team was assembled in the kitchen when he
arrived. Ruletka fussed over Keira's wavy violet hair,
teasing strands here and there for extra volume.
Deliverance, chattering about nothing, bounced on his
seat as usual. Pinball appeared tired and subdued. Arms
crossed, he leaned against the fridge and took in the
scene, his eyes cool and focused. Like Rauch, if today
went right, Pinball would become a rich man—rich
enough to build himself a whole fleet of Rictors and
Sins, if he so chose. But unlike Rauch, he had a lot to
lose. He'd devoted his most beloved creations and at
least a year of his life to this plan. He had the right to be
tense.

And then there was Frank who sat there, winding a
clear plastic straw through his fingers. His gaze darted
back and forth between Deliverance and Ruletka, and
every few seconds, his nervous expression smoothed
into a stoic mask as if he kept reminding himself to play
it cool.

"Ruletka should know, too," he'd said, after Keira
had stormed from the bedroom. "Otherwise, what's he
gonna think when he sees the bags of money? How will
he react? It's an unnecessary and possibly dangerous
variable to leave hanging. He needs to know."

Rauch agreed. Two days ago, he'd thought the
same about Frank. But he patted Frank on the shoulder
and reassured him it was part of Keira and Pinball's
master plan. He and Frank just needed to ride the wave,

and everything would turn out fine. Then they went and got more beer.

"My, don't you look dapper today." Keira crossed the room to straighten his tie, cinching the loose knot tight around his neck.

Rauch twisted away. "Will I do?"

"You'll more than do."

Ruletka begrudgingly concurred. "Very nice. You do clean up well."

"Thank you. I'm sure that hurt to say."

Keira wore a short black cape wrapped and pinned at the shoulder. As she moved, the hem fluttered and revealed a purple satin lining and a peep of shimmering hosiery, which disappeared into her thigh-high boots. Rauch wasn't sure if he should be disappointed or relieved by the modest attire.

"I thought you were anti-cape."

She laughed. "I am totally anti-cape—for crime-fighting."

"What about for crime-committing?"

Deliverance stopped chattering, plunging the room into silence. Frank's straw popped into the air, and Keira's smile disappeared.

"The cape is for dress-up, Rauch. For cosplay. I'll take it off when I get to the convention center. I know it's Vegas, but I'm a lady, and ladies don't walk around town in what amounts to S&M gear."

"Shame." He winked at Frank, donned his best swagger, and sauntered toward the door. "You ready to get your game on, lady?"

****

Rauch figured he had until the count of ten before Keira laid into him. He gripped the steering wheel and counted under his breath. He made it to six.

She fastened her seat belt with a vicious click of the buckle. "What the hell was that about?"

Rauch kept his focus on the flat road ahead. "Just planting a seed. Frank's worried Ruletka might be shocked useless when he sees the money. He's so very moral, you know."

"Frank needs to let me worry about such things, and so do you. I'm the brains of this operation. Ruletka didn't used to be so upright in his younger days. Shoplifting, truancy...I did my research. I've spent more time probing Ruletka's psyche than you or Frank would ever want to."

"That's for damned sure."

"I know exactly how Ruletka will react."

Rauch's lips twisted in a sardonic grin. "No one ever knows exactly how a man, or woman, will react under pressure. It's like cornering a stray dog. Some will whimper and some will bite, but rarely will you find one that follows commands."

"Thank you, Dr. Rauch, for that brilliant insight. And I had you pegged as a desperado street punk."

Rauch's eyes narrowed. "Don't get too cocky, princess. That's all I'm sayin'. I may not have a degree from a fancy schmancy university, but I know a thing or two about survival of the fittest."

She lapsed into stone-faced silence, broken only when she was forced to give him directions to the conference center. Customized vehicles, tricked out to sync with their owners' costumes, packed the lot.

He slipped the new rental, a sporty roadster in a rocking shade of red, between a 1960's Batmobile and a two-wheeler replica of the Hell Cycle from *Ghost*

Rider. Rauch clambered from the low-slung car and turned in slow circles, taking it in the mind-blowing scene. "Sweet."

A trio of candy-colored furries flounced by and sniffed with disdain at Rauch's plain suit. He grinned. "The cheese is strong with these people, and I love it." A wave of giddiness crashed over him. A month ago, he expected to die on the streets of Philadelphia as a penniless man. Now, here he was, standing in the glitter capital of the world, wearing fancy duds, driving an awesome car, and escorting a gorgeous chick. He shook his head. Lady. Woman. Whatever. Keira was smoking, no matter what label she preferred.

Impulsively, he grabbed her by the hand and pulled her close to his side as he weaved through the cars toward the entrance. "C'mon, Psylocke. We've got a con to rock."

"Rauch, wait. Stop." She tugged her hand free. "I want to leave my cape in the car. And also, you're my bodyguard. No smiling like an idiot, and no hand-holding. You'll need both your hands free if Jack shows up and pitches some sort of hissy." With the flourish of a bullfighter waving a muleta, she unpinned her cape and twirled it off her bare shoulders.

A waft of her spicy perfume tickled his nose and sent his head spinning. Rauch had seen her in costume in the photos on her phone. But it was a whole different level of sensory experience with her standing a mere foot away, moving the way she moved and smelling the way she smelled. He blinked as if he'd suddenly realized the brightness of the desert sun.

She slammed the car door. "Okay. That's better." She cocked her head at his expression. "What? You've never seen in a girl in a black leather bodysuit before?"

Despite her sarcastic tone, her sullen mood softened, and Rauch thought he detected a hint of a self-conscious smile. She tossed her hair, which glowed like a violet veil in the harsh yellow light and smiled for real. "Come on, big guy. Let's give it a go."

Chapter Thirty-Two

Frank couldn't help himself. Every ten seconds or so, between bites of Ruletka's ought-to-be famous meatloaf, he questioned Pinball with his eyes. *Now? Is it happening now? If not, when?* Pinball rolled a single, perfectly round pea around the edge of his plate and avoided Frank's gaze.

They finished lunch and cleared the table. Pinball wiped his mouth with his napkin and oh-so casually stretched his arms overhead. "I hope y'all weren't planning on taking the day off. The boss left us a revised scenario to run this afternoon. If the team passes, you each get an added bonus with your comic con registration—a ticket to tomorrow evening's meet-and-greet with the *Avengers*."

Deliverance dropped his dirty knife. It hit the concrete and bounced, spattering bright red globs of ketchup over the kitchen floor. "Sweet mother of God."

Ruletka narrowed his eyes. "Who determines if we pass?"

"Yours truly, with some minor assistance from Sin." Pinball flashed a wide, toothy grin. "Follow my orders like obedient little heroes and you'll do fine. But remember, Sin and I will be watching. I own a red pen, and I'm not afraid to use it."

Ruletka flicked him with a dish towel. "Tico, you know I adore you, but you're so full of crap."

"Maybe, but without me…" He spread his arms wide and deepened his voice to a low rumble. "…You shall not pass!"

Deliverance giggled. Pinball winked and dropped his arms. "She's even hired an actor to assume Rauch's role as the driver. Should be fun." He glanced at the time. "Don your costumes, heroes. We leave in twenty."

Deliverance zoomed from the room with Ruletka tut-tutting at his heels.

Frank lingered behind. "Man, you're so bad, you're good."

"Thanks." Pinball paused, and his smile faded. He lowered his gaze to the sullied floor. "I'm glad she told you, Frank. I wanted to tell you myself, but—"

"I know. Forget about it. Rauch is my best friend, and he didn't bother to tell me, either. I'll just be glad when it's over. I'm ready to go home."

"I live here, and I'm ready to go home, if that makes any sense. Two hours. In two hours, it'll be over and done."

"Deliverance is going to take it hard when he realizes there is no Heroes2B." Frank wiped the ketchup from the floor.

"There are only two good things about preacher boy: He's an excellent shot, and no one will believe his babble if he decides to rat. Dude's bat shit crazy."

"Now you sound like Rauch." Frank frowned. "Ruletka would not approve."

"If Ruletka were any more sincere, he'd collapse under the weight of his own convictions."

"He genuinely cares about the team."

Pinball's chair screeched over the concrete floor as

he pushed away from the table. "Good for him. No offense, bro, but I'm like Miss Keira—I'm in it for the dough. I have no issues with retiring my costume once I'm a millionaire. What about you?"

"Hadn't thought about it."

That much was true. Frank hadn't given the future much thought, mostly because he'd only learned about the money a short forty-eight hours ago. He tried to imagine a life without his evening patrols around the hood. He couldn't. Rich or poor, he would always be Lambda Man. After all, Lambda was his real name, as Rauch delighted in pointing out. But maybe with the right amount of cash at his disposal, Frank could channel the need behind the mask into something more. Time would tell. Two hours' worth of time, to be exact.

Pinball watched the emotions shadow Frank's face. He slapped him on the back. "I like you, Frank. You've got a good heart. No matter how this plays out in the end, we should stay in touch." He grinned. "I can teach you how to build your very own Sin."

****

The van's front windows were tinted far past the legal allowance, and for that Frank was grateful. Once the garage door opened, the late-afternoon sun would be blinding. The team could ill-afford a handicap of any kind. He looked at Deliverance bobbing gleefully behind the wheel. They were handicapped enough already.

Pinball briefed them before they assumed their positions. Deliverance driving. Frank hunched in the back seat. Ruletka riding shotgun. Just like last time, boys, only faster, meaner. Tear the rear hatch clean off. Transfer the contents. Return to the hangar, and await further orders. Make Miss Keira proud. Easy-peasy. Pinball said it three times. Frank wasn't convinced.

Their earpieces crackled in unison, relaying information. *SUV approaching pump. Garage door opening now. Awaiting system capture.*

As soon as the gap between the floor and the door was adequate, Pinball released Sin. The drone whirred from the garage to position herself above the target. With capture complete, she streamed video to Pinball's laptop and the small screen on the van's dash. The door rose to a fully open position. Sunlight streamed into the dusty garage. Deliverance revved the engine.

Frank blinked.

Pinball's detached voice echoed in their ears. "All systems ready. On my mark."

Frank's heart skipped a beat.

"Go."

Chapter Thirty-Three

Frank and Ruletka jumped from the car more or less simultaneously, but Ruletka made it to the rear first. Frank tripped over the only decent-sized rock in the entire desert and face-planted in the sand.

"Get up, Frank. Get up." Pinball's voice echoed in his ear. "Ruletka, keep moving."

Frank's boots skidded on the gravely surface as he scrambled to his feet. By the time he reached the hatch, Ruletka had managed to hoist the duffel out by himself and was dragging it through the sand. Frank grabbed an end, and they hurried to the rear of the SUV.

"You're bleeding." Ruletka unzipped the duffel and leveled the equipment on his bent knee while Frank operated the controls.

"He'll live." Pinball sounded tense, and Frank couldn't blame him. They had not allotted time for him to roll around in the sand like a gecko on acid. By now, the SUV's occupants were well-aware the vehicle's navigation system had led them into a trap.

He attached the serrated jaws to the vehicle's hatch and flipped the switch. The SUV groaned as the door popped, then screamed as the metal peeled away from the hinges. A dozen plain cardboard boxes, stacked to the roof, packed the SUV's trunk. Behind them, a steel partition with a tiny peephole divided the passenger compartment from the rear.

The metal partition throbbed with the thumping of the radio's bass, and Frank grinned. Tom Jones. How quintessentially Vegas. At least it wasn't Barry Manilow. Frank grabbed the topmost box off the stack and imagined Jack's Irish heavies, freckled faces purple with rage, staring at him through the peephole. The partition shook with a violent thud, as if one of the goons had slammed his beefy palm against it. Frank jerked backward. The box in his hands bobbled, and he nearly tripped again, this time over the duffel lying at his feet.

He and Ruletka exchanged glances. They picked up their pace, transferring the boxes from one vehicle to the other as quickly as they could move in the heat of the desert sun.

"Deliverance, a distraction please." Another solid thump on the steel partition triggered Pinball's brisk command. Frank started to sweat as he imagined a pair of rabid goons bursting forth to pound the snot out of he and Ruletka. Or worse.

Deliverance pulled Vengeance from its holster and swaggered toward the driver's window. Frank and Ruletka, the transfer complete, detached the jaws from its metal prey and returned it to the black duffel. With a grunt, Frank heaved his end into the air, and Ruletka did the same. Together, they shuffled the weighty bag toward the van's open hatch.

"Deliverance, stop." The urgency in Pinball's voice made Frank and Ruletka pause.

Sin, guided remotely by Pinball's expert touch, buzzed from where she'd been hovering over the armored SUV's roof to whiz over their heads.

"Return to the car," he ordered, some urgency in

his voice. "Frank, Ruletka, get your hustle on."

"Is there a problem?" Frank, wheezing under the strain of the heavy load, staggered to the hatch where he and Ruletka hurled the duffel against the row of boxes.

"Deliverance, I said—" A blast of gunfire drowned out Pinball's words.

Frank and Ruletka dove under the bumper for cover. Two more shots pierced the air. Their earpieces screeched, rendered temporarily useless by feedback.

"Tico, what's happening?" Ruletka reached overhead and slammed the van's rear doors. He and Frank, palms pressed over their ringing ears, crouched under the bumper. "Talk to us, Tico."

Ruletka's voice was calm, too calm. Frank stared at his placid face. *He still thinks this is a simulation.* Frank grabbed his forearm and, through a throat choked with dust, managed to croak out two words. "It's real." Ruletka's serene expression melted into one of puzzlement, then shock as the truth hit.

Sin landed on the ground next to them, and their earpieces crackled back to life. "Get in the car." Pinball's voice boomed from the speaker below Sin's red optical array. "Frank, drive."

"I don't know how to drive. I'm from the city, remember?" Frank crept from beneath the bumper to peek around the van's hulking frame. He recoiled in horror. His head spun, and he screwed his eyes shut, aware he was hyperventilating but powerless to stop it.

A dozen yards away, Deliverance lay face down in the sand. Blood streamed from his wounds, soaking into the parched desert, staining it as red as Louisiana clay.

"Just get in the goddamned car." Sin's motor

whined as she abandoned Frank to return to the safety of the garage.

Ruletka recovered first. "I'll drive." He rounded the bumper to the driver's side, leaving Frank alone. The driver's door slammed shut. The van's engine revved. Frank had to move or risk being left behind.

He opened his eyes, but whether from sand, wind, or the salt of his tears, found his vision blurred. He took a gulp of hot dry air, willed his legs to move, and dashed around the bumper. The passenger door popped open, and he dove through headfirst. Ruletka gunned the engine in reverse. The door slammed against Frank's feet as the van skidded to a stop outside the garage.

Pinball, Sin tucked under one arm and his laptop under the other, ran to join them. He jumped into the back seat. "Off road, wide. Give the SUV a fifty-yard berth."

Ruletka's jaw twitched. "Why?"

"Because they've installed fucking gun ports in the doors, that's why. Once we're past, you can return to the road. Now punch it. Move."

Ruletka stomped on the gas. The van's spinning wheels kicked up a cloud of brown dust as they skirted the SUV in a wide circle.

"Wait—what about Deliverance?" Frank, arms and legs flailing with each jerk of the wheel, struggled to right himself in his seat.

"What about him? He's dead." Pinball opened his laptop and pounded on the keys. "And keep your head down. Just in case."

Frank slouched until his head was below window level. "Are you sure? Maybe he was just wounded."

"I'm more than sure. Sin got a nice, close-up view. One of those shots went straight through his forehead." The frantic typing continued. Pinball's laptop flashed and beeped a ready signal.

Frank wiped the grit and tears from his cheeks. "We can't...we can't just leave him to rot in the desert. It's not right."

"He won't rot. He'll burn. Cover your ears."

"What?"

Pinball punched a key, and the garage exploded into a giant fireball. Smaller explosions rocked the diner and gas pumps, sending the armored car tumbling across the desert like dice on a dirty craps table. Deliverance's body disappeared, engulfed in the spreading flames.

"Oh my God." Frank sat upright and stared at the hellish scene in the side-view mirror. His ragged breath quickened, his vision tunneled, and everything around him dimmed to a hazy shade of gray. He lowered his head between his knees to avoid fainting. "Was this part of the plan?"

"No."

A secondary explosion annihilated what remained of the station. Once the roar abated, Frank raised his head. "All that from one bomb the size of Sin?"

Pinball shrugged. "There might've been one or two more hidden in strategic locations." He flicked open a pair of metal aviator sunglasses and hid his eyes behind their mirrored lenses. "For better or for worse, Jack's men will survive, thanks to the vehicle's armor plate."

Ruletka pressed the accelerator to the floor, and they raced toward the anonymity of the air hangar. Once the black smoke disappeared over the horizon and the first glimpse of the city loomed, he reduced his speed. His gaze remained on the dusty road, but the timbre of his tight voice disclosed his disquiet.

"Someone needs to explain what just happened. Who's Jack, and why was he worth dying for?"

Frank glanced over the headrest at Pinball. Pinball stared at Sin. Frank cleared his dry throat. "No one was supposed to get hurt. Easy-peasy. Isn't that what you said, Pinball? Isn't it?" Fueled by panic and anger, his voice soared to a shrill screech.

Pinball flinched. "Miss Keira will explain. This was her plan, not mine. I'm just the tech wizard."

"And an expert at deflecting blame, from the sounds of it." Ruletka's fingers twitched on the wheel. "I don't care what kind of explanation she gives. Deliverance deserved better."

"Funny, I seem to recall you saying a few days ago that he was a liability who should be purged from the community."

"Purged, not slaughtered. The difference is more than semantic."

"He'd have been fine if they hadn't installed those gun ports. They weren't there a year ago."

Frank glanced in the rear view mirror as if expecting to see a legion of Irish thugs bearing down on them. "Don't you think you should call Keira, let her know we had a…a…problem?"

"I already texted her." Pinball squeezed his phone and frowned. "She hasn't texted back."

Chapter Thirty-Four

Rauch and Keira stood in the registration line between a Silver Surfer and a Wookiee. As the wait stretched, he succumbed to temptation and reached to stroke the costume's luxurious brown fur with his fingertips.

"Rauch, really?" Keira slapped his hand away before he made contact. "Not cool." The Wookiee, unaware of the drama at his back, gathered his brochures and lumbered away.

They breezed through registration, and Keira perched on a vacant bench to study the map and schedule of events. Rauch stood guard, or more accurately, stood and gawked at the menagerie of costumed creatures beginning to assemble in the convention center's great hall.

Behind a statuesque woman sprayed from head to toe in glittery blue body paint, he glimpsed—or thought he glimpsed—a familiar face. His stomach tightened. He craned his neck, struggling to see over the woman's cerulean shoulder and through the undulating horde. Two burly men in expensive suits parted the crowd. Rauch grabbed Keira by the elbow and hauled her to her feet, but not soon enough. Jack's angry green eyes met his.

"Hey." Keira, oblivious to her brother's approach, yanked her elbow away with a snarl.

Rauch curled his arm around her waist and directed her through the crowd toward the door. "We need to move. Jack's here."

Keira lurched to a stop. "Okay, so Jack's here. We wanted him to see us. It's our alibi, remember?"

Rauch prodded her into motion. "He didn't look like he was in the best of moods. And his heavies looked even friendlier. I mean, if you really want to chat, we can find a table, maybe order some cocktails—" His sarcastic jabber ended when they found themselves stalled behind a baker's dozen dressed as the Legion of Doom. "Shit."

They did an abrupt about-face and were greeted by Jack's sneering henchmen. Keira's phone buzzed, signaling a text. Jack stepped forward and waved a bejeweled hand. "You should get that. I'm pretty sure it's important."

****

Jack actually had four bodyguards. While Rauch waited for Keira to engage her brother in verbal combat, his senses, overloaded by the tremendous amount of input from his insane surroundings, regained their focus. The background clamor dissipated into a muted hum, and his peripheral vision sharpened, allowing him to recognize that two additional thugs were closing in from the sides to prevent his and Keira's escape. But why did Jack think they had reason to run?

Rauch studied Jack's face for clues. The mobster's attention was focused on his sister, and his eyes blazed with such hatred and contempt that Rauch's skin prickled beneath his suit. This was no typical sibling rivalry. As far as Jack was concerned, Keira may as well be the gum on the sole of his shoe.

She made a big show of reviewing the text before nonchalantly deleting it. "Bummer. The salon canceled my manicure. Nice to see you, too, Jack. Didn't know cosplay was your jam."

"Little people playing dress-up hold no interest for me. I don't believe in disguising who you are."

"Then you're in the wrong place."

Jack snatched the phone from Keira's hand.

"What do you think you're doing? Give it back." She reached for it, and one of his bodyguards stepped forward.

The muscles in Rauch's forearm rippled as he clenched his fingers into a tight fist. "The lady said to give it back."

Keira shook her head at Rauch and crossed her arms while Jack scrolled through her messages and contacts.

Jack showed the screen to his bodyguard, who laughed. "Looks like your manicurist's name is 'Pinball,' and he says you have a problem. You need to learn to empty your deleted messages, too."

"What do you want, Jack?"

"You stole something of mine. I want it back."

"Yeah? Welcome to the club, baby bro."

Her mocking tone hit its mark; Jack's face tightened with barely contained rage.

Rauch suppressed a groan. Deny and run would've been their best option—if she hadn't just shot it clear to hell. She'd better have a contingency plan or else they were royally screwed. If a plan existed, she hadn't bothered to share it with him.

"You know what? Excuse me, Mr. McConnell."

Rauch held up a finger. "I know you two have some unresolved family issues, but Miss Keira's running late for the..." He glanced at the schedule dangling from Keira's fingers. "...Grrls Rule: Evolution of the Female Superhero panel. Maybe we could finish this conversation tonight at the bar—"

"Maybe you could shut your fucking mouth." Jack's lip curled, and he waved his ring at the goons hovering over his shoulder. "Escort them to the car. Feel free to shoot him if he gives you any trouble, but not fatally. I need them alive, at least for now."

I need them alive.

The tension in Rauch's shoulders relaxed slightly, thanks to Jack's spillage of too much information. Emboldened, he decided to stall, although he didn't know what he was stalling for. Hopefully, Keira was working out the details for the both of them.

"Look, bro, I tried to be nice about this, but we're not going anywhere. First of all, your guys have a serious case of the uglies. I mean it; it's bad. No offense or anything. Secondly, in case you didn't notice, we're in a public place. What are you gonna do—drag us through the crowd kicking and screaming? These geeks are dying for a chance to be the heroes they're pretending to be. You wouldn't make it ten feet."

Jack burst out laughing. "Oh, no. Look out, boys. We might get collared by Captain Farticus over there." His heavies snickered.

Jack leaned in close—close enough for Rauch to smell his expensive cologne. "Here's how it's gonna work, asshole. I'm gonna walk away. You're gonna follow them." He hitched his thumb at his goons. "My boys may be ugly, but they come nicely equipped. Sort of like gun ports on an armored car, right, Keira?"

Her face froze, and the squad of heavies tittered again. Jack grinned. "If you run, scream, or otherwise make a scene, my boys will zap you with fifty-thousand volts. You'll twitch, drool, and fall to the ground. They'll toss you over their shoulders and carry you to the car. The whole process takes less than a minute. And as far as Captain Farticus knows, my men are security."

One of Jack's bodyguards dragged a neon lanyard from beneath his collar and waved an official-looking ID in front of Rauch's nose. *What is it with goons and their lanyards?* He opened his mouth to tell the tale of no-neck Skinny but reconsidered after one of Jack's bodyguards brushed his jacket away from his hip and rested a hand on his Taser. Story time was over. No more stalling. Rauch glanced at Keira for guidance.

She shrugged. "Fine. You're such a drama queen, Jack. Lead on."

Instead of fear, Keira projected annoyance, which Rauch presumed was intentional. Her eyes, however, scanned the room continuously as if searching for options.

They navigated the sea of costumed creatures, the two heavies in front acting as icebreakers and the two in back as escort ships. As they walked, Rauch leaned to whisper in Keira's ear. "'Fine. Lead on.' That's the best you could do?"

"I'm thinking. You could help."

"You don't pay me enough to think, doll. This is your party."

She shot him a furious glare.

They strode through a series of glass doors and into

the attached parking garage. Jack's thugs directed them down the stairs to the lowest level, which was reserved for contractors. A smattering of white box vans and other utility vehicles claimed the spaces closest to the elevators. The bodyguards headed the opposite direction to a sleek SUV parked in a poorly lit and otherwise empty corner.

The reality of their situation hit, drying Rauch's mouth to a plate of sand. This was worse, much worse, than when he'd met the don in Philadelphia, and he'd expected to die then. He licked his lips and again whispered in Keira's ear. "You prepared for something like this, right? You have a plan?"

"This wasn't supposed to happen."

"You don't say? This mole of yours—the one who told you Jack was moving the money early—is it possible she's playing both sides?"

"It's possible. The only way Jack could've found out about the heist this quickly is if someone tipped him off and he prepared in advance. Pinball was supposed to keep the armored vehicle's communication systems blocked for two hours, long enough for us to return to the hangar and prepare to blow town. Something went wrong, hence the text."

"Something's about to go even wronger."

"Wronger is not a word."

"It is today."

"Shut up, you two." Thug number one plucked a pair of zip ties from his pocket. His partner frisked Rauch from behind.

Rauch jumped. "Whoa, there. Watch it, sweetheart. I don't even know your name."

"Sure you do." Thug number two gave Rauch's ass

an extra squeeze. "I think you called me 'Ugly.'" He removed Rauch's gun from its holster and dropped it in his pocket. "Now the fun part—the lady's turn."

Keira's face contorted with revulsion and rage. "Touch me, and I swear to God I'll break every bone in your ugly face, and if I don't, someone else in the Family will. I'm a McConnell."

Ugly stepped forward. "Your baby brother's the one giving the orders now, bitch."

"Oh, boy. Now you've done it. Don't ever, ever…" Rauch shook his head and paused, which made Ugly pause.

That was all the time Keira needed. She twirled and threw her right elbow into the bridge of Ugly's nose. The crack echoed throughout the underground chamber. Ugly cupped his hands over his bleeding face and collapsed to his knees.

"There's one." Keira kicked him in the face with the heel of her boot before his partner could haul her away. Another sickening crack bounced off the walls. "There's two."

Rauch wasn't sure what he was thinking, or even if he was thinking. But he knew one fourth of Jack's team was now on the ground, which improved their odds dramatically. Three to two. If only the three weren't so heavily armed.

He lunged at Ugly's partner, flattening him against the SUV in a tackle worthy of an NFL contract. The vehicle's side panel crumpled like aluminum foil under their combined weight. They toppled to the cement, grappling and trading punches, their motions hampered by their sports coats.

Footsteps raced across the cement, and a flash

filled the dark corner with an intense white light. A strange pop followed by a long, slow hiss made the hair on his arms stand on end. The man beneath him froze. Rauch tried to let go but could not. He stared at his rigid hands until even his brain seemed to spasm. Coherent thought stopped.

Keira's distressed face swam in and out of view, as if he were suspended beneath the surface of a pond with her bobbing above him in the murky water. Her purple hair floated like seaweed, choking out the sun. He gasped for breath and tried to focus on the narrowing tunnel of light, but it faded into oblivion, allowing the darkness to swallow him in a haze of purple and black.

****

When the fog cleared, the first thing Rauch noticed was that his muscles ached. As in, *all* of them. Some he never knew existed shouted their displeasure. Even his scalp hurt.

His second thought was how much he loathed coffee. He hated everything about it, and wherever he was, the place reeked of burnt beans and stale brew. His stomach lurched. He forced his quivering lids to open, expecting to see the green logo of a certain coffee chain—his own personal Hell on Earth.

Zip ties held him to a chair stationed at an oblong conference table, the cheap kind with a thin laminate top. White heat stains marred its surface—rings of shame, he suspected, from those nasty cups of joe. Keira sat to his right. Her green eyes were open but unfocused, and her dazed expression suggested she'd not yet recovered her wits.

The conference room was otherwise empty. Despite its shabby furnishings and crappy beige walls, tinged yellow by the harsh fluorescent lights, the space managed to feel simultaneously bland and menacing, as if an alien monster were about to burst from the sagging dropped ceiling.

The air conditioning kicked on, rattling the screws in the wall vents. Rauch jumped. The blast of cold air rustled Keira's hair and awakened her from her stupor. Her head flopped to the left as she struggled to control her neck muscles enough to turn her gaze toward his.

"You okay?" Rauch sounded like he'd swallowed a mouthful of hot sand. He coughed, tried again. "Keira?"

She shuddered and grimaced as the zip ties cut into her thin wrists. "Yeah. I'm working on it."

"They zapped you, too?"

"I did not go quietly." She succeeded in straightening her neck, and Rauch's breath caught in his throat. Her lower lip was split, and her right cheek glowed with a shiner as bad as any he'd seen, and he'd seen and had quite a few.

Any time Rauch saw a woman with a black eye, he thought of Frank's father. Though Frank didn't talk much about his childhood, he'd said enough for Rauch to build a profile in his mind of the type of man who beats a woman with impunity—a man who preys on the weak or dependent of any sex or species. The image never failed to make his teeth clench and his chest burn with rage.

Rauch understood the laws of survival better than anyone, but that didn't mean he had to like them. A fight wasn't a fight unless it was fair, and life's battles rarely were. Keira sure wasn't weak, but Jack's goons had a good hundred pounds on her, and that wasn't fair, even without the Taser.

He realized he was staring at her swollen lips and dragged his attention back to her eyes.

She cocked her head. "I'm fine, Rauch. Consider it a badge of honor."

"Honor? Really?" The muscles in his jaw twitched, and he clenched his fists, straining against the zip ties in a futile attempt to bend their plastic teeth.

"For me, not for them. You know what they called me? Frisky."

"Frisky my ass."

"Exactly. That's when I head-butted the shortest one, which earned me the punch and a jolt of juice."

He surrendered the effort to break free from his ties and slumped in his seat. "Any idea what's going on?"

"Jack mentioned gun ports. I think it's fair to assume the entire plan's gone south. Let's just hope no one was killed."

Rauch stiffened. "Pinball didn't say in his text?"

"No." She sniffed the air. "Is that coffee?"

"Yep."

"Yum." She surveyed the windowless room. "Can you see if my phone is in my boot?"

"Jack took it, remember?"

She frowned. "Obviously not, or I wouldn't have asked. What about yours?"

Rauch had tucked his cell into the inner pocket of his suit jacket. He rocked in his seat until his lapels swayed, feeling the weight of the material as it brushed against his chest. "I'm pretty sure it's still there. I can feel it. Guess they didn't bother taking it since I can't reach it anyway."

"I told you Jack was careless. I had Pinball put tracers on the team members' phones. Pinging only triangulates a phone's position, but the tracer gives the exact location."

"You were tracking us?"

"No. I was thinking ahead. It was for emergency use only. I had him put one on my phone, too, if it makes you feel better. As long as Jack hasn't turned it off, Pinball should be able to find us."

"You're assuming Pinball's not dead. Jack may've found him already. You're also assuming my phone wasn't fried from the jolt of juice or damaged from the fight."

"Your optimism is overwhelming." The doorknob rattled, and Keira inhaled. "Here we go. Let me do the talking, okay?"

"Try not to get too frisky with them."

Keira shot him a look that made him grateful her hands were tied.

The door swung open, and Jack strutted in with Ugly and an additional pair of goons at his flank. He tossed Keira's phone on the table. It skidded across the smooth surface and landed on the floor by her feet.

"Pinball, Frank, Ruletka, Deliverance, and Rauch. Your contact list contains quite the colorful cast of characters. Which one's the dead guy?"

Jack laughed at their horrified expressions.

"Guess you don't know either. Doesn't matter. They're all gonna be dead soon if you don't tell me what happened to my goddamned money." He bellowed the last two words and leaned over the table until his face was inches from Keira's.

She never flinched. "Jack, I told you before—all I ever wanted was my fair share. That's it. Let me go, and I'll arrange to have half the money dropped at the location of your choice. Half for you; half for me."

Jack flicked his fingers toward the door, and his bodyguards left. Ugly puckered his lips, blowing Rauch a mock kiss before shutting the door with a quiet click. Arms crossed, Jack paced the coffee-stained carpet, his demeanor surprisingly contemplative. He half-sat on the edge of the table, which creaked its displeasure.

"Your offer is not unreasonable, dear sister. I want you to know that. It provides a quick and easy solution to what could become a messy and costly situation for both of us." His gaze briefly rested on Rauch. "In terms of lives lost, I mean. However, by cutting a deal, I stand to lose a significant amount of credibility in front of my men, and more importantly, in the eyes of the extended family."

He walked behind Rauch and Keira, then squatted between their chairs. His cologne mingled with her perfume. The musky blend hung in the air, replacing the essence of stale coffee. Rauch, confused by Jack's sudden stillness and certain the end was near, strained at his tethers.

Jack brushed Keira's purple hair away from her face and tucked it behind her ear. His left hand clasped hers, and with a gentle twist, he removed the emerald ring from her finger and dropped it in his pocket. "This never really belonged to you, did it?" His lips grazed her bruised cheek. "There will be no deal."

He rose and spun on his heel to stride purposefully toward the door. He looked over his shoulder at Rauch. "And for you, my friend, things are about to get ugly."

Chapter Thirty-Five

Ruletka and Frank unloaded the jaws of life but left the cash in the van as per Pinball's instructions. The tech wizard dashed around the hangar, gathering equipment while shouting orders. "Pack your bags. Rauch's, too."

When Ruletka and Frank returned from their rooms, the van's rear doors were wide open. Rictor burbled hello from atop the mounds of cardboard boxes, partially crumpled under his weight and that of two long duffels stuffed with Pinball's "necessities." They tossed their own bags onto the pile, and Ruletka slammed the doors. Rictor's single red eye peered through the tinted glass.

"Now what?" Ruletka had said surprisingly little since receiving Pinball's terse summary during their return to the hangar.

"Now we wait." Pinball motioned toward a metal table closest to the command hub, where he could monitor the security cameras for signs of unwanted attention.

"Wait? We're just gonna sit here and wait? For what—a pizza?" Frank glanced at the grainy images of the barren stretch of road leading into the desert.

"Miss Keira said she and Rauch would be back by six at the latest." Pinball tapped coded commands into his laptop, and a satellite map of Vegas appeared on the screen. It zoomed in, collapsing around a flashing red pin positioned far east of the conference center's location. He leaned back in his seat. "Huh."

"Huh's right, Tico." Ruletka pressed his lips into a tight, thin line. "Miss Keira's not where she's supposed to be, and she's not answering her texts. She's most likely in trouble."

"I'm confirming her position now." Pinball's phone rang, and the three men jumped. "It's her."

Frank exhaled with relief. If Keira was okay, Rauch must be okay, too. Probably. Maybe.

Pinball held up a finger, signaling them to be quiet. He answered on speakerphone. "Heroes2B. How may I direct your call?"

No one spoke, but the call was anything but quiet. The clatter of dishes competed with a background buzz of laughter and music. The high-pitched whine of a rotary motor transitioned to the whoosh of a nozzle under pressure. The call disconnected, and Pinball powered his phone completely off.

Frank's forehead furrowed. "Was that some kind of a grinder?"

"An espresso machine, I believe." Ruletka's phone buzzed on his hip, and he glanced at the screen. "It says it's from Keira."

"Don't answer it." Pinball held out his hand. "Gimme your phones."

Frank's started ringing in his hand. He dropped it on the table, and Pinball, with a sweep of his arm, brushed all three phones onto the ground and smashed them under the heel of his black leather boot. He responded to their shocked expressions with a grim smile. "Tracking works both ways, you know."

"They have her, don't they?" Ruletka bowed his head to stare at his intertwined fingers.

"I think so. She's supposed to be at the conference center getting her geek on with Rauch. But as you can see…" Pinball rotated his laptop so the others could more easily view the screen. "…They're nowhere near the center. According to my satellite mapping system, they're at an off-Strip café called Bolly Beans, which advertises itself as a locally owned coffee shop with international flair."

"Rauch hates coffee." Frank shook his head, and Ruletka shot him a quizzical look. "I'm just sayin'. You won't find him there sipping a latte. Not even for Keira."

Pinball closed his laptop. "Who's a tea snob, in case you didn't know. I can't think of a single reason she'd go to an off-Strip coffee shop, unless she modified the plan without telling me. If I had to guess, I'd say the building belongs to Jack, who bought it to use as his center of operations. Throw in a couple of legit, albeit, shady local businesses as tenants, and voila—a perfect front."

Frank, too nervous to sit any longer, rose from his chair and paced the room. "What happened to good old-fashioned bars and laundromats?"

"Not yuppie enough, I guess. Sign of the times, just like tracking cell phones. In the past, if the mob wanted to know a thief's accomplices, they'd beat the information out of him. Now they just run the list of contacts, and the hunt is on. Or, if they feel like working a deal, they know who to call."

"But you destroyed our phones. Now they won't be able to reach us."

"Or track us, either. Miss Keira knows how to reach me if she wants to. Gives them reason to keep her alive. Right now, she and Jack are probably negotiating their little Irish hearts out."

"Negotiating?" Frank shuddered. Jack did not, from Keira's descriptions, seem like the negotiating type. Not in the traditional sense of the word, anyhow. And what would Rauch's role be? Frank had no doubt he'd be considered expendable—by both parties.

Pinball guessed the nature of Frank's distress. "It's his own fault, you know. Keira told me he talked you into this. He's been thinking with his nether region the entire time. But the joke's on him. You probably noticed that Miss Keira's not the warm-and-fuzzy type. She'll use him and drop him—"

"Just like the rest of us. Just like Deliverance. Am I right, Tico?" Ruletka, face twitching with suppressed rage, looked up from the table.

"Maybe. She's always played fair with me. Or so I thought—until last night. Come here. I want to show you something." Pinball, his expression inscrutable, cocked his head toward the rear of the hangar.

Frank hesitated, his skin prickling with a sudden sense of danger. The hair on his forearms stood on end. He looked at Ruletka, who pushed away from the table and nodded as if to convey *I've got your back*. They followed Pinball to a utility closet bearing a thick new lock.

"I don't get in here much. It's a junk closet, more or less. A few burner phones, some leftover circuits from Rictor's construction—that sort of thing. Last night while I was tinkering on Rictor, I saw Keira leave later than usual. Then Rictor blew a fuse, so to speak, and I came to this closet to rummage for spare parts. That's when I noticed the new lock. Wasn't there before. Guess Miss Keira thought I was too preoccupied with the heist preparations to notice."

Frank ran his thumb over the fine network of scratches marring the lock's shiny surface. "Did you pick it?"

"Man, you know I did. Wasn't easy. Missed out on my beauty sleep last night. I'm runnin' on fumes." Pinball twisted the handle and the door popped open, revealing a small closet lined with metal shelves. He slid a bin from one of the shelves and removed three phones. "May as well get these while we're in here. Take a look in the bottom left corner."

He stepped out of their way. Frank and Ruletka peered around the door into the unlit space. Stuffed as far into the dark recess sat a small lidded pot.

"Is that—" Frank's question died in his throat.

"A bomb. Sure is. But this one's not mine."

Ruletka backpedaled away from the closet. "Then what are we still doing here?"

****

Ruletka drove them to the convention center's overflowing lot, figuring a van full of spandex-clad dweebs would blend right in. Pinball monitored Keira's position from his laptop.

"No change." He removed his mirrored shades and stared at Ruletka and Frank. "It's decision time."

Ruletka stared back, his expression wary. "What do you mean?"

"I mean, thirty mil split three ways is ten mil each. Thirty mil split five ways is—"

"Six million apiece. I can do math, Tico."

267

"If she set us up, she deserves what's coming."

"How chivalrous of you. That's a massive 'if.' The bomb could've been planted by someone else. Her brother comes to mind."

"Negatory. If Jack knew the location of our base, we would not be having this conversation. His goons would've been lying in wait to reclaim the money."

Frank, stunned by Pinball's proposal, listened to their heated exchange. Rauch's loyalty, despite his assertions to the contrary, had wavered, and Keira hadn't spoken a truthful sentence since they'd first met, but that didn't mean they deserved to die. Still, ten million dollars. With that kind of money, he could afford to buy an entire block of his old neighborhood.

He pictured his old boss, Roy, on the blood-spattered floor of Baum's Books with his belly splayed wide and a jack of clubs near his fingertips. The bile rose in his throat, and he shook his head violently to clear the painful image. "No. No one—no one—deserves the kind of punishment Jack gives. Heroes don't abandon other heroes during their hour of need."

"Rauch is no hero." Pinball snorted in disgust.

"Based on what you're suggesting, neither are you."

"I've been dancing around in spandex longer than you've had chest hair, Frank. The entire city knows I'm a hero."

"Prove it."

Pinball cursed under his breath and reached for the door handle. Ruletka clicked the lock, thwarting his exit. "Frank's right, Tico. We're a team. Until an hour ago, I had no knowledge of the money, and you know what? I would've saved them anyway. Because that's what heroes do. For me, it's worth four million to rescue Keira, look her in the eye, and watch her squirm up some answers about that bomb." Ruletka put his hand on Pinball's shoulder and smiled. "Besides, what's four mil between friends?"

"What is it? It's four million simoleans, that's what is it. Forty thousand Benjamins. A whole lotta dead presidents." Pinball swiped a hand over his glistening forehead. "Shit. You guys know this ain't no video game. No replay, no extra lives, no dry run. Jack's men are as badass as they come. They'll be packin' a whole lotta heat. It's not just about the money. It's about whether we're willing to die for them. Whether we can pull this off without a plan."

"Of course we can. We're Heroes2B." Ruletka revved the engine and threw the van into gear. "I'll drive. You heard the man, Frank, while you navigate, start working on a plan. And for God's sake, make it a good one."

Chapter Thirty-Six

Rauch was gonna need some new teeth. He spat a chunk of clotted blood and heard the clink of enamel hitting the wooden leg of his chair. A second blow hammered the bridge of his nose, and his chair tipped on its side, cracking as it contacted the concrete floor. His shoulder popped out, then back into place, and the searing pain made him puke more than blood.

Jack's goons had dragged him from the conference room to a warehouse behind the coffee shop, where burlap sacks of beans intermingled with boxes of paper supplies and jugs of flavored syrups. He rested his cheek against the sticky, cool floor and hoped for a quick death.

Ugly's phone rang, and he turned away from Rauch's retching to answer it. A cockroach skittered across the floor. It stopped close enough to Rauch's swollen eye for him to see the individual spines on the creature's spindly legs. He waved it along and realized his hands were free.

Ugly and his equally unattractive partner had cut Rauch's zip tie when they'd moved him to the warehouse for questioning. It wasn't until they had him seated in the rickety wooden chair that they realized they lacked a replacement. In a flash of inspiration Ugly deemed "brilliant," they'd cut the twine securing one of the burlap sacks and used it to bind Rauch's hands to the back of the chair. But the spindle broke with the fall, and the thin, frayed twine slid from his wrists. He grabbed the splintered shaft of wood and tucked his hands behind his back as if they were still securely bound.

Ugly shoved his phone into his pocket and waved his partner out the door. "Boss needs help with the girl. I'll finish up here. Save some for me." He grasped Rauch's bloody necktie and hauled him to his feet.

Rauch allowed his knees to sag, forcing Ugly to support his full weight with both burly arms. As soon as the door clicked, he slashed at Ugly with the jagged stick.

"What the—"

Ugly staggered backward, hands clutching his throat. A crimson line appeared across his neck. Rauch adjusted his grip on the improvised weapon. It had broken into a sharp point like a dagger's, but it lacked the strength of a metal blade. It wouldn't last long. Every blow had to count.

His ragged breath whistled through his swollen nose as he again slashed at Ugly's neck. The big man twisted to avoid contact, and Rauch buried the stake between Ugly's shoulder blades. It snapped in his hand. Ugly howled in pain and staggered forward. He fell on his knees and sagged over the open sack of beans, his right arm pushing against the scratchy burlap as he tried to heave himself back to his feet.

Rauch grabbed Ugly by his greasy hair and buried his head deep in the sack of shiny, black beans. Coffee streamed onto the floor as Ugly, arms flailing, slipped on the fallen beans, crushing them underfoot as he struggled to gain traction. The smell of freshly ground beans mixed with blood, and Rauch gagged. Now he really hated coffee.

Ugly's thrashing ceased. Rauch, panting, released Ugly's hair and cautiously backed away. Sweat dripped onto his split lip, and he winced. His mind raced with a jumble of options. Run for help or run and help? Keira was still with her brother. He spat another slippery chunk of blood onto the floor and wondered if he could do much good in his current pathetic condition. Probably not. But that didn't mean he shouldn't try.

Ugly's phone rang, reminding Rauch his own cell rested in his jacket's inner pocket. He fumbled with the buttons. The cracked screen flickered to life, and he sighed with relief. The phone looked as rough as his face, but at least it still worked. The signal strength was weak, though, thanks to the warehouse's thick metal walls. He dialed Frank's number anyway. The call dropped.

He staggered around the perimeter of the space and tried again. After pauses of various agonizing lengths, the calls continued to drop. Finally, he crouched near the door through which Ugly had dragged him and listened for sounds of life on the other side. All was quiet. He dialed again. This time, the call went through.

"C'mon, Frankie, c'mon."

Despite his pleas, his call went unanswered. Fingers trembling, he scrolled through his contacts and punched Pinball's number. Again, nothing. He glanced at the time. Five-thirty. The heist should be over and the team celebrating their success while awaiting he and Keira's return. But Jack said one of them was dead. And if Keira had broken, Jack might've gotten to the rest of them, too.

Rauch's stomach clenched, and he vomited, spewing a noxious blend of blood and lunch onto Ugly's motionless back. He dabbed his throbbing mouth on his sleeve. Safest to assume no help was coming. He was on his own.

He surveyed the warehouse with his left eye, the right one having long since swollen shut. The front door led to a maze of bland corridors—part of an interconnected corporate complex, which included the conference room where he and Keira had been held. Rauch had paid attention during his journey to the warehouse. The hallways had security cameras mounted at both ends, and while he couldn't be certain they were monitored or even operative, if they were, any attempt to escape through the front would end in immediate failure.

Like most warehouses, the back held an oversized garage door leading to a loading bay, which would certainly have a security camera. Overhead doors were loud anyway, and the racket would alert Jack's goons to Rauch's escape.

The warehouse held one more door. Positioned along the south wall and unmarked, Rauch assumed it either led outdoors or to a coffee shop, given the burlap sacks and supplies clustered near its opening. He pressed his ear against its cold surface but heard nothing.

He fidgeted, debating what to do. If this did lead to a public place, where his bloodied appearance was sure to incite panic, it was his best option. With any luck, he could make it through the café and onto the street before Jack's goons realized what was happening. And maybe one of the patrons would dial nine-one-one.

Rauch tugged on the door. It was locked. Stymied, he glared at it with his one eye and raised his fist, planning to pummel it until someone answered. The rush of anger abated, and he paused. What if it didn't lead to a café after all?

Goddammit. His options sucked. He plopped on a sack of beans and buried his face in his shaking hands. Maybe he should just stay put until someone came looking for Ugly. He prodded the dead man with his foot and fingered the cold steel of Ugly's gun. The more he thought about it, the more he liked the idea. Given how outnumbered he was, a good old-fashioned ambush gave him the best odds.

A fully formed plan coalesced, and he dialed Keira's number before he had a chance to change his mind. The call connected, but no one spoke. After a few seconds, the call dropped. He tossed his phone into position and, grunting from the effort, dragged a dozen of the heavy sacks across the floor.

Your move, Jack.

Rauch settled into the nest of beans, placed the gun in his lap, and waited.

****

He should've learned how to meditate. No matter how hard he fought to stay focused, his thoughts kept returning to Keira. The rage returned, fueled by the thought of what Jack and his men might be doing to her. But while bursting into the conference room with his gun blazing sounded enormously heroic, chances are they'd both wind up dead. Besides, Keira didn't need a hero. She was tough and smart—far smarter than he. For all he knew, she'd already talked her way out the door and left him to fend for himself.

The warehouse lacked air conditioning, and Rauch's head grew fuzzy from warmth and pain. The sack of coffee was surprisingly comfortable, conforming to his aching body like a bean bag chair. His vigilance waned with the heat, and his head bobbed. Jack hadn't taken the bait. May as well rest up. Big day ahead.

The door rattled, jolting him awake. He'd spoken too soon. He dove behind a row of burlap sacks, licked his dry lips, and aimed the sight of Ugly's pistol for the mid-chest of whoever walked through the door first.

The glowing red dot landed on Keira.

He exhaled and held his fire. She looked no worse than when they'd parted. Jack, on the other hand, sported a freshly bloodied nose. No wonder Ugly had said the boss needed help with the girl.

She strode in with her head held high and her hands zip tied behind her back. Jack stood inches behind, using her body as a shield. Both he and his sole remaining guard had their guns trained on the back of her head.

The expression on Keira's face gave Rauch pause. She didn't act like a hostage. She didn't appear to be afraid or even nervous. She looked cool. Cool and…satisfied.

They struck a deal.

Rauch's stomach dropped. He'd bet all the dough in Ugly's wallet that deal didn't include him. After all, if she split with Jack alone, she got half the money. The team would cost her two-thirds.

Jack stopped short of the broken chair and Ugly's lifeless body. "Nicely done, Mr. Rauch." His loud voice bounced off the warehouse's metal walls. "If circumstances were different, I'd consider hiring you myself. I offered to pay you double, if you remember, and that was just to walk away. Too late for that now, I'm afraid."

He held what appeared to be Keira's phone in his free hand and punched at it with his thumb. Rauch's phone rang, blasting the *Star Wars* "Cantina Band" theme from behind a pile of cardboard boxes.

Jack's bodyguard grinned and closed in, peppering the boxes with gunfire. The warehouse boomed with echoes as bullets ricocheted off the metal walls, shredding burlap sacks and piercing jugs of flavored syrups. Beans and liquid streamed onto the floor, adding to the chaos. Swirling puddles formed like sticky landmines. The smell of vanilla mixed with the aroma of coffee and smoke. When the gray haze cleared and the noise ceased, Jack's bodyguard lay dead from a single gunshot to the back of the head.

Rauch, sweat dripping down his neck, crouched behind his man-made barrier of burlap sacks and congratulated himself on his ruse. It wasn't elegant, but it got the job done, which was basically his whole life summarized in nine words. Unless Jack called in reinforcements, it was down to the two of them—*mano a mano*, with Keira as the wild card.

The dismay on Jack's face was laughable. Rauch settled for a grin. It was quieter, and any movement of his own face caused him excruciating pain. Totally worth it, though. The mobster looked like he was about to explode.

Jack shoved his revolver against Keira's temple. "Okay, asshole, you wanna play? I'll show you how the Irish do it. You've got three seconds before I blow her fucking brains out. One."

Keira's smug face now registered a modicum of concern. "Jack, I know you're angry, but if you kill me, you'll never see your money. We discussed this."

"Two."

The grip of Ugly's gun grew slick with sweat. Rauch knew Jack was bluffing. He had to be. Keira and he probably planned this in advance. But then why did she look so terrified?

"Three."

Rauch closed his eyes. He didn't want to see if he was wrong.

Chapter Thirty-Seven

Ruletka navigated through rush-hour traffic and followed Pinball's coordinates to the oldest part of Vegas. The downtown area of Fremont Street bustled and glowed with neon, but after a short drive west, the neon faded and the storefronts sagged with fatigue. The team parked a block from a shabby strip mall, its businesses dark except for Bolly Beans, which anchored its southernmost end.

Pinball focused his tracer and pointed to the end farthest from the café. "Keira's somewhere in there. I'll release Sin first and have her disrupt their surveillance cameras."

He programmed his drone and flew her overhead. She perched on the flat roof to stand guard, her red eye glowing in the darkness.

"Even with Sin scrambling their signals, I think it's wisest to enter through the back where there are no traffic cams." He popped the latch to the rear doors, unloaded Rictor, and opened the longest of his black duffels.

Ruletka peeked over his shoulder and gasped. "How did you amass such a small but mighty arsenal?"

"What can I say? It's America." Pinball shrugged. "I usually don't carry weapons on patrol, but sometimes drones aren't enough. Did I say that out loud? Sorry, Sin. Love ya, baby." He blew a kiss toward the roof and claimed himself an Uzi.

Frank dithered over his options. "Deliverance would've had a blast with these."

"Why do you think I didn't show him?" Pinball grabbed a pump-action shotgun and shoved it in Frank's hands. "You're up, Toni. Take your pick."

Ruletka chose an AK-47. "Russian-made, of course. Although let it be said for the record, I disapprove of private ownership of assault rifles."

"Let it be said for the record, I'd expect nothing less." Pinball frowned at Frank, who was awkwardly juggling his weapon. "That thing's loaded. Careful how you handle it."

"I've never held a rifle before."

"It shows."

Pinball dodged as the rifle's barrel swung with his every movement. Finally, Frank propped the shotgun over his shoulder ala Davy Crockett. "I know you and Keira have this thing against capes, but you have to admit one would nice right about now. Where am I supposed to hide this? We're on a public street, for Christ's sake."

"Not for long." Pinball led them around the building, hugging its dark corners until they stood at the base of the loading ramp. He waved at the disabled security camera and paused for a response. Nothing. He exhaled. "Looks like Sin did her part. You guys ready for this? It's about to get real."

Rictor burbled, and Frank nodded. A fortifying rush of adrenaline quickened his pulse and strengthened his resolve. "We're ready. We have to be. And just so you know, I've seen real action before. Back in Philly, I once kicked hoodlum ass while armed only with a couple of smoke bombs and a Taser."

"Good for you. Except these hoodlums are expertly trained and will shoot to kill."

"Bring 'em on." The desert breeze ruffled Frank's hair, and he pictured his nonexistent cape fluttering majestically behind him. "I'm only afraid of two things: movie theaters and the fifth of November." He cocked his shotgun like a badass. "Ruletka, what day is it?"

"It's November thirteenth."

"Pinball, what's this building standing before us?"

"Don't be a moron, Frank. It's a strip mall. You know it's a strip mall."

"Perfect. Then we're good to go." Frank raised his foot to march up the ramp.

Ruletka grabbed his arm. "Not so fast, Lambda Man. It's not just movie theaters and calendar dates. When we drove by the Stratosphere, you said you're afraid of heights, too."

Pinball was equally unimpressed. "And I'd bet if a big old rat jumped from behind that stack of shipping pallets, you'd scream like a sissy. You might even wet your pants."

Frank's bravado fizzled. "Guys, I'm having a moment here. Can't you let me have my moment?"

Pinball rolled his eyes and elbowed Ruletka. "He's having a moment."

"That's nice, Frank." Ruletka patted him on the upper back. "Maybe you should have your moment a little faster. I suspect all hell is about to break loose, especially since you're wearing neon green and standing in the wide-open carrying a shotgun. Thank God it's evening and dark."

The Russian pointed at the floodlight mounted

above the garage's overhead door. "It's probably motion-activated. I know you can pick the lock, Tico, but any idea how to get in without announcing our presence in a halo of light?"

As if on cue, a pair of headlights bobbed around the corner, and a failing engine backfired. Frank jumped, and Pinball nudged him in the back. "Behind the crates. Get a move on, Rictor. Hurry up."

The team ducked for cover behind a teetering stack of damaged shipping crates and discarded wooden pallets. They peered between the slats and watched as Jack's armored SUV, windows broken, roof dented, and rear hatch missing, chugged into view. The vehicle hit a deep pothole, and its dangling bumper sent sparks flying across the asphalt.

"I can't believe it's still running," Frank whispered.

"I'm not. The armor's designed to protect the occupants and the engine. It did its job."

The driver and passenger doors slammed shut. Two battered men, their suits singed and torn, limped toward the loading ramp. Pinball's eyes flickered with recognition. "Those are the guys from the heist. The ones who killed Deliverance."

A muscle pulsed in Pinball's jaw, and Ruletka crossed his arms. "We're not here for revenge, Tico. We're here to save Keira."

Frank eyed the two senior members of the team as they faced off. "And Rauch. Don't forget about him."

The overhead garage light clicked on in response to the men's approach. Ruletka adjusted his mask. "They're our ticket inside. Disarm, but kill only if necessary. You hear me, Tico?"

Pinball glared. "Look, I didn't give a shit about

preacher boy. I was simply pointing out that these are the dudes who shot him. Save the lecture, okay? You're lucky I'm here at all. I've got ten million reasons to be in Mexico right now."

"Guys, please. We're missing our chance." Frank took a deep breath and, praying his team would follow, bolted from behind the pile of crates.

His footsteps on the pavement thumped louder than the SUV's engine. His heart matched their frantic pace. He raced from the safe shroud of darkness into the security light. The two men turned. The driver dropped the keys from his right hand and reached inside his jacket. His partner crouched and did the same.

"Think it through, assholes." Pinball's deep, gruff voice echoed close to Frank's right ear. He clicked his tongue, and Rictor charged to the front. His glowing red eye turned white as it strobed blinding pulses of harsh light at the men's faces.

The men cringed and shielded their eyes with their hands and forearms. Pinball clicked his tongue again, and Rictor's light extinguished. Frank stepped behind the driver and pressed a firm hand against his shoulder.

"On your knees, scumbag." He patted his utility belt and glanced sheepishly at the rest of his team. "Either of you bring handcuffs? Or some zip ties, maybe?"

Ruletka looked at Pinball. "Not me."

Pinball sighed. "Me neither. They're in the duffel in the car."

One of the men lunged from his knees to his feet. With a lightning-quick spin-o-rama, Pinball whacked him across the jaw with the Uzi. He fell unconscious to the ground, blood streaming from his mouth and onto

Ruletka's polished boots. The Russian took a broad step backward.

Pinball grinned. "Sorry about the mess. But at least I didn't kill him."

Frank retrieved the keys from the ground and dangled them in front of the driver's bruised nose. "Which one of these opens the door?" He waved toward an entrance to the right of the overhead garage doors.

The driver hocked a wad of bloody spit at Rictor's electronic eye.

Frank groaned.

Ruletka cringed and looked away.

And Pinball broke his second jaw of the night with an Uzi. The driver's face hit the ground. His body jerked and, with one final twitch, fell still.

Ruletka sighed. "I guess we're doing this the hard way. Eeny, meany, miney mo."

"Not quite." Pinball snatched the keys from Frank's hand. The ring held five keys and a fob for the SUV. He knelt to examine the lock at eye level, rubbed the pad of his index finger over the hole, and held each key to the light for closer inspection. "I'm pretty sure it's this one."

He slipped the key into the lock and twisted. The deadbolt slid without a hitch. Pinball withdrew the key and marked it with a smudge of blood.

Ruletka wrinkled his nose. "Eww, Tico, that's not very sanitary."

"It's not like I'm gonna be licking it."

"You're beyond gross."

"Sorry, but I left my felt-tip marker at home next to my pocket protector." Pinball wiped beads of sweat from his brow. "Okay—just like we discussed during the drive. Rictor goes into the warehouse first. Once he locates Keira and Rauch, we rush in using standard formation."

"We have a standard formation?" Frank wrinkled his forehead in confusion. "I don't remember discussing a standard formation. Did we discuss a standard formation?" He looked at Ruletka, who shrugged.

Pinball exhaled between his teeth. "Just follow my lead." He strapped his submachine gun to his shoulder to free both hands. With one, he booted up Rictor's software on his phone. The other he rested on the door handle. "Ready, Rictor?"

The drone's fan whined as its processor picked up speed. Pinball cracked the door just wide enough for Rictor's rectangular body to scoot through. "Go get 'em, boy."

****

Pinball, Ruletka, and Frank huddled over the screen as Rictor zipped into the warehouse. Except the door didn't lead to the warehouse. It led to a drab hallway the color of sweat stains. A security camera sat mounted high on the far wall.

Pinball froze Rictor in place. He thrust the phone into Frank's hand and unclipped a second phone from his belt. "Hold this. And for the love of God, don't touch anything."

"What are you doing?" Frank cradled the device in his palm, afraid to allow his fingers to so much as twitch lest they trigger Rictor to do something unfortunate.

"Making sure Sin in still in place and has the security system hijacked. Otherwise, this is going to be a short attempt at a rescue." He tapped on the screen, and his tense shoulders relaxed. "We're good."

He reclaimed his phone from Frank. "It's tough to control them both at once on one phone. On the laptop, it's no problem, but things get a little hairy on such a small screen. And I have fat thumbs, which makes texting commands difficult." He opened the door wide. "Shall we?"

Frank stared dubiously down the brightly lit hall. The walls were bare and unbroken until they dead-ended in doors on both sides. Every first-person shooter game he'd ever played flashed through his mind. The plainest hallways always held the most terrifying monsters. And this hallway was pretty damned plain.

"One of us should stay here so we don't get trapped. If those doors won't open and Jack's men wake up, we're tigers in a cage."

"I'll get the doors open." Pinball zoomed Rictor's lens on the unimpressive lock. "But you're right. Ruletka should stay here and cover our rear." He synced his phone with Ruletka's. "I'll stream the video so you can follow the action. Stay alert for any unwelcome company."

Ruletka eyed the bloody men on the ground with obvious distaste. "Why me?"

"Because you're carrying the faster weapon. You can fire ten shots to Frank's one. We have no idea how many of Jack's men might join the party."

Ruletka conceded with a nod.

"We won't be long. Nice and quiet now." Pinball advanced with Frank close behind. As they neared the end, they heard the clatter of dishes from the door to their right. Pinball typed on his phone.

—Cafe kitchen?—

Frank nodded.

With a few more taps, the flashing red dot of the tracer map advised them to bear left. Pinball gently pushed on the handle. The door was locked. He repeated the steps he'd followed with the outer door, but this time, he only had four keys from which to choose.

Once again, he chose wisely. Frank gave him a double-thumbs up, causing his shotgun to bobble from his grip. Ruletka gasped from the opposite end of the corridor. Frank recovered control of his weapon and flashed the Russian an embarrassed grin.

Rictor slipped through the opening. Frank and Pinball monitored his progress on the small screen. The drone weaved around pallets, boxes, and jugs lining the perimeter of what appeared to be a large warehouse. After skirting a line of burlap sacks, the drone stopped short, and its camera auto-focused. Rauch's bruised face swam into view. Frank stifled a horrified gasp at his friend's battered appearance. He looked worse than the dudes outside, and they'd been blown up by a bomb.

Whatever Rauch was watching had him frozen in place. Left eye wide, mouth forming a silent "O," he was so transfixed, he failed to notice Rictor's approach. He aimed his gun over a burlap barricade. Pinball reversed Rictor's path, guiding him around the barrier in an attempt to see what Rauch was seeing. Rictor's lens widened; Frank gaped at the grim scene. He questioned Pinball with his eyes. *What do we do?*

Pinball's thumbs pounded out a command.

—Rictor go boom—

Chapter Thirty-Eight

Jack's gun clicked, and Rauch's heart stopped. Keira ducked and dodged to her right. The toe of her boot caught on a pallet of sugar, and with her hands still bound behind her, she landed hard on the concrete floor. Something broke. The sickening crack—loud enough for Rauch to hear from his position against the opposite wall—hung in the sultry air. Wild-eyed with pain and terror, she struggled to her feet. Jack's maniacal laughter echoed off the ceiling.

Rauch, pulse pounding in his ears like a drumline during halftime at a Penn State game, aimed his gun at Jack's chest and stared through the sight. His shoulder throbbed; his hands shook. Dammit, he needed a smoke. How long had it been? Weeks? Months? The red dot bounced uncontrollably. He closed his eyes, rested the gun against his damp forehead, and took a steadying breath.

When he opened them, Jack had moved to shield himself behind Keira. Rauch cursed under his breath. His clean shot was gone. He had his chance, and he blew it. A soft electronic hum distracted his attention. He glanced to his left. A glowing red eye met his. Rictor. What the hell was he doing here?

Jack's antics worsened Rauch's confusion and added to the pounding in his head. His attention bounced between Rictor and Jack, who had the barrel of his revolver pressed into Keira's ribs. She winced, and her flushed cheeks blanched with pain.

"Did you know you're never supposed to dry fire a gun? It's bad for the chamber. But it was worth it, dear sister, just to see you squirm." He yelled into the warehouse. "That was a warning, Mr. Rauch. The next round is real."

Boom. The concrete floor vibrated. A resonant wave sent the spilled coffee skittering across the floor like Mexican jumping beans.

The door behind Jack opened. Two beefy men, scowling with concern and guns drawn, charged in. Rauch recognized them from the conference center.

"Everything okay, boss?" The larger of the two moved to Jack's right. The other protected his left.

With Keira shielding the front, Jack was safely surrounded. Rauch shook his head. If Pinball had planned to use Rictor to worsen their odds, he'd succeeded admirably.

Boom. A second wave thundered closer to Jack and Keira's position. The goons flinched. The warehouse floor shivered as if a thousand cockroaches had scattered into the corners to hide from impending disaster.

"This is your last chance, Mr. Rauch. Show yourself. Whatever trick you're trying to pull will fail. You're badly outnumbered. You can't win." Jack waved his gun in the air.

Keira's pale lips stretched into a brittle smile. "That's not Rauch. It's Rictor. And you're now in dire need of reinforcements."

****

Rictor burst into the open from behind a stout sack

of beans. He zoomed to the feet of the goon farthest from Rauch and lurched to a stop. His electronic eye targeted a red dot over the man's chest.

"What the hell is that supposed to be?" Jack glanced at his guard, who shrugged his broad shoulders.

Keira nodded at the drone. "Rictor, meet Jack. Jack, meet Rictor. He's my hero—one of them, anyway." Her gaze shifted around the dark corners of the warehouse. The droid kept his sight fixed on his target.

"You mean to tell me that bucket of bolts is here to save your day?"

She smirked. "You're more correct than you could possibly know."

Jack laughed, and his men joined in his merriment.

The trapdoor below Rictor's eye slid silently open. Rauch tensed his muscles and trained his gun on the other bodyguard, the one closest to his position. Whaddaya know? Pinball had a plan after all. Rauch steadied his hands. He wasn't exactly sure what that plan entailed, but this time, he'd be ready.

In a flash of sparks, the laughter stopped. The blast took Jack and his men by surprise. But not Keira. When the bolts, nails, and ball bearings erupted from Rictor's mouth, she broke free and, clutching her broken ribs, staggered toward the rear of the warehouse. The barrage of shrapnel caught one bodyguard square in the chest. In a single shot, Rauch took out the other. Both men dropped to the floor. From somewhere near the rear, Frank screamed his name. Rauch ignored him and pressed his eye against the gun's sight. The next bullet belonged to Jack.

Chapter Thirty-Nine

Frank, shotgun aimed at Jack's chest, burst through the door with Ruletka at his heels. He screamed for Rauch. Pinball grabbed Keira by the shoulders and escorted her to the safety of the rear hallway. Rictor, following Pinball's lead, whizzed by Frank's feet in full retreat. Another shot fired. No one fell. Jack abandoned his wounded men and ducked through the front door, slamming it behind him.

Frank stormed after him, but Ruletka grabbed his arm. "Leave him. Let's get who we came for and get out. Keira and Tico might leave without us."

The thought made Frank's blood run cold.

They twirled, weapons at the ready, at the sound of movement from behind a row of burlap sacks. Rauch shuffled into view, hands held high in the air. "Whoa, whoa, guys. It's me." He mumbled like he had a mouthful of marbles. "You have no idea how happy I am to see you, Frank. Even you, Commie."

Frank threw an arm around his waist. "Can you make it?"

Rauch grunted, and together they limped toward the rear of the warehouse. "I missed him, Frankie. I can't believe I missed the shot."

He sagged in Frank's arms.

"Don't worry about that right now. Concentrate on moving forward." Frank nodded at Ruletka. "You run ahead. If they try to leave without us, shoot their tires out. We'll figure it out from there."

"I'm on it." Ruletka's jaw tightened. "If they're smart, they'll wait. The van's out front. As far as we know, Jack is, too. He and his men could be lying in wait. We're stronger together."

"Stronger, but more expensive, and Keira doesn't like to pay." Frank stumbled as Rauch's knees buckled. He hoisted his friend back to his feet.

"If she leaves, I'll find her, and she'll pay." Ruletka's voice faded as he sprinted down the beige hallway. "The McConnells may play spin-the-bullet, but we Russians invented it." With a whoosh, he disappeared out the door.

Rauch tried to whistle but failed. "I didn't know Commie had it in him."

"For the love of God, Rauch—I told you before. Ruletka is not a Commie. He's as noble as they come."

"I'm not convinced anyone on this team has honorable intentions. Present company excepted." Rauch, struggling to match Frank's pace, snuffled through his blood-encrusted nose. "Glad to see you're not dead. Jack said someone was killed."

"Deliverance. They blew him away. Looks like you were slated to be next."

His swollen lips twisted in a gross facsimile of a smile. "I look that bad? You should see the other guy."

"The one with the stake sticking out his back like a goddamned vampire? I noticed." Frank's bad shoulder began to ache. "I know you feel rough, but can you hurry it up a little? We've got a ride to catch."

They burst through the outside door and into the cold, dry air. Jack's fallen men and the armored vehicle's burnt-out carcass were gone. The loading bay was empty and eerily silent. They stepped over the patch of dried blood at the entrance, and the motion sensor light clicked on, freezing them in their tracks. Frank strained against the silence, but heard nothing except his friend's ragged, whistling breath.

"This way." He feigned confidence as he steered Rauch away from the lighted ramp and into the darkness. "The van's a block down."

"What if they're gone, Frankie? What then? Here we are halfway across the country with nothin' but a couple of dead bodies and a pair of stolen weapons."

"Ruletka would never leave without us." *Not willingly*. Pinball and Keira, on the other hand…

Frank and Rauch continued their slow trek to the corner of the building and peeked down the block to the street. With a roar, the van, its headlights off, careened into view. Ruletka motioned from the back seat. Frank gave Rauch a nudge. "C'mon. Let's go."

Pinball dropped the driver's window and grinned. "Did somebody call for a ride?"

Chapter Forty

The day Frank returned to Philadelphia, he scheduled an appointment with Roy's attorney to check on the status of Baum's. He'd always thought of the attorney, who'd drop by the shop from time to time bearing a bottle of Irish whiskey, as a distinguished, educated man, but now that Frank was aware of Roy's underhanded business practices, he was wary. For all he knew, the lawyer's stylish office and expensive suits were subsidized by the mob.

His concerns seemed unwarranted, however. The gray-haired attorney greeted him with the same kindly smile as always. He rose from his leather seat to shake Frank's hand with genuine enthusiasm. "It's all yours, Frank. The store and everything in it. Everything except what the police confiscated from the back, of course."

"Do they still think I'm a suspect?"

"Pfft. They never did, really. They know it was the mob. They just don't know which soldier. Can't arrest them all, and even if they could, there'd be a dozen more waiting in line. Say what you will about the mob, but they pay their people well. They never have a shortage of willing employees." He thrust a stack of papers in Frank's hands. "Here. Sign them so Roy can rest in peace. He worried about you more than you'll ever know."

Frank's eyes welled with tears. He ducked his head

and pretended to review the documents page by page before signing on the dotted line with the lawyer's custom fountain pen. With a sigh, he placed the pen and documents on the antique cherry desk.

The lawyer folded the documents into a parchment envelope and handed it to Frank. "This has the deed, the spare key, and Roy's bank account information, which has been transferred to your name. You have everything you need to reopen." He walked Frank to the door, shook his hand again, and paused before adding, "If anyone bothers you, you let me know, okay?"

The giddiness hit the next day. Frank took the heist money, which he'd planned to spend on Baum's, and bought Julia's apartment building instead, with the intent to renovate the entire space—including a penthouse apartment for himself. In the interim, he moved into the only vacant room the building had available—a dark and scummy apartment he shared with the roaches. But it was his, and it was there that he hung his cape, far in the back of a closet the size of a child's coffin. He didn't need it anymore. Besides, a wise man once told him that capes were impractical, and now he knew why. He could make more of an impact on his neighborhood with money.

An infusion of dollars here, a well-timed donation there—he was determined to resurrect his neighborhood one block at a time. Every small project he funded, every tiny bit of progress, brought another glimmer of hope. He felt it on the streets. He'd become the hero he always wanted to be.

He visited Roy, his mother, and Joey on Christmas day, placing his mask, a dozen roses, and a teddy bear on their graves. Julia, wrapped in a warm new coat, walked him home, deflecting his melancholy with chatter about her upcoming enrollment in school. She needn't have bothered. Life was good. He finally understood why fate or karma or God had chosen him to survive that first horrific November the fifth. Because of him, others could now thrive, starting with Julia. Roy would be proud.

Rauch called from time to time when he wasn't too busy island-hopping. It never failed to give Frank a thrill to hear his friend's voice and know he hadn't been forgotten.

"Happy New Year, Frank. How's life in the hood?"

"Cold. What exotic locale are you gracing with your presence now?"

"Aruba, where it's sunny and warm. You're welcome to join me for a visit."

"Thanks, but I'm stuck in Philly until I hire myself an employee for Baum's. I'm trying to convince Ruletka to buy in as a partner, but he's got his heart set on opening his own gym."

"Excuses, Frank. Nothing but excuses."

"Maybe. Speaking of visitors, a guy came into the shop yesterday asking for you. Said his name was Skinny. Then he asked me out for a date." From the length of the ensuing pause, Frank thought the call had dropped. "Hello?"

"You're kidding, right?"

Frank chuckled. "Only about the date part. He wanted to know where you were. I told him you were in Jamaica with some chick named Keira McConnell. You should've seen his face."

Rauch's tone remained uneasy. "Guess I won't be going to Jamaica any time soon."

"Aruba, Jamaica—he didn't seem the sort to know the difference. I doubt he's been any farther than Jersey."

"Listen to you. One trip to Vegas, and suddenly you're a freakin' globetrotter." Rauch's voice hardened. "He's bad news, Frank. Almost as bad as Jack, but not as rich. Be careful. Let me know if he comes in again."

"So you can do what? Swoop in with your island tan and save the day? Don't worry about it, Rauch. I've given Baum's some upgrades, including the security system. I can handle it." Frank paused. "You still hanging with Keira?"

"Not at the moment, but funny you should ask. She just invited me to her spread on Grand Cayman. Now that her ribs are healed, she's back in fighting form. Said she's got a new scheme to discuss. Six million doesn't last long these days, you know. She's still sore about Ruletka forcing her to divvy up the money."

"Speaking of bad news…"

"Oh, come on, Frank. She's not so bad."

"She planned to rook us out of our fair share and then blow us up in our sleep."

"Maybe or maybe not. She told me her intent was to destroy the facility and remove any traces of evidence. We were not the targets."

"And you believe her?"

"Yes. Yes, I do. She and I, we're two of a kind, Frank. And you know what that means, don't ya?"

"I'm afraid to ask."

"It means the con is always on, and that's just the way I like it."

A word about the author…

J.L. Delozier has practiced rural and disaster medicine for 25 years. For inspiration, she turns to science that exists on the edge of reality—bizarre medical anomalies, new genetic discoveries, and anything that seems too weird to be true.

She's published three thrillers, the first of which was nominated for a "Best First Novel" award by the International Thriller Writers organization. Her short fiction has appeared in the British crime anthology, *Noirville: Tales from the Dark Side*, in NoirCon's official journal, *Retreats from Oblivion*, and in *Thriller Magazine*. Her first sci-fi short story won the "Women Hold Up Half the Sky" prize of the Roswell Award and appeared in *Artemis Journal*.

She lives in Pennsylvania with her husband and three rescue cats.

See more at:

www.jldelozier.com

Thank you for purchasing
this publication of The Wild Rose Press, Inc.

For questions or more information
contact us at
info@thewildrosepress.com.

The Wild Rose Press, Inc.
www.thewildrosepress.com

CPSIA information can be obtained
at www.ICGtesting.com
Printed in the USA
LVHW081337040220
645810LV00009B/235